A DETAILED MAN

David Swinson

DYMAXICON

Published by Dymaxicon
An imprint of Agile Learning Labs
San Francisco, CA

First Edition
ISBN 978-0-9828669-7-9
www.dymaxicon.com

text set in Calluna by Jos Bivuenga

A DETAILED MAN

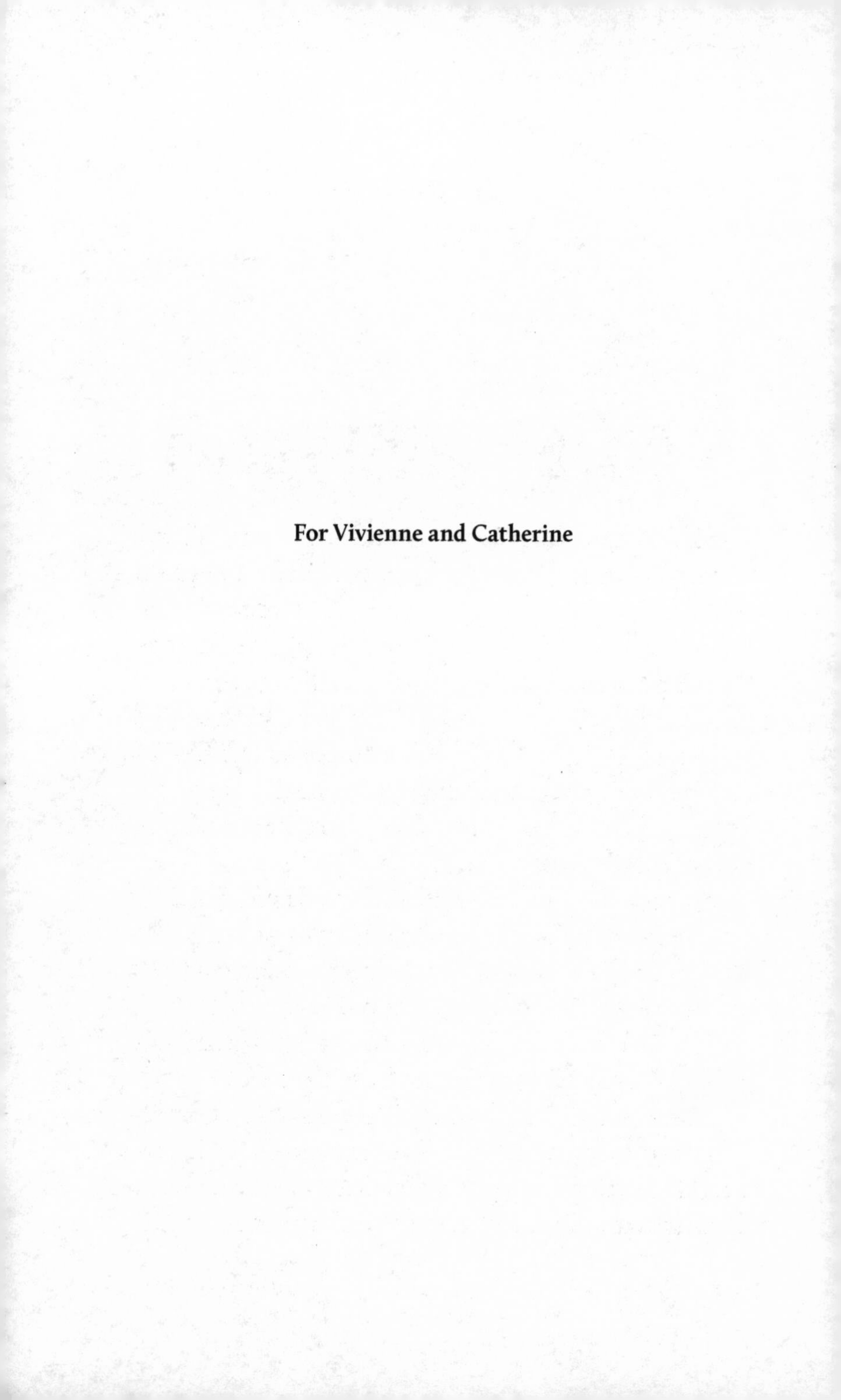

For Vivienne and Catherine

ONE

PEOPLE THINK I'VE HAD a stroke. They say, "That's what happens when you work too hard." I've given up convincing them otherwise. I don't deny I used to work too hard. Even the doctor suggested that as a possible factor in the palsy. Years of unpredictable days and long hours had to have some kind of negative effect on my body. But I don't like the idea of some slaps using my condition to justify their low work ethics. The ones that say, "Look at Simeon. See what this job'll do to you?"

I check the progress on the left side of my face. I still can't blink my left eye and have to wear a patch when I sleep because it won't stay shut. How odd to dream with one eye open, like having one foot in reality. That's what makes dreaming dangerous and why I moved my gun farther from the bed.

I wear sunglasses whenever I'm outside, even when the day is darkened with overcast clouds. This protects me from foreign objects that might find their way into my unprotected eye. I've also grown a goatee.

It conceals the part of my lip that droops because of the paralysis.

I do not follow the doctor's orders to massage the muscles of my face to quicken the healing process. Instead, I raise my brow a couple of times, force a half Joker smile, wink and brush my teeth.

My officials gave me a choice—limited duty and answering phones at the Fifth District detectives' office or burn more sick leave and hope for a quick recovery.

Limited duty. That would be like chasing the wind for the remainder of my career. It can easily turn into purgatory for the working cop. Once that paperwork is stamped by the police clinic you'll find yourself climbing the walls and moving closer to hell than heaven. Fortunately for me, I still have a few friends in high places and I'm not ashamed to admit I used them, made a couple of calls. That's how I was detailed to Cold Case.

It's not a bad gig. There's little to no supervision and just a handful of detectives, mostly old-timers. I'm the only detailed detective.

It's supposed to be a time for me to regenerate, to heal a body beaten down by fourteen years of hard work, barking victims, thugs, officials and a pager that triggers migraines.

After I wash away all the toothpaste pasted on my goatee, I turn on the news and drink two cups of coffee with a straw. I drink everything with a straw so most of what I try to swallow won't dribble down my chin. Today's news is the never-ending conflict in the Middle East, potential terrorism on the home front, the newest line of unsafe toys and the body of a woman found murdered along the Anacostia River late last night. I wait for the weather, and then turn off the anxiety channel.

The winter wind snaps my face and my eye stings and quickly tears. The sunglasses hardly help at all. I decide that today I'll stay in the office—a beautiful day, though. The heavy wind has cleaned the sky and the trees and allows the sun its full strength. But even that's not enough to cut the wind chill. I'm a block out and my cheeks and the tips of my ears feel like they're being slowly sanded off with fine grain.

Winter.

My favorite time of year.

Down the long Dupont escalator and into the depths of mass transit. Soon I'm sitting next to an overweight suit with uneven sideburns. Three stops to Judiciary Square, where I badge my way through the exit. The wind sands away my ears again for the short walk from the escalator to Headquarters. I see a couple of familiar faces and show recognition with a nod.

I enter the code to gain access into the secured area of the third floor that houses Cold Case, Intel, Sex Crimes and a few other specialized units. Once anyone could pass through these doors, until a man walked in armed with a Tech-nine and a vengeful heart, taking out two FBI agents and the Detective

Sergeant this building's named after. You'd think, given the work done on this floor, someone would've anticipated such a thing. Shame, how we're sometimes forced to learn.

In the office I replace the old battery on my handheld for a fresh one. I hook the radio on the left side of my belt behind my clips. I don't know why I do this anymore. I rarely use the radio. Force of habit based on a conditioned sense of security. I hang my suit coat on the back of the chair at the desk. There's no one here to pass the time with. Most of the guys are on committed "use or lose" leave through the holidays. It's just me sitting in this paint-peeled, water-stained office with the day already weighing heavy as a tight blanket over restless legs.

I LOG INTO THE computer, check my e-mail, then sit back and work up enough courage to pick up a case coffin. Most of them are the usual drug-related shootings, the bodies found by members of district patrol then transported by DC Fire Department Ambulance to the nearest hospital where they're pronounced. No witnesses. No usable evidence. The case I pick up reads like a typical Death Report:

> *The scene of the death is Howard University Hospital. The scene of the shooting is at the intersection of 7th and O Streets, Northwest, where the body was found by members of the Third District, fallen face down on the*

southeast corner and suffering from what appears to be multiple gunshot wounds to the chest and head area. The scene was processed by Mobile Crime. 9mm spent casings were recovered along the street toward the southwest corner of the intersection of 7th and O Streets, Northwest, by Mobile Crime. One live expended round was recovered in the gutter area of that same corner.

Detectives John Scanns and Robert Smitt responded to Howard University Hospital to view the body. The body was observed wrapped in a white plastic bag tied at the feet, laying on a hospital gurney. Inside the plastic bag the victim was observed nude with entry wounds to his mouth, left eye, chest and abdomen area. The eyes were fixed and dilated and the body warm to the touch. The victim had a small bruise just below the neck on the left side of the shoulder. The victim had a plastic tube in his mouth.

A Death Report's no literary masterpiece of criminal observation. The subsequent investigative reports are just as vague and unhelpful. What can I do with this case? Nothing, so I slip it back in a box and move on to the next case.

These are my days and how I fill them. I don't have long here, so what's the sense in getting wrapped up in something I can't finish? I'll be back to robbery soon enough and picking up about forty cases a month. Details don't last. I hope command will forget about me, like the dead files I've been burying myself in—decedents who'll never find rest. Row after row, stack after stack, dead and buried in their case jackets; on the floor, in drawers, closets, the bathroom, and if you sit too long—on you.

And that's what happens when I find another one resting on my lap.

I open it.

"I know this kid," I mumble while looking at the death photo. It happened a couple of months prior to the Death Report I just read.

Dante Grimes.

Just like that, right on my lap.

"Dante Grimes," I repeat aloud. Why didn't I hear about this one? It was almost two years ago and in my district. I go back with this guy.

I hadn't seen his face in years. It hits me, something like a sinking heart, but not a feeling that comes with grief. More like failure. I worked plainclothes back then, had a softer heart, something I carried over from my public school days before this place. I had not spent enough time on the job to have the soft parts rubbed out.

I always called him Grim because he never smiled, even when he was happy. I knew when he was happy. Those were the days I gave him a break, let him walk, not for information passed my way. Grim wasn't a Snitch. And I never expected anything like that from him. I just let him walk, petty crimes like smoking blunt, tossing dice or an open container. An arrest would only have been enough to disrupt his day, nothing more. Grinding his blunt or the zip of weed into pavement was punishment enough. He wasn't so stupid to ever hold what he was known for selling, which was mostly weed. He always had a stash somewhere else or a crack head to hold for him. What I liked about Grim was the respect he gave me and my partners. It didn't hurt that I knew him before he could talk. I had a job to do and nothing more. Grim knew that.

"You get me good one day Sim and I ain't gonna fight ya. Hell, I won't even run," he would laugh.

The area he worked was my beat while in uniform and a neighborhood I grew to care for and pain over. I spent most of my days in plainclothes there. I got to know most of the players and most of their clientele. That's where I honed my skills, learned how to talk to people. I knew a lot of mothers too and a lot of kids like Grim who used to walk and talk like little kids should. I watched most of them grow, some not. They all learned how to walk like Grim and all the other big boys who trailed behind him who were slinging dope on the corner every day. And talking to most of them, they all knew their time was short. Even the somewhat decent mothers knew it was bound to happen.

It paid the rent. It bought the food. It never lasts.

Dante's boys called him Black, a common street

name, but one that fit him. He was dark as polished coal.

I continue reading.

It was a drive by. 1500 hours, on a Sunday. A black four door sedan with tinted out windows and unknown temporary tags was the only look out. Unknown how many occupants. New York Avenue is a busy street every day of the week, and not one witness stepped up. They didn't even get a partial on the temporary tag from the shooter's car. The front passenger side window opened and an arm stretched out. Grim was tossing around a football with a group of young kids, at a place on the corner the District called a park. Shots rang out. Two little boys hit, but not critical. Grim three times, the last shot knocked him off his feet, ball in hand. He died on the scene like a pro.

Not much to work with here either, except for the boys I know he used to hang with, if they're still alive and willing. I'll run with this one. Doesn't matter to me that there's nothing to work with. I liked Grim.

This is the season of hope after all.

Winter.

My favorite time of the year. Oh, yeah.

And so it goes. And so I go when the clock finally makes its way to 6 p.m.

Time passes too quickly outside of work.

A COMFORTABLE CLUTTER OCCUPIES the rooms of my two bedroom apartment, all memories that have been recently placed with calculated effort to recapture an otherwise lost civilization. I am settled here. I find solace in the room I have made my office, shelves of books beside books upon books, boxes of framed accomplishments on the floor, Pez dispensers, papers, notes, odd trinkets and mementos—a subterfuge, a sanctum, a museum, and a place where I can safely face the rising spirits.

I turn on the anxiety channel, mostly for the weather, which will determine what I wear the next day. More war stories, but this time a report follows of anti-war protestors clashing with Capitol Police. *Violent acts for the sake of peace.* Then there's a little more on the woman who was murdered. An "inside source" at the Police Department this time, and now they have more information. She lived in the Adam's Morgan area, but her body was discovered at an undisclosed location along the Anacostia. She was an escort, which means she charged $490 more than a street whore. *That's a case that'll never go cold.* In my career I know of a hundred murdered prostitutes, but none who lived in that neighborhood full of organized community associations, whose biggest concern is cops parking in front of fire hydrants and being able to walk their dogs without leashes. Now they have a murdered neighbor. I'd hate to be the detective on that one.

After a couple of hours I ready myself for bed. Sleep is a painful process. It is not something I look forward to. I have to sleep on top of the covers with a thin blanket draped over me or I feel like a body wrapped in an ace bandage, stuffed in a coffin. It is a condition my doctor suggested is stress-related, but I blame it on a cheap mattress.

4:30 a.m.

The gusting wind sounds like it's racing through a thin tube outside my window. Left side of my jaw's throbbing. Despite the darkness, my hand finds its way to the container of prescription ibuprofen on the nightstand and the glass of water with a straw. Sleep has fled me once again and so I find escape in that tube, riding on the whisk of wind.

Daylight eventually seeps through the pulled blinds and my routine with it. Down the long Dupont escalator once again and into the depths of mass transit. I step into the train to standing room only, wedged between sweet migraine perfume and a man with a thin paisley tie and a few missed whiskers under his chin. The skin on the left side of my face feels like a tight shoe. I look down, conscious of my appearance, until the train eases to a stop at Judiciary Square. I get to the office, have my coffee and muffin and after go and find myself a cruiser.

NOT MUCH HAS CHANGED along North Capitol Avenue between P Street and New York Avenue. They still call it The Pharmacy. Old timers, drug thugs, boosters and the walking dead clutter corners, making obvious hand to hand transactions—heroin, crack, weed and every pill on the market from Oxy to

Viagra. It's an area the city wants to desperately consider up and coming. To discerning eyes, it is far from that.

Grim used to live in the large housing complex on New York Avenue and North Capitol. As a plain clothes officer, this was the hot spot. We were called "jump out" because that was about all we could get away with doing back then—driving to the corners fast and jumping out, stopping everyone in our path. It was as if the landscape was designed to prevent the detection of criminal activity. Surveillance locations were next to impossible. They had lookouts on bikes and old addicts on corners with binoculars. There was virtually no place to set up and everyone was so well known and established that introducing an undercover was difficult, but not impossible. We did have our moments of glory.

This was Grim's territory. It was good land. Something worth holding on to. He held on for twenty-two years and I include his birth.

I pull the cruiser up to North Capitol and Hanover Place. It's not something I'm supposed to be doing because even though I am not considered limited duty, I am unofficially on "non-contact." I don't really know what that means other than maybe not being allowed to touch bad guys harder than a friendly tap. It does not take long for me to be recognized. The ones that are stupid and dirty scatter like frightened squirrels. The ones who don't have the need to feed hold their ground.

Familiar faces don't stray too far from comfortable territory. I see a fat fingered old timer sitting on a milk crate.

"I remember you, old man. You lost some weight," I lie.

"I remember you, jump out man. You been missin' for a minute." He notices my face and figures he doesn't have to ask why I've been missin'.

"I got promoted to detective, reassigned."

"Jump out, you ain't got your boys to back you up."

"True," I tell him. "It's not like I need back-up when I'm here to help out, right?"

He turns slightly and spits gelatin-like milky saliva that sticks to the wall behind him like glue. That usually pisses me off. It's rude. That's why they do it.

"Black's murder," I tell him.

"I know three Blacks that'd been murdered," fat fingers tells me.

"You know which one I'm talking about. Dante. He's the only one I knew that goes by Black on this corner."

"Dante. That name supposed to mean something?"

"Only if you care. And don't play me. You know I wasn't about that. Looks like you still got the same crate from years back, and I never tried to kick that out from under you."

He lifts a brown paper bag, takes a drink from a bottle tucked inside, testing me. It's a fifth of something hard. Spitting bothers me more.

"They came looking into that a long time ago, a

couple of detectives, and they got nowhere. Why you want to try?"

"I got different interests. I liked Dante. I knew him since he was born."

"Yeah," he says and his eyes move up as if directing me to the front of the liquor store at New York and North Capitol.

I back turn away from him like I want to look at my car and notice a group of young ones huddled like they're ready to call a big play. One of them has a familiar face.

"That boy over there wearing the Avery jacket, what do they call him?" I ask.

All I get is a slight shrug.

I walk toward the corner. They don't scatter so I know they're not holding or they just don't care.

"I know you," I say to the kid wearing the Avery.

His boys slowly move away as if telepathically directed to do so. They stay close to their boy, though. I position myself so I have an angle on them as they watch me talking to him.

"I know you, too. You're officer Sim," the kid says.

"I'm a detective now, but yeah, I was an officer here a while back. You would've been pretty young back then. How do you know me?"

"Hard not to know you, and all your jump out boys the way you used to tear this corner up. It's been peaceful since you been gone."

"No other jump outs ever come around anymore?"

"Naw, man, just some uniforms every once in a

while."

"Like I said, you would've been pretty young, what, seven, eight years old?"

"Somethin' like that. Black was my brother. You used to buy me sodas. You was all right for a cop."

Dante's brother. I smile. "I knew you looked familiar. I work homicide now. I just learned about his murder. I was looking through some unsolved cases, and was sorry to find one on Dante."

He nods upward. He is dark skinned, but not as dark as his brother. He has short dreads and twists the ones behind his right ear. His tennis shoes are expensive, whatever the latest wear is. Not like his brother. Grim wouldn't draw attention like that and he would have bought those shoes for one of the neighborhood kids rather than for himself. Robin Grim Hood.

"I used to call him Grim. What do they call you?"

"I like Grim," he says not willing to give me his first name. Doesn't matter. It'd be easy enough for me to find. I know his last name and where he lives.

"Grim Junior, then" I counter.

"Naw man. I ain't no junior."

"No, you're no junior. Your brother used to call me Sim. How's your mother, you all still stay at the complex over there?" I motion across the street with my head.

"Yeah. She's fine."

"Grim, I'm looking into who killed Dante. I want to be the one to take him."

"He been dead for a bit. Why you want to do that now?"

"I got a special interest."

"Yeah."

"Yeah, I liked your brother. He was smarter than all this. I didn't care much how he earned his money. I've seen him give back a lot of what he earned, mostly to some of these kids walking around here now looking like they're little big men."

He looks at me with dead eyes. "So you think you're gonna catch the guy, put your cuffs on him and be a hero in the community?"

"I could care less about being a hero, Grim. You work your corner and I work mine. Back then, part of this corner used to be mine. Maybe I could've had it all if I stuck around and didn't get myself promoted. Maybe I should've locked your brother up all those times and he'd still be alive right now."

Dead eyes.

"We know how to handle our own business. Your boys didn't do much of anything back then except ask foolish questions about nothin'."

"Maybe they just didn't ask the right questions," I tell him. "How do you handle your business, Grim?"

"'We take care of our own just like you cops do." He nods then walks slowly toward his boys.

That might be what *Law & Order* calls probable cause, but unfortunately not us. That's not even close to being circumstantial. He turns one last time, spits on the ground "7th and O, Sim. That was the business that got handled." He walks away.

I let him go and it doesn't take me more than a second to realize what he not so subtly admitted to. He's either really stupid or very sure of himself. Or both if it's possible.

I STOP BY THE coffee shop at the corner before I make my way to the office. I buy a medium coffee, black, and a cranberry muffin. Before I can leave, I run into Scanns. We survived the academy together, something that binds you throughout a career. I was the best man at his wedding, but we were closer before the burdens of work overwhelmed our lives. He's a good guy. Lanky, off-kilter sort, with a shaved round head and funny rectangular glasses with light blue rims. Made detective a couple of years after me. His suit is wrinkled and he has that glassy-eyed, thousand-mile stare that can only mean he's been working straight through, having caught a case. He tells me that I'm looking better, "Definite improvement, Sim," and "How's the detail?" Then it's my turn to inquire, and that's when I learn he caught the case involving the Adam's Morgan escort.

He moves in a little closer, as if to speak confidentially. "After she was strangled, a rolled up newspaper soaked in some kinda flammable liquid was inserted in her vagina and then set on fire. Not pretty."

I tell him that I reviewed a cold case a while ago involving a murdered crack head prostitute. I remember her name was Evelyn Jackson. It was among the first stack of cold cases I picked up. Happened about a year ago, her body discovered in a vacant row house in Northeast. The suspect used a rolled up newspaper. Similar MO.

Scanns says he's checked with one of his boys at sex branch, and according to him there've been some rapists who have done that sort of thing before—setting fire to the victim's vaginal area. Says that when a suspect does something like that it's not just an attempt to destroy DNA evidence, it's an indication of extreme hatred toward women. Not typical but not enough to suggest we've got some sort of serial killer out there. "You know there's no such beast in this city, anyway, right?" Scanns adds.

"Of course I do," I reply, then we knock knuckles. "Hey, you remember that scene you and Smitt were on quite a while back—the dude that was shot at 7th and O?"

"Yeah, that was a long time ago. Another drug related dead-end case."

"You didn't find any witnesses, no leads on the black sedan."

"*Nada*, brother. Why, you got something?"

I smile because I actually do have something. "No, I just read the report, that's all and I have to act like I'm doing something. Get some rest, or you'll end up looking like me."

"I got Grand Jury."

"I'll give you a call later," I say. "Let's try to get together."

He nods. "Like old times, buddy."

As I maneuver between pedestrians and oncoming traffic, I glance back to Scanns, still standing where I left him, his body not having caught up to his mind's signal to move.

A day of solitude and its diminishing moments once again before me. From the window beside my temporary desk I can see the old Mayor's building, and north on the next block, the U.S. Attorney's Office and then the FBI's Washington Field Office. My attention's deflected over the buildings beyond the police memorial, where I lose myself in the distant and dark clouds on the horizon. "It looks like snow," I whisper and half-smile at having said it aloud.

I start thinking about Dante and the 7th and O case. I could pursue it if I wanted, probably get one of Grim Junior's boys to roll over on the 7th and O shooting. Those guys aren't that difficult to work. We used to do it all the time when I was in robbery and to a certain extent when I worked plainclothes. Once they got rolling on each other we would spend the following days drafting affidavits and kicking down doors. Those were fun times. We made some good cases. This one might be fun, too. Just like the old days.

The afternoon is sudden, like the overcast sky, and so I go to Jack's Deli for a sandwich. It smells like snow now. I grab a tuna melt, medium coffee and a couple of straws to go. Tuna's an easy chew and easier to wash down with liquid. My left lower lip is still healing from the constant accidental biting. There's no muscle control on that side, and when I chew that portion of lip always finds its way between my teeth. A couple of chomps have almost gone clean through. I don't like the taste of my own blood on rye.

❄

BACK AT THE OFFICE, I find the case jacket involving the crack head I told Scanns about. I give it a second go-through while I eat.

The man that discovered the body was also a crack head and quickly ruled out as a suspect. Considering the amount of drugs and alcohol he put in his system over the years, he'd have been no more a rapist than a eunuch would. Doesn't mean he's not a killer, though. This one occurred over a year ago. No substantial evidence, or if there was, it never made its way into this jacket. ME's report does indicate that a swab of her interior anal area did reveal trace amount of apparent semen. Third degree burns inside vaginal area and around inner thighs. *Glad I wasn't at the autopsy.* Cause of death, asphyxia. Manner, manual strangulation with fractures of the Hyoid bone and Thyroid cartilage. Looks like the fire was postmortem. *That was kind of him.* Area canvassed for witnesses with negative results. No family. That is, no family that cared. A typical scenario. She was an independent. No pimp would have her. A five-dollar girl and too far gone to be worth anything more. Why would someone torch her down there unless it was to dispose of evidence? And then why would any guy in his right mind have unprotected sex, forced or not, with a dirty—more than likely HIV-infested—girl like her? Maybe he's already got AIDS and doesn't care. Maybe he did use a condom, did the rest for fun and the recovered semen belonged to some other John. Maybe it was a message from another pimp or a drug dealer. A lot of maybes here.

I soon find myself sitting on the bench at the Judiciary Square metro. The digital message board reads, "Delay on track." Shortly after, I see a couple of Metro detectives and a uniform, followed by Scanns and his squad making their way down the escalator and toward the tracks. *I don't think I'll be taking the train home.*

They walk into the tunnel and disappear into darkness. I head that way, because curiosity gets the best of me sometimes. I walk up, my badge already hanging on my neck. I nod to Scanns and a couple of the other guys I know and ask what they got—even though I already know there's going to be a body in there somewhere. I tag along.

A uniform transit officer leads us through the dimly lit tunnel, shining his department-issued stream light. The transit officer hops off the catwalk and climbs ladder stairs that lead into the first car. Power's off. The cars are deserted and the only available light that filters in is from an occasional low-watt bulb in the tunnel along the way. The light bounces off the gray walls diffusing existing color. Black-and-white world, like something out of *The*

Twilight Zone.

The last car is packed with uniform officers, fireboard, EMT and a couple district detectives. Salty Dog is one of the detectives. I don't know the other one. Looks like a rookie. Fresh Military haircut, clean shaven and wearing a name brand navy blue suit with a crisp white shirt. Then there's Salty Dog, wearing this '80s-style double-breasted gray suit with a wrinkled blue shirt and a tie with golf club patterns. He's been called Salty since I can remember. Why? I don't know. Its meaning would depend on what side of the fence you're on. He's worn and torn by the work he does, or rather by the work he once did. Maybe that means something. Now, he's worthless, doing his time with as little effort as possible until his longevity kicks in, then he'll burn whatever leave he's got and live on his eighty percent. Salty has a way of staying with you, like some character out of Dickens but not as likeable. He's always been the butt of someone's joke or the lead in some great story. He greets us with, "Looks like an industrial accident, but then you guys're the experts." He looks at me and asks with no great concern, "You had a seizure or somethin'?" I tell him no and give him the condensed version. "Oh," is his only reply. He walks toward the end of the car, "Right out there, can't miss it. I'd recommend going out the sidecar to the catwalk, though. Better vantage and less to accidentally step in."

I allow Scanns and his guys the lead. It's their

scene. I get that old achy feeling deep in my gut that comes from unwanted expectations, the mind preparing itself for an unnatural image. It's something that instructors at the academy say you get used to. You don't. At least I haven't.

The body's between a train track and the catwalk that curves and extends along the metro tunnel between stations. His legs are stretched wide apart and his torso is bowed between the spread limbs, like some awkward gymnast's pose. The face is kissing the deep red blood that paints the cement from between his legs to the gutter about two feet from the tracks. Two flaps of skin on the head fold away from each other, starting from the bridge of the nose to the nape of the neck, like little dorsal fins. The brain sits about twenty feet from the fallen body, perfectly intact: a large silky larva prematurely expelled from its cocoon. The gap between the two flaps of skin on the head is a dark void. Life also expelled. The blue overalls and orange visibility vest suggest that he was a metro rail worker.

"The driver's at the clinic taking a piss test," Salty announces from the catwalk. He'd never chance messing up his twenty-year-old suit by following.

"One cf your guys with him?" a detective in the squad asks.

"No, just Metro detectives," Salty replies.

"You notify the ME?"

"Yeah. On the way."

Some of the detectives, including Scanns, pull

on their latex gloves. Two Mobile crime officers are in the near distance, canvassing for body parts and possible evidence. Each one knows what he has to do. Evenings always catch the cases. That's why they rotate every two weeks. These guys look tired. Especially Scanns. I won't talk to him about looking through that cold case involving the crack head. Definitely not a good time. He glances my way, and I know he wonders why I'm not home. He'd be, if given the chance. He bends beside the body, stares into it like he has x-ray vision. A body and mind rendered insensible by exhaustion. I decide to leave, having no desire to get caught up if this turns into something other than an accidental.

Salty greets me as I enter the train. "Looks like his head took a big albino crap, don't it? Like some kinda alien, huh?" I force a smile and tell him I got a long walk home.

So I walk 5th Street to H and head west through Chinatown. I used to make time for long walks, as important as a balanced diet and a good book. But those things don't play much of a role in this life anymore. I feel like this neighborhood—afflicted with dilapidated, vacant row homes and thriving Asian-owned liquor stores. The streets are dark for lack of working lamps. But the liquor stores shine through like beacons. The wind must like the space outside my bedroom window. It does not pass any other window except this one, and only at night when I lay my head against the pillow. I will not say aloud that it's a comforting sound for fear that the wind might find someone else's window to pass. I lose myself again in its lullaby and move into that pause of time just before the fall. And when I do, I find myself in a dream.

EEEE! EEEE! EEEE! I snap up and feel like my brain has slammed into the back of my skull. "Where am I?" I whisper. EEEE! EEEE! EEEE! The awful noise keeps on, and I realize it's my pager. I grope for it on the nightstand, push the button, stop the pain. The clock on the nightstand reads 6:04 a.m. Hours have passed me by.

The message on the pager reads:

CALL FIFTH DISTRICT DETECTIVES OFFICE ASAP!

It takes me a couple of minutes to shake away the dream before I call. When I do, an old 5D buddy, Detective Ronnie Scott, tells me that Scanns is dead.

THE POLICE DEPARTMENT DOES not consider it Line of Duty and so he'll have a quiet funeral—family and close friends. In the end it doesn't really matter how hard you work, even if that hard work causes your death.

In the end all Scanns will be remembered for is where and how he died.

After his squad caught the accidental at Metro, Scanns wrote up the death report and then advised his partner to hit him on the pager if something came up. He was tired and needed a little nap. Instead of going home to his wife and kids, he went to the apartment of a girlfriend. He took a nap on the sofa and never woke up. His girlfriend found him there a couple of hours later after she returned from the grocery store. The doctor said he had a clogged artery and it was a miracle he survived as long as he did. Once they opened him up they realized the portion of his heart the clogged artery once fed was now dark and useless. He was only thirty-eight years old. None of us saw it coming. Even when I last saw him and he had that glassy-eyed stare, I never would have recognized it as the look of death. I've seen that enough times to know, but never on a friend.

He was married with two boys—Bobby, eight, and Michael, eleven. I always thought he had a good marriage; never knew he kept that girl on the side.

Even though we had lost touch with one another for a while, I always considered him one of my closest friends on the department. It's like Clem, my one girlfriend in California. We could lose touch, and when we did finally get together it would be like old times.

Clem and I go back to my freshman year at UCLA. "Literature into Film"—a class that met every Wednesday afternoon for three hours.

The moment Clem and I met, we were meant for friendship, at least that is what I convinced myself and so we were spared those awkward moments that came from forward attempts. I was smart enough then, even in youth, to realize the difference between a look of admiration and possibilities and the friendly arm-in-arm of a wonderful female companion. I am not saying that is what I would have chosen, but that is where it led and where it stayed. There were awkward moments, but she would never realize them. At least I hope she wouldn't.

Even setting that aside, Clem's mind was fixed on a goal. There was never anything else for her to consider, especially getting involved with anything or anyone that might hinder her destination. That meant me or any other guy for that matter. She is a great friend, though, the only friend that stayed with me through the hard times back in Los Angeles, long before this job. Clem filled that part of my life that was taken when Priscilla and I divorced. Priscilla, my first love. We married young. She was the first for most everything in my young adult life, including the first and only girl I was ever destroyed by. I never gave anyone else a chance after her.

Clem fulfilled her goal and still lives in that self-condemned land of unsightly highways, perpetual traffic and endless construction. I do not miss that un-natural place and its lack of seasons. I need the divisions of the year and a changing climate. I need the pockets of communities and the history that exists within an unyielding design of grids and circles. Clem, on the other hand, is forever trapped within the wake of some Hollywood feeding frenzy. She's VP of development for a major studio and speaks a language I have long forgotten, but I still call her friend.

Scanns was like that. He was my east coast Clem,

but without those initial awkward moments. He sat behind me in class at the Academy along with this other buddy of ours, Adam Rucker. Scanns was a goofy sort with a likeably obnoxious charm, to a point, who was well known for those funny rectangular glasses that didn't belong on such a round head. The three of us got lucky, and after graduation were assigned to the Fifth District in Patrol. After about three years in patrol, Scanns put in for homicide and was reassigned. I was eventually assigned to the Fifth District Detectives Office. Rucker stuck it out in patrol, and after a few years made Sergeant, then up the ranks to Captain. When they eventually announced new vacancies at homicide, I put in for it but wasn't accepted. Later found out my application never made it past my immediate command. Made them look too good where I was. That's what was said. At least that's what I'd like to believe. Point is, Scanns got caught up in his thing, and I in mine. We lost touch, aside from the birth of his boys, the subsequent congratulatory calls and the frequent run-ins at court.

He met Celeste, his wife, in an after hours club. Not a place you'd think to meet the future mother of your children, but they fell for one another, nevertheless. He wooed her with that obnoxious boyish charm. And then they married. Poor Celeste. She'll never know where he was found. Those of us who do know have promised to keep the secret. Maybe she already knew about the girl on the side, but maybe not. Regardless, she didn't have to know about the place where his eyes closed for the last time. Why burden her with such an image. Let the life rest in chosen memories. I will.

Celeste is sitting in a pew a couple of rows in front of me, her arms gently wrapped around Bobby and Michael, holding them against her on each side. Her parents and other family members sit beside them. It's a small, modest Presbyterian Church in Alexandria, Virginia. A sizable wooden cross is centered on the wall behind the pulpit. White candles with curiously still flames line the edge of the stage. Large, colorful floral arrangements rise above in back, and at the head of his closed casket on the floor, which is centered between the two sets of steps that lead up to the stage. I'm wedged between older people, maybe distant relatives. My tender sinus membranes tingle at the sharp commingling scent of pine and roses.

Despite the funeral's lack of all the customary trimmings that come with a traditional police ceremony, it is still crowded with family, friends, and officers dressed in their Class A uniforms., everyone huddled together according to their tribe. I recognize a few of the officers and detectives from the Fifth District, and some of the guys from VCU. I'm also surprised to see a few high-ranking officials, dressed discreetly in dark suits, squeezed together in a corner pew, near a back exit door.

Scanns should have been allowed a Performance of Duty ceremony. As hard as it is looking at Celeste sitting there with the boys seemingly clueless, the department should have overlooked where he was found. They can't, of course. I even know that. But I'm concerned for her wellbeing, not theirs. The department's motives are different. "On-duty homicide detective found dead at the apartment of his mistress." With all the murders going on in this city, that kind of media attention is the last thing VCU needs. Every official at VCU will find a teletype with their name on it, reassigned to places like ID and Records, or Cellblock. What is Celeste thinking right now? What did that cluster of suits sitting in the back tell her, to relieve them of the duty of giving Scanns a proper police send-off? Johnny wasn't a slap. He was a hard working detective. Did the job suck the life out of his heart, or was he dead before he started, a condition one of his parents passed on to him. I'm only a year older than him. I need to get a physical. I've been to too many funerals on this job. I've known a few of them, but not like Scanns. It's an unfamiliar feeling I have, knowing his dead body is in that closed casket a few feet away. Knowing the person that once occupied the body makes a difference.

The Pastor is on the stage behind a podium above his casket, reading a passage out of a large Bible. I feel mentally off balance, and the words are lost to me. Other people begin to line up and stand single-file below the steps on the right, to follow one after another and share other passages, or some infamous Johnny Scanns story. I was asked, but respectfully declined. I certainly have stories, but nothing I want to share.

❄

IT'S STRANGE HOW SILENT this evening is. The city is quiet for lack of sirens, horns, loud people and the sound of their bottles breaking in nearby dumpsters. I hate funerals. I've never understood the custom of viewing the dead. Cremate my human remains and if there's a need for any ritual just keep the ashes in a clean pickle jar on a shelf beside your favorite book. I won't have anyone charged with such a burden as arranging burial. You can count on that.

I haven't moved from this couch since I got back from the funeral. That was about four hours ago. I feel the loss but not the pain. The dead grieving the dead. That's how I feel and why I will sit here, all night if I have to, in an effort to find real tears.

'A weary lot is thine.' Yes. It surely is.

TWO

LIEUTENANT HATTIE'S IN CHARGE of a couple of the squads at homicide—including the one Scanns was on. He's a likeable guy with a decent reputation. I've got more time on than him but won't hold that against him. A lot of these guys are going up the chain too fast, not spending enough time in patrol, but Hattie, he did about five years on the streets at the Seventh District before making Sergeant. And doing time there is like in dog years. He was assigned to my district as a Sergeant, in patrol. Did about two years there then made Lieutenant and a little over a year later, got assigned to homicide. No real detective experience but a good administrator with a lot of time to go before retirement. Company "yes" man all the way. That's what the big boys are looking for, someone young, eager and like silly putty in their god-hands. It's the detectives and a few of the sergeants who do the real work, anyway. Guys like Hattie, well, they just have to know how to swim with the big fish—choose the right words, and make nice colorful charts.

His suit looks like he pulled it right off the rack at JC Penney, like that rookie I saw at the accidental at Metro. Heavy starch on the porcelain shirt. The skin on the back of my neck tingles just looking at it. He needs to get that thing tailored is what I think. He's a top-heavy guy like he lifts weights but doesn't work the legs. When he walks he gives the impression he's about to fall on his face. He shuts the door behind him, looks around the office, and I assume the smile is the result of all the vacant desks and lack of bustling activity before him.

"They got you running this whole place now, Detective Simeon?" He asks, not expecting an answer. "You're looking better."

"A little better, thanks. How're you doing?"

"Good." He walks to the window ahead of my desk, looks out as if for effect. "I'm sorry about Scanns. I know you guys were buddies. I wish I could've made it to the funeral." He sits on the window ledge. His neck tightens, stretches further out the stiff collar. "You know how it is."

A pause, and I wonder if he expects an answer.

"So what's up, Lieutenant?"

"You know things are changing since homicide's been re-centralized?"

Again, does he expect an answer? I choose no.

"My understanding is you put in for it some time ago but they wouldn't let you go. Not enough manpower where you were or some story like that, right?"

"Something like that."

"Your officials have a lot of respect for you. Your closure rate can't be beat. Damn, you closed a lot of cases in my PSA back when I was Sergeant, and that was a while ago."

"Closure rate's gone down since my detail here."

"How do you like working Cold Case?"

"It's a break."

"Well, you know one of the changes at VCU is McDermott's gone and Rucker's in."

"Rucker's commanding homicide now?"

"Yes."

"Where'd they send McDermott?"

"Promoted him to Commander. He's at the First District."

"Who took Rucker's old spot?"

"I don't know about that one. But you know with the way things are set up at OSD now, they can pretty much do what they want. At the blink of an eye we're re-assigned. Same goes with detectives."

"Is this where you ask me or tell me I'm being transferred?"

"Neither, it's already a done deal. They're calling it a detail for now, but you know how that is. I was just in the neighborhood and thought I'd give you the good news before the teletype hits."

Good news? I think and then say, "So I don't have a choice?"

"Everyone has a choice, and if you choose to fight it, it'll be from a desk at VCU. Listen, I know this isn't how you wanted to get there."

"That's an understatement. You want me to take his desk and family photos, too?"

"No need to be so morbid, detective Simeon." He stands. "If Captain Rucker hadn't of come in you probably wouldn't have been the choice. Someone else would be getting it. Someone else would have brought one of their boys in. At least Rucker knows you're about work and so does everyone else. He wants you to take over Scanns' case load. My guys are too overwhelmed with what they already have. So far, the way the bodies have been coming, we're going to take the 'Murder Capital' title again this year."

"Lieutenant, with all due respect, I put in for Homicide a few years ago, and they never let me go. I like it where I am now. If I can't stay at Cold Case, then I'd rather go back to Robbery. You can find a hundred detectives who'd jump at your offer."

"I understand the circumstances are rough, but Rucker wants you, and he outranks me. I'm not going to stand here and argue the point. If you want, go through your chain of command. So, unless I get a memo stating otherwise, you've just been notified."

"When am I going?"

"Effective next pay period. Sunday."

"What about the cases I'm working here."

"Someone will take care of it. They're Cold Cases," he says almost too calmly. "Take leave for the rest of the week if you want. Report to me 0600. Copy?"

"Sir," is my acknowledgement, but not what I really

want to say. He's a man of orders and set rules. He walks out different than when he walked in, this time like a shy man in a crowded room. I've got that kind of effect on some people. I've got enough sense than to try to fight this. I know how this department works. The last thing you want to be known for is a whiner.

The last thing I do before I pack up and leave is pick up the 7th and O Streets case jacket and mull it over for a bit. It's a closed case and no one on the department will ever know about it. I know Grim Junior and his boys were behind it. Street justice. It's not a murder that is likely to warrant any attention and suddenly reappear as a blip on one of those big screens in Operations Command. Odd as it is, I actually like that feeling. I have a good lead based on a solid statement made by his brother, but I'm not going to pursue it. Why? Because I can, and I'm pissed off. I also sort of like the brother, Grim Junior. Let him have his little corner. Just like all the big and little thugs on all the corners throughout this fine city, their lifespan is short. Hopefully, he'll last a little longer than Dante did.

I TAKE FOUR DAYS off, including my regular Saturday before I have to report in. This detail had me with weekends off, so now I lose Sunday. I'll be low man on the totem pole at VCU—even if I do have more time on than a lot of the guys there—so that means I'll probably get stuck with Sunday, Monday and Tuesday as my days. Doesn't really make a difference: Sunday, Monday, Tuesday—Thursday, Friday, Saturday. It's all the same. Four-day weeks, ten-hour days, with three days off. That might not be so bad. They got those guys rotating all three shifts, though, and I hate midnights. It'll be like the walking dead for me after three months of that. Not true. I'm already like the walking dead. How much worse can it get? Shouldn't say that. It can get a lot worse. Breathing is what keeps it from getting real bad.

❄

REST AND A LIGHT work schedule haven't really helped my face or this haze that's been clouding my mind lately. I droop less and think less, but that's about it. I resolve to read, rest and not watch the news for the four days I've got, maybe take a couple of walks and get back into the city I once loved to explore. I don't go out much anymore. It's my vanity. Looking in the mirror too much has made me self-conscious. I am the opposite of Narcissus, catching his glorious image in the clear, pool of water. So why do I still find myself drawn to the mirror, and the image I see reflected there? I certainly don't want to kiss it.

It does not take much before I fall back to my old self and start thinking about the job again, and it doesn't take long to realize the only reason I'm going to homicide is to be detailed long enough to put a dead friend's case load in order. And one of those cases already hit the news. Not something to look forward to.

Whatever feelings of intense disillusionments I've been having as of late, I've kept to myself. I start thinking about Rucker and Scanns. The three of us, we used to be pretty tight way back when. Rucker was the first to lose touch after he became a part of the "Big Boy Club." I was the first to say that it went to his head. I think that pissed him off. Now he's the "Man" at homicide and I'm finally going there, but I don't like how I'm going, and I'm not real sure I'd want to go, even if it were under different circumstances. I'd much rather find a place where I can disappear until retirement, like Cold Case. That's the place to be. But what can you do? Things never go the way you want them to. And Rucker, well he probably thinks he's doing me a favor.

So the first thing I do after convincing myself to accept things is to browse the shelves of books in my office for a good read. I pull one I've been meaning to read for about two years—a bio on Dickens by Chesterton. I found it at a used book store on P Street. It's not thick and looks like a quick read so I place it on the nightstand in the bedroom, near the clock so I won't forget to pick it up tonight while in bed. Then I put a patch over my bad eye, go to the sofa, pat down one of the pillows at the end and stretch across for a nap. I lift the patch just a little and slide the eyelid shut with my finger. I'm positioned with a view through the living room window. Puffy blue gray clouds have gathered. Before I know it the haze that shrouds my mind is like cement over my eyes and I'm gone.

I wake up to falling snow outside the window, coming down in wafers. It's already late afternoon, and my first day is near gone. They'll fly by. This I know. As hard as I've tried in the past, I can't prolong days off. I've resolved to take it easy today. Time can fly over my outstretched body if it wants to.

And that's what it does.

THE VIOLENT CRIME UNIT is located on Pennsylvania Avenue in Southeast, hidden behind what looks like a ghetto strip mall. *Only in* DC, I think as I drive across the parking lot and then roll to the back and see all the marked and unmarked cruisers parked in an open lot in front of an entrance that should house H&R Block, not Homicide. Money had to be the motivation behind this spot. It certainly wasn't discretion. Inside, there are long, clean, narrow hallways that lead to secured doors and a large room with several cubicles for the detectives. The cubicles are mansions compared to what we have to work in within the districts. Each one has its own computer and phone. Living large here. Back at 5D I had to share a computer with a detective who was on the same shift and mostly liked to play Mahjong. The phone's receiver was always slippery from the remains of too much hand lotion. These guys here got a pretty good setup for interviews—two small square rooms with clean walls and little cameras at a high angle positioned over rectangular tables with two chairs. The adjacent room has the recording equipment and 13" viewing monitors for the audience. We have rooms like this at most districts but none of the equipment works and most of the rooms smell like public bathrooms gone especially bad. We're talking years of vomit, blood, urine and who knows what else, soaked into those walls and carpets. Our cleaning crews won't even go in. Most of us carry our own cans of Lysol or scented candles but usually the prisoners are cuffed to a chair with wheels and rolled to a cubicle area for the interviews. I give this new building here five years before it starts crumbling away like all the other ones. But they'll probably have this place sold to H&R Block by then and send all the detectives back to the Districts as they've done a hundred times before.

I see Tommy Maynard and his partner, Yvonne forget-her-last-name, sitting at the second-row cubicle area. They're a couple of good detectives who made a name for themselves a few years back on a RICO case that closed a string of murders and put some Southeast boys away for life. They know most of the crews like the backs of their hands. Doesn't matter what quadrant they might be from. They know the players. When you need to put a face with a nickname you go to one of them. I've called them on more than one occasion. Most of my robbers were drug boys who needed a little extra Christmas money or had a little too much to smoke and needed to work it off with some adrenalin. They've helped me put a couple away. And so they welcome me with congratulations and a couple of handshakes, and I have to remind them it's just detail.

"You know how that is," Yvonne tells me.

"They're not gonna keep me here," I say. "Not real sure I want to stay anyway, the way I hear they been working you guys."

"You got that right," Tommy says.

Yvonne gets a concerned look on her face and asks, "Did you have a stroke?"

I give her the Bell's palsy spiel and she still looks at me the same way, like I'm making it up. I assure her that it's not like that and then talk a little about the seventh cranial nerve, but all she does is nod and smile. She has good skin, a rich olive complexion that makes her look younger than she really is. A sincere smile and I think I'd hate to be the one sitting across from her in one of those interview rooms. I'd give it up just to make her smile. Tommy's a detective first grade. It's common knowledge that he lives the job, and that's about all that's known about him. I don't even know if the two of them have a life outside the job. The cluttered desks they occupy suggest that they don't. Not even a hint of a life off-duty. They might be married to each other for all I know. They remind me of some good Hollywood couple that you never read about in the tabloids.

Scanns' desk is across from Tommy's. It's still cluttered with personal effects. A framed picture of his wife and boys leans against a stack of books. Two color-by-number drawings done by his boys are tacked against the cubicle wall over his desk. One is a man and a little boy fishing, and the other is what looks like it should've been a giraffe. The boys used every color in the spectrum and wrote "Love," then their names as best they could, on the bottom. Case files are stacked at the corner surrounded by Baltimore Orioles and Redskins plastic drinking cups. The computer screen still has the "Locked by WSCANNS" message on it.

"His wife hasn't been by yet," Tommy says. "We don't want to box anything up, either. That wouldn't be right."

"Yeah," is all I can say.

"They did a good job on him at the viewing," Tommy continues and then with an awkward smile, "He looked good."

"He's with the Lord," Yvonne says.

"Sometimes these morticians can make them look real puffy and sometimes miss some of the scars from the ME," Tommy says and looks down to a report on his desk.

"You got to do roll call here?" I ask.

"0600," Tommy tells me.

"It's the room down the hall to your right, but not for about twenty minutes," Yvonne says.

"I'm always early," I say and then, "Where's Hattie's office?"

"I'll show you," Yvonne smiles and leads the way. I shoulder my briefcase and follow. Tommy shoots me a nod.

❄

HATTIE'S ON HIS CELL phone when I appear at the open door of his little seven-by-nine whitewashed office. He motions me to take the seat against the wall in front of his desk. Yvonne winks and walks away. Hattie's talking about some triple shooting that occurred the other night in Northeast. I wouldn't know about it because I was faithful to the commitment I made to stay away from the anxiety channel. *The big boys get started early.* As I sit and listen to him, obviously talking to a superior because every other word's "sir," I realize that he reminds me of an up-and-coming film producer who has one hit behind his name. Unfortunately, he has about ten studio execs above him, and it sounds like he's dealing with one of them now. Based on his responses, it sounds like the latest release was a flop. And you know he's one of the young "make-a-difference" new bloods assigned to his seven-by-nine office in this H&R Block building. So why was there a triple shooting? And why do they keep getting killed in the district? You know we don't want that "Murder Capital" title again. It's got to be his fault. Who else are they going to blame? When a movie busts out the first weekend and the numbers don't look so good, you think the one at the other end of the line is kicking himself in the ass? I don't think so. The guy at the other end of the line is mentally kicking Hattie's right now, between all those "sirs" I've been hearing. It doesn't matter where you are.

Everything always rolls down hill. I almost feel bad for him, but only for a second. He rolls his eyes and does the "Yak yak yak" hand-puppet thing with his free hand. I gotta smile, but mostly out of politeness.

So this goes on for a while as I mentally twiddle my thumbs. It's about time for roll call when he ends the call—or rather when the party on the other line ends it.

"Welcome," Hattie smiles, quick to have brushed that mess off his shoulder.

I let out a nervous chuckle that sounds more like an involuntary release of trapped air. I've seen prisoners at debriefings do the same thing after they realized they've just screwed themselves with something they said.

"Roll call's at 2200 hours. We have a couple of minutes. I'm afraid you'll have to try to make do without a space of your own for a while. They're supposed to add some more cubicles in the next couple of weeks. In the meantime you can share a desk with someone who's on another shift."

"That's fine."

He grabs three case jackets sitting on the right side of his desk and hands them to me. One's getting pretty thick. The other two are light. "These were Scanns' open cases."

I look at the names on the lips of the jackets. The thick one has NOYES written in black permanent marker along with the "HO" number. Hattie says, "That one is going to need a lot of attention. The media is on it like bottom-feeders."

One of the thinner case jackets has the name, Tomlinson on it, and before I check out the other one Hattie continues, "The most important thing I want you to know and to follow is to write, write, and write some more. You knock on a door and no one's home, you put that in your notebook. I don't care how small the detail, I want it note-booked. Time and date everything. CYA. Got it. That's what will keep you alive here."

I nod. I'm anal about doing that now and don't need the rookie Lieutenant telling me. That's basic stuff but not so necessary on a lot of the cases you pick up at the district level. Here, the smallest thing'll come back to bite you, sometimes years later. I've seen it first hand, guys I've known whose names hit the papers after the littlest thing screwed up a major case. Next thing they know they're bogged down with domestic violence cases at the Seventh District. I should be more irritated having Hattie telling me this. Actually, I am a little but don't show it.

"I know I don't have to tell you all that," he says as though he read my mind. "I've checked your jacket and know you've been to all the advanced courses. We had to fight your officials just to get you detailed here. They were expecting you back at 5D. So are you feeling rested?"

"Yes."

"Good. I don't have the schedule worked out yet, so for now, you'll get Thursday, Friday and Saturday.

That good?"

"That'd be good."

"We'd better get to roll call."

He stands and scoots around the cramped space. I stand and allow him to pass, and then I follow as we walk to the roll call room.

After roll call's finished, Sergeant Barnes introduces himself as my squad supervisor. I don't know much about him, but he looks like another old timer. Real laid-back demeanor, an approachable type. I follow him to his desk in a room filled with other sergeants' desks. He leans on the edge of what I assume is his.

"It's too bad about Scanns," he says.

I agree.

"The only desk we have available right now is his. I know his wife hasn't come by yet..."

"I'll box his personals up for her," I interrupt. "So she doesn't have to deal with sorting through all that."

"That'd be nice," he tells me.

"After she picks his belongings up I won't have so much of a problem using his desk. All the files are there anyway."

"Two of you were in the academy together, right?"

"Yes, also the best man at his wedding, way back when."

"I didn't know that. So you were close."

"Fell out of touch, you know?"

"Happens, especially with this job. I hear you got a reputation for being the 5D robbery man."

"I've been trying to live that down recently."

"My cousin had Bell's Palsy," he tells me.

"Yeah?"

"Woke up one morning and thought he had a stroke."

"How long before he got better?"

"I think a couple of months."

"He's lucky. I'm well past that and only a little sign of improvement."

"I think he did some kind of massage therapy or needles stuck in him."

I nod like I'll look into that.

"I'll talk to him if you want," he offers.

"Sure."

"Listen, I'm going to pair you up with Paul Mather, just 'til you get settled. You know him?"

"Not really. Maybe by face."

"He'll help you get acclimated. Everyone's paired up here but they work their own cases and mostly we all work as a squad, at least initially. You know what I mean?"

I nod, then he says, "C'mon, I'll take you to Mather."

Mather has a nice private corner spot behind the detective's in-box with nothing but a wall behind his cubicle. Prime real estate. I recognize him from the metro death, walking in with Scanns. He looks mid-thirties, slim with a shaved head. He's focused intently on the computer's keyboard as he types, looking at the monitor once or twice. You can just barely make out a bald patch on that spot at the top of his head, where a lot of guys start to go. Looks like he forgot to shave his head and the patch is more apparent. If you put little rectangular glasses on him he'd pass for Scanns' brother. He's wearing a black V-neck sweater, like something from J Crew, olive green pleated slacks and expensive Patagonia hiking shoes. Looks like he does all his shopping in Georgetown. He's got several 4x6 color photographs of white sand beaches with crystal clear water, landscapes and cityscapes, pictures I'm sure he took himself to remind him of the spots he loves to get lost in. His desktop is strewn with "cop" memorabilia, tin paddy wagon, ceramic figure of "Officer Friendly," things like that. I don't see anything that would indicate a family. He looks up from the keyboard when we approach.

"Sarge," is his acknowledgement.

We're introduced. He stands to shake my hand and politely welcome me. Barnes advises him that he'll be working with me for a while and to get an extra key made for the cruiser that we'll be sharing. After Barnes leaves, Mather sits down again, saves his file using the mouse.

"You worked robbery in 5D, right?"

"Not for a few months. I've been detailed to Cold Case Review for a while."

"That's cush, man, retirement spot."

"Yes it is."

"It's not all that bad here. The books say ten-hour shifts, but as long as you stand by your pager and take care of your cases, you can go off and do what you got to do."

"I need some coffee, but not what they got around here." I say.

"I'll take a drive with you. Just let me finish up with a couple of things here first."

I tell him I'm going to go through some of these files the L T gave me and to come get me at Scanns' desk when he's ready. He throws me this weird grin that I think was meant to be a smile.

THE CASE JACKET I open is the Adam's Morgan Call Girl. Amy Noyes, *not a name that suits the profession*. Funny how life comes back to bite you sometimes. And I don't mean her. I'm talking about me taking over this case—when I said "I'd hate to be the guy who caught that case." And now here I am. I go through the pictures that were secured in an evidence envelope. Despite the petechial hemorrhaging on her face and both eyes and the bruising around her neck, my opinion, she was attractive in life.

Scanns' Initial Case Resumé reads:

> POLICE REPORT:
>
> *At approximately 0900 hours, members of Park Police were dispatched to assist Fire Board at a once accessible boat ramp located in Southeast,* DC *along the Anacostia River. The location does not carry an address (see MapQuest printout). Once on the*

scene, Ambulance Technicians, ROBERTS *and* SALAS *advised that there was a deceased female along the river's edge. The decedent, later identified as* AMY NOYES *was found nude on her back with her head slightly sunken in mud and her legs spread apart. According to the reporting officer,* DARIN REID, *of Park Police, discovered the body while on routine patrol.*

Upon inspection of the body, there appeared to be a contusion on the right upper cheek and around the neck; severe petechiae on the facial skin and both eyes; slight dried and caked blood mixed with mud on back of head due to blunt force; what appeared to be charred remains of rolled up paper inserted in vagina and apparent second and third degree burns around genital area with the presence of ash on upper thighs. The decedent was removed to the DCMEO *for the purpose of autopsy.*

Mather interrupts my read with, "You want me to come back?"

I close the jacket, "No. I'm good." I grab my overcoat draped over an adjoining cubicle's chair. "You mind if we make a stop at the decedent, Amy Noyes' apartment? I may as well jump right into this mess. I know this good spot for coffee near there."

"No problem."

I slide the three case jackets in my briefcase, snap it shut, then shoulder it.

On the way we make a quick stop at a "police friendly" locksmith located on the lower end of 3D. It's only a buck, so we get two copies made. I pay. It's the least I can do.

Back in the car and driving north on 9th, Mather says, "It's getting harder to avoid these potholes around here."

I smile my Joker half-smile instead of a reply. What's on my mind is Scanns' write-up. Pretty thorough is what I think. Most of the 854s I read don't come close to the kind of detail he had in his. I tend to write books, too. That's all right, as long as it's not a work of fiction. The more detail the better, just so you remember when you get to the stand. A year down the road if it ever goes to trial you're not going to remember half of what you saw or heard on the scene.

"So, is it true you were a Hollywood screenwriter before you were a cop?"

"No. Where'd you get that?"

"Captain told me you were getting detailed here, said you guys used to hang together. He mentioned it. Talked you up like some Hollywood star."

"He was pulling your leg. He knows I never wrote scripts. I taught high school English and lived in La La Land, that's all.

"High school teacher. Public or private?"

"Public."

"What made you want to come do something like this?"

"Wanted to be a cop since I was a kid, and I didn't want to get too old and not have given it a shot. 'Sides, there wasn't much to leave. It wasn't all that." I told him as I was not about to divulge the sordid details that actually led me here. I don't know him like that.

"You married?"

"Divorced," I say with hesitance—like shame. "What about you?" I recover quickly because he's trying to uncover those details.

"No, not in the foreseeable future, either."

"Married to the job, huh?"

"I do love this job, but it doesn't go to bed with me."

Good comeback. I want to tell him that it's only a matter of time before the job finds its way into his bed, but I don't. "You were partnered with Scanns, right?"

"Yes. He was a loner, though, didn't like to roll with anyone."

"How much time you got on?" I ask. "Going on nine years."

"When'd you make D2?"

"About four years ago. Got my shield at Youth."

"Hard place to get out of, Youth Division. Once you're there, they don't want to let you go."

"I know. I got lucky and put in for Homicide when the last announcement came. I begged my Commander to sign off on the 681."

"You got to be what—thirty?"

"Thirty-one."

"You have a ways to go. You plan on doing it all at

homicide?"

"I like it enough. You never know." He turns to me, "You know, I think that thing you got going with your face gives you character."

I blow air like a laugh.

"It just gives me more years than I want. Like I'm forty-two on one side, fifty on the other."

"Forty-five in the middle," Mather smiles.

"Hah! So you think I look older than I am on two sides then?"

"So you're forty-two?"

"Let's say forty. I like forty. It's a good age. It'll stay with me for a while"

"Fair enough. I'm okay with thirty."

"It's a good age," I tell him. We roll up 18th and find a parking place across from my coffee spot. Best coffee in the city, strong, but not thick and oily. Mather ordered a Latte and that's how I figure he's not a coffee drinker. I was raised on the dark brew, had my first cup when I was about ten. We decide to sit in the car, parked on 18th while I drink the coffee and he the coffee-related drink. It's Sunday and still early and not much going on. The air outside smells fresh, like something new. *Maybe snow.* Occasionally cars cruise by, mostly cabs and club-goers made zombies by the night's end. We're monitoring the 3D zone on the cruiser's radio. It's that time that brings with it a dead silence and what you hear is the eerie sound of filtered crackly air passing through broadcast space. Relief has already been called for midnights and they're probably well on their way home, like those zombie club-goers. *What a life.* But one I chose. This is why I can't stand day work or midnights. You have these spaces in time that push out too much thought. I sip the coffee, still burning hot. It stings the tip of my dry tongue. Mather slurps his Latte with an "ahhh" after each tilt. Too much of that kind of stuff and I'm going to be thinking I'm not really up for having a partner. But like the Sarge said, we each got our own cases to work. That means the other guy's there for back-up when you need him and the squad mostly for the first forty-eight hours after you pick up a case. I don't need much back-up going through a cleared crime scene in Adam's Morgan, though.

MATHER HANDS ME THE keys to the building's entrance and the apartment as if it were a diploma on graduation day. We take the stairs four flights up and then down a hall to 403. The dark gray residue of fingerprint dust covers most of the door's exterior and frame, with rectangular patches revealing true paint color where latent prints were peeled away with clear tape. Looks like Mobile Crime took their time here. The living room carpet's been pulled, more than likely trying to find evidence of blood or clean-up. That dark gray dust everywhere is like a home decorating show blunder.

"You see the crime scene report yet?" Mather asks.

"Not yet. Saw it in the jacket—looks thick."

"I went through it. About a hundred and fifty items

seized. They got a lot of DNA to work, both here and the primary scene, but then she probably had a lot of customers. My thought was she took one of them to that place at the river.

I look out a living room window. A couple of bundled-up people are walking their dogs in the park. "You know if she owned this place?" I ask.

"No. This area's expensive, though, whether you rent or own."

"If they only knew what we know, huh?"

Another "Ahhh," as he sips his latte. She did have to make some money to afford this place. A certain high profile congressman lived right across the street—not suggesting that increased property value, but it's a popular part of town for people on the Hill and young upwardly mobile types. Every one of them will make the victim list at one time or another. Unfortunate for this girl who made the ultimate one.

On the mantle surrounding the fake fireplace are framed pictures of her posing with friends, smiling big. She's in several pictures with the same girl—black female, light complexion; long thin face with high cheekbones. They all look like wannabe models made into strippers and escorts. The furniture's a combination of antique mix-match to Ikea contemporary with Pottery Barn accessories. This definitely looks like her spot and not a place she'd bring a John back to. Maybe that special someone, though.

The bedroom floor is wood, area carpets probably taken. The mattress is bare, looks comfortable. A few more framed photographs of the decedent and her friends. *No men or anyone that looks like family.* I don't worry about moving around or contaminating anything. The scene's already been worked. I open a couple of drawers knowing I won't find anything, but I do it anyway. Scanns was thorough. I've said this before. If anything was missed here, I'd be surprised. This is what I'm expected to do, though and that is why I'm here. Merely something to notebook and that's what I do:

> WALK-THROUGH OF SCENE CONDUCTED. DETECTIVE MATHER ALSO PRESENT. (GO THROUGH EVIDENCE REPORT.)

I look out the bedroom window to the pot-hole ridden alley and its overturned empty garbage cans, the trademark of a recent garbage collection. I turn back to Mather who is gazing at his image in an oval-shaped vanity mirror, nursing his Latte.

"I got to get a haircut," he says when he realizes I see him.

"I'm ready to get out of here," I say.

"You sure?"

"Yeah, I'll come back. I should go through some of the stuff back at the office."

"All right."

I drive the car back as Mather reclines in the passenger seat with one foot on the dash. The radio cackles and calls are dispatched. It's turning out to be a busy Sunday for members of the Third District.

I turn the radio to the City-Wide zone.

❄

SEVEN MORE HOURS TO go on this first day and I realize when I get home I'll probably have to take a nap and then end up staring at the ceiling when it's really time for bed. I find one of those paper boxes with a good cover and slide it under Scanns' desk. *I'm not going to do this now.* I log into the computer instead and change my location on the command box to get my profile moved to this terminal. After that, I open the other two case jackets for review. It's your typical Boo Boo shoots Shorty because Boo Boo looked at him too hard at a go-go one night. No witnesses, a hundred suspects, the same kind of crap I had to deal with in robbery. I re-open the Noyes jacket and find the paragraph about the autopsy. It states the following:

> *Dr. Goshen performed the autopsy. A sex kit was used on the decedent and hair was removed from her pubic and anal area; head and left hand. Dr. Goshen made the following observations: There appeared to be one blow to the back of her head to the occipital area with contra coup contusion. The hyoid bone was broken and the thyroid cartilage fractured. Dr. Goshen stated that the suspect would have had to apply significant pressure to the neck for this to happen. The major arteries in the neck were intact but there was*

significant injury to the tissue of the neck.

I shuffle through the other papers in the jacket in an attempt to locate the autopsy report. It's not there, more than likely hasn't been picked up from the ME yet. I write in my notebook to check with the ME for the report. The way my brain's working lately I have to write everything down or I'll forget. There was a time when a mental note was like an alarm clock. Those days are long gone, though. I do find an investigative report, PD 854, concerning a videotaped interview with a guy named William Bergine.

As I sit here I wonder what they expect of me. Am I just maintaining his case load until someone else is freed up? Probably. But the way I figure it, I'm not doing this for them. If it weren't for the circumstances I'd be fighting to get out of this detail right about now. The buddy I lost touch with is the only reason I'm sitting here and trying to muster the motivation to do what I have to do. As I contemplate this I remember something else. I open my note book and write: GET THE EVELYN JACKSON JACKET AT COLD CASE—REVIEW AGAIN.

THREE

THE REST OF THE first day was a struggle to maintain focus. Shifting has a way of doing that. The squad didn't catch any cases. They've picked up a homicide the last four Sundays on day work, but not this one. Yvonne said I'm good luck for the squad. My response is a smile because I know better than to put a jinx on it.

Amy Noyes is on my mind for the ride home. Her red-dotted petechiae face is an image I've seen many times in the past, but the photograph seemed to have had more of an impact. It took strong hands to cause the hundreds of pin-hole sized hemorrhages in her skin. Was he raping her at the time? I wonder. Was it even rape or was he paying for it, and the choking was an afterthought, something spontaneous? Someone who does that kind of thing doesn't stop. That I know. I remember a case I had with this nineteen-year-old kid I got on a warrant about five years back. Had him on three armed street robberies. He beat the male victim up pretty bad in one of them, used the butt of the BB gun to bust his eye socket out. The guy that got busted up was with two girlfriends, so the kid wanted to show him he wasn't such a big deal. I got a search warrant for his uncle's home where he was living at the time, recovered a couple of previous crime mementos he had stashed under his mattress, a cell phone and a class ring, two stupid things to keep around. A guy that does that has got to be a little slow in the head or subconsciously wants to get caught. I know he didn't want to get caught. The young ones never do. It didn't take much effort to locate the owners of the property under the mattress. Both of them had been raped, by the way. I debrief the kid in B1 at the U.S. Attorney's Office and without hesitation, he tells me that one day while walking around trying to find a victim to rob, he saw a girl walking toward her car in an alley. All of a sudden, he thought, "I can have her." So he did. Just like that. No internal debate. No fear of consequences. Just had a sudden urge. So he took her right in the alley between her car and an ivy-covered fence.

That's how they're bred nowadays. Guy started by busting into cars when he was twelve, then snatching purses by the time he was fourteen, using BB guns shortly thereafter. It goes just like that. Nothing new. Most of these kids were made by fathers whose lives were spent behind bars, left to some baby mother addicted to crack. And this one in particular, wearing his undersized orange jumpsuit with white socks sliding down twig-sized ankles, sat there shackled, in that little square room in the basement of 555, in the presence of his attorney and the AUSA, and said with no expression at all that he "took her in the rear between her car and a fence." The next one was easy. There might even be a dead body out there somewhere. Who knows? He was stupid, but not so stupid that he'd give up that kind information. I remember his face clear as day, little sociopath. He had a round baby face, with a clear complexion, big eyes and thin eyebrows, the kind of look that'd make him someone's little toy inside. I don't get pleasure out of saying that. Believe me. It's just going to make him tougher—meaner. If he ever does get out, he'll be a new breed of monster. Hopefully, I'll be long gone by that time. But the guy that murdered Amy Noyes, he wasn't made the same way. This aching gut tells me Amy Noyes wasn't his first, either. My luck, he's probably a congressman.

❄

I DECIDE TO STOP by my spot on M Street, between the two strip joints and grab another bottle of Lagavulin, then get a couple of Coronas from the cigar shop next door. It takes a little mental convincing to get the cigars. The left side of my fallen face makes it harder to draw in the smoke. I make these embarrassing puckering, sucking sounds and don't get enough draw for flavor.

All this really does is make me salivate too much so I have to pat the tip of the cigar dry. I have to take baby sips from the glass of scotch too, or most of it'll drool down my chin. But what can I do, use a straw? How would that look? Just a few months and I can already say these are things I have grown accustomed to.

It's about five in the afternoon by the time I get home. I set the bottle of scotch on the bar that separates the dining room from the living room then tuck the cigars in the unfit humidor that sits on the edge of the bar. The curtains are drawn, and it's like a dungeon in here. I'm too tired to enjoy these vices now. If I nap I'll never get to sleep later on. I dial my number to check for messages, and, when prompted by the recorded voice, I enter my password. Two messages. One is a new bank and I qualify for a platinum card. Before the guy who calls himself Bill can finish, I press the number that deletes him. The second is Clem. She left a message that she'd be in New York next week and in DC for the weekend. *Two visits in one year. That's something new.* I place the phone back in the charger and kick off my shoes. I don't feel like calling her either—maybe later.

I help myself to a glass of Lagavulin and a cigar from the unfit humidor; sit at my desk to make love to the past. I find an odd sense of comfort in this. Life becomes a series of intrinsic seasons and this is my Fall.

The phone rings before this mind carries me too far into self-indulgence.

I recognize the number. It's Clem again. My mood has changed. I decide to answer.

"How's my Two Face?" she asks.

"No improvement."

"What does your doctor say?"

"That it takes time. I think it gives me character. No wrinkles on the left side of my face, like Botox. People your way would pay big money for that."

"That's a good idea. I should quit my job and open Bell's palsy clinics along Wilshire. Paralysis: the natural way to stop unwanted wrinkling." We both chuckle.

"Did you get my message?" she asks.

"Yes, I was going to call after I settle a bit," I lie. The truth is I don't want to talk really, tell her about Scanns and then fall into a lengthy conversation I'm not ready to handle.

"I'll be in New York next week—maybe drop by DC for a day or two."

"That's what the message said. You'll stay at the Mayflower?"

"Of course."

"I'll notify the bellhop to start stockpiling that blue-bottled sparkling water you like to waste your money on."

"Very funny. We're getting ready to go into production on our next project and I have to charm a hideously rude financier in New York. And, speaking of financing, I put a bid on a loft in Santa Monica."

"View of the ocean, I hope?"

"A gorgeous view. And close to work."

"Clem, *nothing* out there is close to work." I pause,

not wanting to ask the next question but knowing I have to.

"You seen Priscilla around?"

"About two months ago, at Canters."

"She doing all right?"

"She seemed fine."

I realize I'm doing what I always do, so I don't ask the next question in the series—if she asked about me. If she's still with the guy she left me for. I already know what the answer will be. The end of my first life was the day she left. I was alive some twenty-four years before my death but those years were more like birthing pains. Even now, years later, my mind will inadvertently recall a torturous moment, pulled from the shallows of the grave where that first life rests.

I knew that Clem did not like Priscilla. It was obvious by her avoidance and lack of interest to motivate my interest in seeing her again after I first met her. But Clem being the friend she was would not dissuade a lonely lovesick, virgin heart and so she never expressed her true feelings about what she thought of Priscilla until well after the split. I think Clem sensed the destructive spirit hidden within the beauty. I don't think Clem realized how far it would go. If she had, I know she would have spoken, but there are blinders on the eyes of youth.

"Countless the shades which separate mind from mind"—a quote I committed to memory because of those moments.

Priscilla and I married about two years after we

met. I was twenty-one. She was twenty-three. We were never apart during those times. Her life was my life. I would lie in bed beside her and slide my lips against hers just to take in her breath while she slept. It was like an addiction—such a sweet natural fragrance. I couldn't get enough of it. We eloped to Las Vegas one weekend and returned to surprise everyone with the news. Clem was taken aback by it, but expressed nothing other than concern for a friend taking a major step in life at such a young age and having so many possibilities yet to be discovered. I understood Clem, or so I thought, but she knew it was destined for disaster. So did my mother, but she believed every marriage was destined to fail just because hers did. My parents divorced when I was seventeen. My father, well, let's just say, other than the occasional seasonal greetings, or belated birthday calls, we don't have much to say. He was always a distant, uncaring man.

Priscilla and I moved into a two bedroom with large windows and a nice balcony, a few blocks from Canters Deli. Vinyl records ruled her life along with cassette and demo tapes. We're talking hundreds and hundreds of records and shoe boxes filled with cassettes. The shelves could not hold the number of records she had, so they were lined open along the walls in milk crates. Other than a worn sofa, a reclining chair, a fifties style dining set in the kitchen nook, a small television and an incredible stereo system the apartment was barren of the things that would constitute a home.

That is where my musical education really began, though. I thought I knew music, but I soon realized I didn't know anything. I loved Social Distortion, Black Flag, Shattered Faith and so many others. Priscilla introduced me to another side of the scene: Nick Cave and the Bad Seeds, Television, Wire and a lot of the great talent that was coming out of the East Coast at the time. I was a babe in the woods musically. She lived and breathed music and that Indie label along with a tattoo-ridden boss, and an over-aged, bleached blond punk rock woman who called herself Fly. It did not take long for me to realize that that existence went well beyond a simple career. It quickly devoured everything in her life leaving no room for me.

The nights were booked with gig after gig, one band after another that was a must see. I went every night for the first few months with her and that punk sensation wannabe boss of hers, whose name I will never allow myself to remember. It soon wore me thin and I had a hard time keeping up with my studies. I had to drop out of her scene. That never stopped her from going every night, though. Always a different club and a new or familiar band to see—night after night after night...

Yes, the beginning of the end for us was that independent label with seed money that was quickly squandered until there was nothing to show for it.

I would become a teacher a couple of years after the corpse was buried and made a meager salary that allowed us a comfortable life. I chose the public school system because I had this simple hearted notion that I had something I could offer the kids who were closer to the street—the ones that were harder to reach. Private schools were too much like green grass and picket fences. Those kids were not the ones I wanted to stand before. I wanted the tough ones, the ones that fought and the ones with cement for front yards. The public system was more than happy to have a UCLA man and so I got my wish. It didn't take me long to learn that most of those little men called kids didn't want what I had to offer.

I was hit with real drama the night Priscilla told me she was leaving me. She wanted a divorce.

"It was a mistake," she said. "Everyone was right."

I stood there and heard the words, but did not comprehend the meaning.

"Our life together—it doesn't mean anything."

"What is it supposed to mean?" I asked naively.

She hesitated and then I knew what, or rather, who was in her heart, but did not want to hear it.

"I have to move on," is all she added.

It was a thunderclap. Call it the beginning of my intuition—the gut feeling that has stayed with me to this day. There was a great silence, but I broke it with a sudden outburst and a demand for more—an explanation, even though I knew it was not something I wanted to hear. I didn't want to hear that she had fallen for that Joe Strummer wannabe boss of hers. He was nothing more than a simple dope head. And she left me for that?

Yes, Clem is the closest thing I know to a saint—if I still believed in that sort of thing. She often came by my mother's, where I stayed for a short while after the break-up and forced me into the light. We sat in rickety lounge chairs in the large rectangular back yard, smoking cigarettes and sipping scotch while she read the worst screenplays she could excavate from the stacks of hundreds sent to her. Truly bad scripts were her comic outlet. But while she read, all I could do was sit and obsess about Priscilla. Clem would sit there all the while and her words were carried away into that ineffable landscape of mind.

Our break-up reminded me at the time, of my parent's divorce. Those childhood memories tend to stay and fester until you have a well calloused internal boil. When those hard times fall on you, like they did on me, the puss will tend to work its way out and ooze just enough to conjure up those repressed feelings. It was oozing a little too much for my comfort.

I thought about my younger years growing up in DC. My father, the big Ben Simeon, had officially become Special Agent Ben Simeon, of the Secret Service. I held his badge after he first got it. It felt heavy in my hand, and under that shiny yellow, blue and white exterior, there was something very grand, and even mythical about it.

I thought about all those years prior to the divorce, as if they had merged into one great hour, when my mom and dad always had their parties. My sister

Emily, and I, were always like sideline ornaments—little burning candles. The parties were packed with new friends—agents and cops from other jurisdictions with all kinds of badges and guns. They sure loved to show them off. I loved it, though.

My father was always gone between parties, on some assignment or another, sometimes for days, or even weeks. I imagined all kinds of adventures. I can't pinpoint the time the ugliness at home began, only the day it ended. It was a few years later.

After the divorce was finalized, Emily and I went back to Los Angeles with my mother, where we first started, back to where my dad worked midnights as an armed security guard for a big construction company, while attending UCLA full time. My mother, sister, and I, went back. That was the beginning of my messy life.

The callous had hardened again, and I regained myself. I decided to pursue the one career in life I always knew in my heart I was meant to do. I did not want to follow in my father's footsteps. God forbid. Being a federal agent was the furthest thing from my mind. I think that all those years hanging around cops, holding badges, and hearing the war stories had more of an effect on me than I thought. I decided that I wanted to find my own little corner and work it, just like a public school. It was as drastic a change as I could have made at the time.

I loved DC as a kid. I always considered it home. I grew to hate Los Angeles and so I applied. After a few months, I found myself packing as little belongings as I could and boxing up the rest, boxes of which mostly contained books. I stored them at my mother's home. There were a few I could not be without like, my Dickens collection, a few by Thomas Hardy and Graham Greene. They were tightly packed in a suitcase with other necessities, like underwear and socks. I shook the LA dust off the bottom of my feet and caught the next flight to DC to attend the Metropolitan Police Department Academy.

I remember being on the plane headed for DC and gazing through the little window down over the landscape. That was when I swore to a God I could no longer see that I would never return to that place.

Clem and I spoke about two months ago. That's when she had called about her latest project and was pissed to hear about my condition. But mostly Clem calls because she needs someone she can depend on to listen to her and to endure her occasional rants. Today's conversation is on the lighter side, which is fortunate because of the state I'm in and especially so with the oncoming single malt buzz.

My mind suddenly snapped back to our conversation.

"You sound tired. You getting rest?"

"I'm not on the street as much. And I'm forcing myself to slow down a bit."

"You never slept much. I bet your condition only makes it worse."

"It's not that bad." And before she can respond I say,

"I have to go Clem. I'm tired."

"Well, I'll call again before I come out."

"I hope you get the condo."

"Yeah, me too," she says.

"Love ya, C."

"Love you too."

I worry about cutting her off, but I don't call back because it's time to fall into self-absorption again.

For some reason I'm inspired to read, maybe try to finish the book I started. I recline on the couch, get through a couple of pages before the words start to join together, and, before I know it, I'm out.

I AM SLOW TO awaken, and when I do it's dark. No dreams that I remember. I pull myself off the couch and stumble to the bedroom. The clock reads 2:10 a.m. In less than two hours I have to start getting ready for the job. Day work. Not a morning person. I watch the clock for the next couple of hours then shower and put on something casual. I leave early so I can stop by Cold Case and pick up the other case jacket in the event I can't find a cruiser at VCU. That's the life of a detailed man. You never have anything of your own. Everything's borrowed, even the time.

I get to VCU about twenty-five minutes before roll call. The lights in the detectives' area are off. What I hear is snoring and the occasional squeak of a chair as someone shifts body weight. *Midnights,* I think. Unless you're rolling all night, those last two hours'll always get you. Finding sleeping midnight detectives is a good sign. It means an uneventful night before. I tread lightly to Scanns' desk, set my briefcase on the next cubicle's chair. An older, heavy-set guy with a familiar face is a couple cubicles to my right, reclined in a chair with his feet propped on another. His head is tilted upward, mouth open, and there's a deep saliva gurgle snore coming out of him. I log into the computer. The fluorescent lights flicker on moments later followed by the sound of several squeaky chairs and a snort, then, "Mornin.'" I recognize the voice as Tommy's.

Some sleepy guy at the other end huffs, "What you got to do that for?"

"Get on home," is all Tommy says.

"I got court," the sleepy guy responds.

A back row of fluorescents turns off, dimming the room.

"Night, night," I hear Tommy say and then see him shortly after.

"You look fresh," I say.

"Give me a couple of hours." He sets his briefcase on the floor beside his chair, looks at the still gurgling guy across from him, "That's a Polaroid moment if I ever saw one." He opens the storage area above the desktop, grabs a Polaroid camera and checks it for film. He walks across and angles over the sleeping man. There's a flash of light and the picture is pushed out as the man snaps up, almost out of his chair.

"What the—?" he growls.

Tommy goes back to his area and drops the

developing picture on his desk.

"You got yours coming, boy," he tells Tommy. "What time you got?"

"Almost six," Tommy says.

He glances my way, nods with recognition. I nod back as he straightens himself to sit up, rubs his eyes with both hands.

Day work arrives. *Changing of the guard.*

Mather checks in on me and says we should go to that coffee place on 18th again. They had good latte. I tell him they'll be open in about an hour. That'll give me time to go through the case jackets again, including the one I just picked up at Cold Case. But before we can make it to roll call the Sarge pops in.

"We just picked one up," he says so everyone can hear.

And there goes my good-luck status.

SO IT'S A VARIATION of "Boo Boo shoots Shorty 'cause Shorty looked at him too hard at a club one night," but the end result's the same. This time we have a family of good witnesses and every one of them wants to give the suspect up. After about three hours on the scene, they were transported to VCU for statements. One of the victim's cousins is sitting beside me as I type her personal information into the computer on a 119. Timone's her name. She has a figure like a bowling ball, with a disproportionate array of beads and shells dangling from her unkempt hair. Her legs dangle from the chair because they're too short and stubby to reachthe floor.

"You can adjust the seat if you want," I say.

"That's all right."

I open up the narrative portion to begin the Q and A. I've already explained to her that I'll ask questions, then type while she's speaking. "I'm a fast typer," I tell her. She taps her toes in the air to some tune that must be stuck in her head and says that she's learning about computers. I smile the half-smile and finish typing in my first question, then read it back to her.

"This office is investigating a stabbing that occurred on today's date in the 1400 block of Fairmont Street, Northwest. Were you at the location at the time of the stabbing?"

"Yes, I was there."

I type the next question then read, "Tell me what you saw and heard?"

"When she stabbed him or the whole thing?"

"Everything you remember, from the beginning."

And then she goes off, and like a well-programmed machine, my fingers find the keys.

"It started we were all standing in front of 1401 by the fence near the steps, and his baby's mother was there too, and everyone was laughing and talking. My cousin Renee asked him was he ready to go to Target? And she said, 'Yeah, let's go,' and his baby's mother asked where he think he's gonna go without her? Then Renee said, 'Who you think you are? He don't have to check in with you.' And she just say, 'Whatever, girl.' And then Ty says, 'Excuse me, but this here is my cousin and I don't have to check with no one when I want to go somewheres. I run this here.' And then she starts to go off on Renee and say that he don't need to be runnin' nowhere but with her right now, and then Renee get in her face and say, 'You think you run this block?' Then Ty step in and say, 'I run this here.' And then she's in his face and they sayin' words back 'n forth, and then I hear her say, 'you ain't gonna do nothin' to no one out here.' And that's when he throw his beer to the ground and then they start swingin' at each other. So Renee and Niecy pull them two apart, and Niecy take him up the steps just to get away. My other cousin take Renee away because now them two start goin' at one another, and my other cousin tells her to go on about her business and that's when she start swingin' on him and he say, 'You stop swingin' on me 'cause if you keep swingin' on me I'm gonna have to hit back.' And that's when she goes to her car and sits inside. She was like, 'Whatever, man.' And then we all was back at the stairs and I was like up there too with my Grandmother when I hear, 'What you gonna do, Niecy?' and then his baby's mother is goin' at it with Niecy and Niecy was like, 'Don't put your hands on me, quit grabbin' me,' and she say to Niecy, 'Whenever I see you, we gonna fight, me and you are gonna fight.' And then she like go back to her car and sits down inside and my cousin –

"Which cousin?" I interrupt, because at this point my fingers are jamming up.

"Her baby's father, Ty. He goes to her and says, 'Since you have so much mouth, why don't you get out and swing on me?' and she tries to close the door back and then he says, 'So you getting' out?' And she tries to close the door again but he keep pullin' it back up, and her hand swings out and I don't know if it hits him, but then them two start goin' at it in the car. My Grandmother asked why they fightin', and I say because she has no reason jumpin' up in everyone's face like that all the time, and my Grandmother is like, 'Oh' and that's when they stop fightin' and he starts walkin' to the steps and I see he's holdin' his side. And I hear Niecy screamin', 'She stabbed him, that bitch stabbed him.' And that's when the police came."

She stops.

I look away to take a breath, then type the question and ask: "Did you see Ty's baby's mother stab him?"

"No, but Niecy say she did."

I stop typing, "That's some memory you've got there."

"Yeah," is all she says.

"Give me a second so I can review what you said, okay?"

She nods, taps her toes against air, and I read through what she said, then type follow-up questions. After each one I read them back to her for answers.

"Do you know what Ty's baby's mother's name is?"

"Angela."

"Do you know her last name?"
"No."
"Where did she go after she stabbed Ty?"
"She went in her car and turned right on 14th Street."
"What kind of car was she driving?"
"I don't know. I think Ford or somethin' like that. I don't know for sure."
"Can you describe the car?"
"Black—maybe four doors."
"Did you see the tag?"
"No. I think it was a Maryland, though."
"Who was the 'other cousin' you referred to, who told Angela to go about her business?"
"That's my cousin Julius."
"What is his full name?"
"I always known him as Julius is all."
"He's your cousin and you don't know his full name?"
"No."
"Who is Niecy to you?"
"She's my Uncle's niece but we always known her as just Niecy."
"Is she the one that the officers brought you here with?"
"Yes."
So it goes like this for a bit longer until I have about seven pages. I print it out and have the witness review it and then sign. I hand the original to Tommy. He's picking this one up, easy closure.

When Mather finishes with his witness, the Sarge asks us to go back to 1401 Fairmont and canvass the building for the "other cousin" and see if we can get anything else on Angela. All these witnesses, most of them family, and the most we know about the girl who had a baby fathered by one of their own is her first name and that she drives a black Ford Escort. Go figure, but not bad considering most of the time it's just "Shorty," "Boo," or "Black," and they live out in Southeast somewhere.

We make a quick stop on 18th to grab a coffee and Mather's latte. I sip it hot so I can try to finish most of it before we get to Fairmont. It's moving toward 10:30 in the morning and traffic has eased down to its normal struggle. I hate the way they drive in this city. It is difficult at times to maintain composure, even in the passenger seat. But we manage to make the five or so blocks without spilling coffee or jumping out of the car. We park in front of the building beside a fire hydrant. I place the bubble light on the dashboard.

We show our badges to the overweight, scruffy SPO working the front door. Mather asks him if he knows anyone by the name Julius who is a relative to the guy that just got stabbed. He says no, but asks if we knew that the girl who stabbed Ty came back and asked what hospital he was taken to.

Mather looks at me. No surprise.

"How long ago was she here?" I say.

"Not even five minutes before the two of you got

here," says the Scruffy.

"You tell her he was dead on the scene?" Mather asks.

"Dead? I missed all that. I just told her that if he was stabbed and taken by the ambulance, probably went to Howard or GWU. Those are the closest hospitals."

We tear out of there, Mather on his hand-held advising the dispatcher to have units respond to Howard, GWU and be on the lookout for the suspect and the vehicle she drives. I take the coffee from the console's cup holder, attempt to chug down the last bit, but all it does is spill out the left side of my mouth and down my chin. I'm thankful it missed my clothing and seeped into the edge of the car seat staining it instead. I look for a napkin but can't find one, so I settle for wiping my goatee with my left hand. Mather notices all this, but doesn't comment. I don't bring up that we probably would have nabbed her had we not made the stop on 18th. Spilling what coffee I had left pissed me off. On the car's mic I advise the dispatcher to get a cruiser to Georgetown Hospital just in case. Officers answer up for the assignment. We code one to Howard, thinking that'd be the first place she'd go.

Before we get four blocks out, a unit over the air is advising that he has a vehicle in sight that matches the description. It's parked illegally along a curb in front of Howard Hospital's emergency entrance. We tell him to keep an eye on it and the entrance. The officer on the scene is heard running the vehicle's tag over the air. By this time our Sarge is hitting Mather on the Nextel. He tosses the phone to me and I fill him in.

The unit on the scene at Howard comes over the air. They have the driver of the car detained. The dispatcher acknowledges and then says the tag comes back to an Angela George. "Nothing current," the dispatcher advises concerning her criminal history.

We get there minutes later. Three cruisers are in sight surrounding the Black Ford Escort with Maryland tags. They got a girl stopped. She's cradling a tiny baby in one arm.

❄

BACK AT VCU THERE'S not much for me to do with this one. Based on everything we got, if Tommy doesn't get a confession out of her, I'd say it's time for him to put in his papers and call it a day.

Rucker walks in. We do the familiar shake with the one-arm hug, and the next thing I know, I'm sitting in a comfortable leather sofa in his office.

He signals me to hold on for a second while he takes an in-coming call, punctuated with "sir," just like the Lieutenant. No doubt, about this morning's homicide. I realize right after I hear him mention my name, along with Mather's, during the course of the conversation—locating Angela at Howard hospital. "Great job." "Teamwork." "Coordinating effort." These are just some of the words I hear.

His office is decorated like he thinks he's going to

stay for a while. Framed photos hang on the wall behind his large oak desk and ergonomic chair. I notice a picture of him with the U.S. Attorney, probably after an award ceremony. Rucker's dressed in his class A. Even from this distance and with my failing eyes I notice our academy class photo from way back when. We're all gathered on the steps of the Lincoln memorial. I'm the one in the third row with the big snicker on my face like I don't believe I got that far. Scanns, looking all goofy, and Rucker dead serious in the last row. Plaques, certificates of commendations and community awards are well-positioned along the wall, too. There's nothing to suggest a new relationship in his life. I doubt he'd have photos of her on his desk even if there were. In fact, not much personal here, except for some police memorabilia, collectables and coffee mugs displayed on the book shelves. But then, that would be expected. Once you make rank you got to have that kind of stuff around. I do notice the cedar fifty-cigars humidor Scanns and I went in on for him after his last promotion. It's on the third shelf. Thing cost about four hundred bucks. I walk over and open it. Empty. I shake my head and glance his way. He shrugs. It used to be a regular thing, the three of us getting together at the Mayflower or Shelley's, depending on the mood and what kind of outfit Scanns was wearing. We'd always have the best cigars, mostly Cubans from our State friends. We'd hold them the way you're supposed to, with an occasional roll between two fingers while checking out the burn like the connoisseurs we thought we were. Silly guys, is all I remember, playing the role we were expected to play. Like the movies. No, more like cable. Bad, late-night cable. I miss it in a way, and feel bad we all lost touch.

He hangs up the phone.

"Whassup?" he says.

I fall back on the sofa. "Just trying to get through."

"Good job this morning."

"Good luck, more like it."

"Whatever it was, it's a closure." He sits in the ergonomic chair, reclines back a little. "I looked for you after the funeral, thought maybe we'd go for a drink, but you were gone."

"I was around, probably just missed me. So you got moved in pretty quick, all nice and efficient."

"When you get the rank you learn to pack efficiently. Who knows where I'll be tomorrow."

"I'm happy for you. This is a good position. Comes with some headaches but probably a good move on your part."

"Yeah, well." He sits up, not so relaxed. "I spoke with Celeste the other day."

"She doing better?"

"Yeah. Man, what can you say? She has a lot of family and friends by her side. She'll be fine. It'll take some time, but she'll be all right."

"Did you know about that chick he was seeing on the sly?"

"Yeah. I told him he was a dope, but you know how

he is—was."

"Who is she?"

"Just some young law student, an intern at the U.S. Attorney's Office. She did a ride-along with him a few months back, and then it went on from there. He loved Celeste. He would've never left her."

"She doesn't know, does she?"

"I don't think so, but you know how women are, especially when you're married to one. But probably not. He had this crazy schedule anyway, know what I mean?" Rucker pauses awkwardly for a moment as if realizing this was like a stab at me.

"So Hattie told me you're responsible for getting me into this mess?" I ask, changing the subject for his benefit.

"I thought it's what you wanted? But if you want out, just say the word. It won't look bad."

"Naw. I'm good. I need the change. It might even grow on me."

"I'm serious, Ezra. All I need is for you to put in some good time and get these cases in order, hopefully close a couple. Then you call where you want to go."

"Quit the foreplay, Ruck. I've had my chain yanked too many times. I know how these things work."

"I got you to cold case, didn't I?"

I don't say anything because I know it was 'he helped me' get to cold case. He didn't make it happen. I admit he was one of the calls I made in an effort to get out of limited duty. He didn't have the authority to make the decision on his own like he wants me to believe. He might have more clout now, being the man at homicide.

"Give me a few months until the next graduating class and you call where you want to go," he continues. "I'm tight with the boss. But I'm hoping you'll want to stay here and play."

Sounds like he does have a bit more clout.

"So you're saying 5D will let me go? I mean a detail is one thing, but something permanent might ruffle their feathers. They're short on detectives as it is."

"If we didn't know each other like we do, I'd throw your ass out of here for having to make me repeat myself."

"I just like to hear it a few times, like I really do have a choice. What's been going on with you, other than this nice new office?" I ask changing the subject.

"Not much to speak of. Haven't got the time for much of anything outside of the job."

"That's not healthy, but who'm I to talk. I'd-a thought you'd be married by now. Seeing anyone?

"Was but it didn't work out, know what I mean?"

He gets that little awkward look again. His foot might get stuck in his mouth the next time

"Like I said, I can't find the time." His text pager chirps and he slides it out of the holder on his belt, reads the message. "Give me a second," he says. He types a text message into the pager. "Listen, man, we got to get out some night, grab a couple of fine cigars just like old times."

"That'd be good."

"I've got to roll, some meeting with the chiefs. They've got us doing two of those a day. Like all of us getting together in one room is going to lower the crime rate."

I stand. "I'll catch ya in a bit." I say.

"Have a good turkey day if I don't see you."

"I forgot about that. But thanks, I'll try to remember."

He smiles. "If you need anything, see me, aaright? And I meant what I said before."

I nod, and then walk out. *My boy's changed.* But then, rank'll do that to you. It's like becoming a parent. When you got the children to look after, you forget that you used to be one yourself. It was nice of him to give me a choice, though. I'm not saying I believe it. He could just be telling me what he thinks I want to hear—thinks he'll get more out of me that way.

I SLIDE OUT AND drive to Amy Noyes' place. I want to do another walk through. I park illegally at the end of the block along a cross walk. I have the case jacket with me and a fresh coffee. Inside her apartment, I set the coffee on the window sill in the living room and lean against the edge to look through the case jacket. I don't even know what I'm looking for. I find some notes that have about thirty phone numbers written down. As I read, I learn that they are numbers Scanns recovered from her cell phone. They're broken down into categories: Received, Called, and Saved. Most of the saved numbers have either names or nicknames associated with them. I find Aletheia Wynn's number. According to the case resumé, she was a close friend of Amy's. I look at the photos on the mantle and wonder which one she is. I'm guessing the one with a light complexion, who's in most of the photographs. I'll need to talk to her. Actually, it's something I should do now, and so I grab my cell from my inside coat pocket and call. It rings about four times and then kicks in to the message, "I'm not available, but I will return your call, but only if you leave a message." *Sweet voice.* I'm sure that's how she makes most of her money. I leave a message that I'm on the case now and for her to give me a call as soon as she can. I slide my cell back in the pocket and then examine the numbers again. Amy had several received calls the day the body was discovered. Three of the numbers were from Aletheia. No doubt, wondering why her friend wasn't returning her calls. I decide to wait and check into the numbers back at the office so I don't blow up my own cell bill. I can write it off at the end of the year, but I still don't like having to dish out that kind of money on a monthly basis. That's the life of a detailed man. I don't get the perks, like a cell phone. That comes with an assigned job, and district detectives never had that luxury.

I sip the coffee—still hot. A little drips down my chin and I do a little avoidance dance before it hits my shirt. I set the case jacket on the sill and grab my coffee, walk into her bedroom. Odd feeling, this presence of death. The specter-like feeling is more intense because of the manner in which the life was taken. I kneel down to look under the bed, but do it in an awkward way so my knee doesn't touch the soiled floor. Nothing's there. *What do you expect,* that there'd be that missed bit of evidence that would lead to the killer? Yeah, that's what I thought. Keeping that in mind, I look under all the furniture. When that's done, I sip some more coffee, but this time carefully. My cell phone rings. I slide it out and flip it open. "Hello?" I say.

"This is Aletheia Wynn, you just called me."

"Yes."

"I didn't recognize the number so I didn't answer."

"I appreciate the quick response."

"I thought Detective Scanns was investigating this?"

"He was, Ms. Wynn, but he passed away a couple of days ago so it was reassigned to me."

"Passed away? You mean he died?"

"Yes. Heart attack."

"Geez. He was so young."

Geez?, I think. "I know that it's hard on you, but we're going to have to go over everything again."

"Okay."

"I'd like to do this as soon as possible. Are you available to meet with me today?"

"I'm just getting up."

"It's something we need to do."

"Can you give me about forty-five minutes?"

"That's no problem." I quickly look in the case Jacket at the Initial Case Resumé. "Are you still at the address on Connecticut Avenue?"

"Yes. Apartment 605."

"I'll see you in about forty-five minutes then?"

"Okay."

Sweet voice, just like the message.

I wander around the apartment for about thirty minutes and then leave. What little I've been able to learn about her does not suggest escort call girl type. Frightening, in a way. I mean that I could probably meet someone like her at the Mayflower or the Whole Foods in Georgetown at the produce section and maybe even muster up the courage to talk to her about apples and never know what she was into. I saw the WALES and NCIC on her and the girl doesn't have a record. She's never been locked up for solicitation or anything. She's lucky, or just has good business sense.

Aletheia Wynn is in unit 605. She buzzes me in. It's another nice building in an equally nice neighborhood.

I knock on her door. She answers quickly, like she was standing there waiting. I was right. She is the girl with the light complexion. Prettier in photographs, though. She looks at me in the way I've been accustomed to being looked at for the past few months. The comforting thing is that those awkward looks are less and less frequent.

"I have a slight condition, but nothing contagious," I say with my half-smile. "I'm Detective Ezra Simeon."

"Oh." She offers her hand. "I'm Aletheia." We shake and she allows me in. Her eyes are puffy and cheeks sunken. Too thin, either alcohol or drugs, but just as likely grief or a bad diet. She's tall, almost as tall as me, wearing a white terry cloth bathrobe and spa sandals. I smell the fresh soap on her skin, Dove or some grocery store bought bar like that. I smell fresh coffee, too and it also smells like some grocery store brand. Probably bought from the same place as the soap. She doesn't seem too uncomfortable with the nakedness under the bathrobe. At least I assume naked. She did say she was taking a shower. *Maybe I didn't give her enough time.*

"Do you need time to change?" I say.

"That's all right."

Her place is small, probably a one-bedroom apartment, matching rattan furniture, Oriental rug over hardwood floor and framed rice paintings on walls. The living room opens into the small dining room and attached kitchen. We sit across from each other at a round four-chair cheap wood dining table. Not the decorating sense her friend had.

"So, has there been any progress?" she asks.

"I'm just getting started on this, but Detective Scanns was able to put some things together."

"So, do you know who murdered her?" The word "murdered" wasn't a comfortable word for her to say.

"I'm afraid not. Not yet."

"Do you want some coffee or something?"

"Sure. Thank you."

She stands and grabs another cup from a cabinet and pours, then tops hers off as well. I notice she has a small tattoo of a cross on the inner side of her left ankle, just over the bone. That must have been a little painful. She sets the coffee on the table before me and sits. *No coasters.*

"Thanks," I say.

She sips her coffee like it was tea. I do the same because they're cups, not mugs. It tastes like Folgers or some crap like that. I don't want to be rude so I take another sip.

"How long've you lived here?"

"Going on five years," she says.

"From where?"

"California. San Diego area."

We have California in common but I don't share it. I would if she were a suspect. "How long have you known Amy?"

"Almost five years. We met just shortly after I got to the city. Same modeling agency."

"That the Sally Stein Agency?"

"Yes."

"How long the two of you work there?"

"I told the other detective all this. He didn't write it down?"

"Ms. Wynn. Like I said, a lot of what we're going to talk about you've already been through, but since I'm new on the case, I'd rather treat it like it's fresh from you instead of something I'm getting off a report. I'll be more effective that way. Please bear with me."

"Okay. I'm sorry. I just don't want to go through this again. We were good friends, you know?"

"Yes. I'll be out of your hair in a bit."

"What was your question?"

"How long the two of you work at the modeling agency?"

"Till about two years ago."

"I'm also going to have to ask you some personal questions, so don't take it the wrong way, all right?"

She nods and slurps the coffee.

"Were you in the same business with her after the agency?"

"You mean escort?"

"That and whatever else came with being an escort?"

"We worked together. But it was mostly looking out for each another."

"Anyone else work with you?"

"It was just us. We didn't have a pimp, if that's what you mean."

"No, it's just that I know some of the escort services also have an agency or an agent who hooks them up with the clients."

"No. We got started on a fluke. Just the two of us and then word of mouth. Next thing we know, we're full-time and pretty busy. We don't advertise or anything like that. Everything was done through referrals and over our cell phones. We don't—didn't use the Internet or anything like that—attracted too many creeps and too much attention. In fact, it's all over with now. I'm out of it. I disconnected my business line the other day. I don't want any part of it anymore."

"None of your clients know where you live?"

"No. Of course not."

"What about Amy? Did she entertain clients at her place?"

"No. We're not stupid."

"I don't think you're stupid, but I've known some who do the massage thing out of their homes."

"Listen, we were mostly escorts, but if it ever came to that, we'd be smart enough to get to a hotel or something. We rarely even went to their places."

"Did Amy have a boyfriend?"

"No. I mean she saw some guys regularly that didn't pay, but nothing serious."

"Do you have their names?"

"I know one guy she liked whose name was William Burgan or something like that."

William Bergine was one of the names from the cell phone list and the guy interviewed on video tape. "You meet him?" I say.

"Once. He seemed like a pretty nice guy. He didn't know anything about what we did. I told the other detective about him."

"I know. You talked to him since her death?"

"No. He wouldn't know how to get in touch with me."

"Do you know how they met?"

"No, I don't...maybe she told me...I just don't

remember."

"You were good friends, though."

"Yes, we were."

"So you must have talked about this William then."

"Like I said, just that she liked him. I don't think she wanted to get too excited about it yet."

"When was the last time you spoke to Amy?"

"About two days before she was found." She hesitated before saying 'found'.. It was about eight at night. I forget what the day was."

"What was she doing?"

"She said she was just going to relax, maybe rent a DVD. I tried to call her the next day and then several times after that when I didn't hear from her."

"That's when you decided to go check in on her?"

"Yes. I have a key."

"I know this must be hard."

"We're close and I have a key and she has a key to my place."

"Did anyone else have a key?"

"Not that I know of."

"Go on."

"Well, when I got to her apartment, I knocked and no one was home. I used the key to enter

"Okay," I say as I force myself to drink a little more coffee. It has cooled quickly, and the bitter flat taste that comes with cheap coffee churns my stomach.

"When I opened the door I called for her, but she didn't answer."

"Was there anything you remember that was

unusual?"

"Not really. Nothing looked different inside her place.

"So you said you quit the work you do?"

"Yes."

"What are your plans now?"

"I have money saved. I don't know. I have skills believe it or not. I'll maybe go back to college."

"I think that'd be a good idea." I look at her and feel bad. I don't know why. She's probably got enough money stashed away to put her whole building through college. It was just the way she said, 'Go back to college.' I don't know. I can't stand the way I think sometimes. "Did Amy use drugs?" I ask.

"Amy? No. She drank, smoked a little weed maybe, but she wasn't into heavy drugs."

"What about you?"

She hesitates but not the same kind of hesitation as before. It's a suspect's hesitation. "Me? No."

"She ever talk about her family?"

"All the time. They live in Virginia. I met them a few times. They were very close."

"They know what kind of business she was in?"

"No, not that I'm aware of."

"Do you know if she ever introduced them to William?"

"I don't believe so, no. I don't think she was ready for that yet."

"So, during the course of your careers, either of you ever have any guys bother you—stalker, anything like that?"

"Me? No. As far as I know neither did Amy. Like I said, the only contact we had with any of those guys was through our business lines. I mean, we met some real creepy guys, but nothing we couldn't get out of."

"And none of them knew where you both lived?"

"I don't see how."

"All right. Would you mind writing down the names of your other friends and business associates and a way to contact them?"

"Like I told the other detective, we didn't really hang out with a lot of people, unless Amy had some secret life. And we don't have business associates. I'll be glad to write down everyone I know. The other one—the detective I mean, never came back, so I assumed..."

I slide my notepad across the table and hand her my pen. "Whatever names and numbers you have will be helpful," I say.

She writes down about seven names but only four with phone numbers. Some of them I recognize from the list Scanns put together from the cell phone's address book. I thank her for the list and the unfinished coffee, then advise her I'll probably need to talk to her again at some point. She shows me out.

I take the stairs going down.

A waft of cold air folds across my face after I pull open the front entrance door. My overcoat flies back like a cape. I button it in the middle while I walk toward the car, and I'm suddenly overcome with depression. Not really depression. It's more like sadness but not overwhelming, just a sudden withdrawal. I question the interview. *Did I miss something?* I know I did. I'll come up with more questions and call her back. I didn't even take notes. Well, I took a few, but nothing substantial. Note-taking's an essential element of the job. I'm usually good about taking them. I never take notes during an interview with a prisoner, usually videotape the session. A witness or a victim, though, they're different. They need to think that what they tell you is so important that you have to write it down. Prisoners are just the opposite. They want to feel like you're really listening. When you break away to write something down they start thinking too hard about what they're saying. That's not good. Aletheia Wynn didn't say much of anything that was important enough to write down. The names and numbers were the most important thing she could provide.

I START THE CAR and let it idle in park until the heat kicks in enough to defrost the front and rear windows.

As I watch the warm air dissolve the frost from the front window, I think it's the weather that's making me feel down, like a movie I once saw. I forget which one. It was a chilly first week of Spring, just like this one. And the character equally discontent.

I decide to call Amy Noyes' family, so I pull out my cell. Her father, Robert Noyes, answers, and I fill him in on the course of events beginning with the death of Scanns and then apologize for not having been in touch sooner. I ask if he's available for me to come by. He says they're leaving town for a few days, but he doesn't mind a few questions over the phone. I begin with asking a few background questions—information I already know, and then because of a fading cell battery and either a disheartened man, or an uninterested, impatient man, I move on. *I choose disheartened.*

"Did she ever mention to you that she was seeing someone?"

"No. She did not," he says. "But I imagine she was seeing a lot of men," he says, like I am partly responsible.

"Did she ever mention anyone named William to either you or your wife?"

"Not to me, but let me ask my wife." I hear shuffling and the sound of muffled conversation in the background.

No. Is he the one responsible?"

"Sir, he's just one of several people we're looking into right now, and I'm sorry for having to ask you these questions, but did you know what she did for a living prior to hearing about it on the news?"

"No. We did not. And I want it known that it was an awful thing to have to hear about that way. My wife was almost destroyed."

"I'm sorry, sir. They have their own resources, those people, and often times they don't consider the consequences.

"Why did your daughter come to the District?"

After a moment he says, "She had some money saved up and she wanted to continue her education. She liked George Washington University there."

"What about work? Did she have a job lined up?"

"She said she was working in a club as a hostess –"

There's a pause and I sense he was hit again with what she really did for a living.

"Well, that's what she told me anyway," he continues. "She said she was making enough to take a few classes here and there."

"What did she want to major in?"

"She wanted to get into communications."

"Do you or your wife know of any friends from back home who she stayed in touch with?"

"No. That's actually something the other detective asked and we honestly didn't know."

"Did she have a lot of friends in high school?"

"She stayed to herself. She was never any trouble. She was an awkward teenager, but by the time she graduated, she had grown into a beautiful young girl. I don't think she realized it—how beautiful she had become. Excuse me," he breaks away and after a brief moment, "I'm sorry. This is difficult."

"I'm sorry, Mr. Noyes. I just have one other question. Did she leave any belongings at home with you—address book, notebooks, diary or anything like that?"

"No, she took everything with her—everything," he repeats.

I give him my cell phone number. "You can reach me at any time."

He thanks me and I hang up.

'She grew into her beauty', I think to myself.

She was probably shy and insecure and met up with someone just like her. Aletheia Wynn. Together they probably realized what they had—easy money and perhaps a goal in mind.

Sad how a life can turn.

I pull out into traffic, narrowly missing a car with an angry horn. At the signal, I hang a u-turn and head back toward Adam's Morgan.

I drive around for an hour or so, mulling things over in my head. I drive down 18th and through the narrow side streets, just like the old days when I was in plainclothes and looking for trouble. Far from my intention this time. The more I think about it the more I'm frustrated with being thrown into this assignment. It would have been better years ago when I had the energy. Nowadays, I often wonder how I make it from one place to an other. The time between is lost in this foggy uncertainty in my head, like I kick into some kind of internal auto-pilot and then all of a sudden I'm where I'm supposed to be. It is especially frightening when you're driving, headed to the office or something, or maybe going home, and the mind will go off into this far-off place and then you find you're where you're supposed to be. As I drive, I'm aware of my surroundings, and I'm overwhelmed with increasing frustration. I want to pick up the cell phone and call Rucker and tell him I want to go back to the District. At least there, I'm not under the gun for immediate results, unless a spree of robberies starts to occur in a politically active neighborhood. Then I'm under the gun. That's when you find you've got about twenty bosses, from the District Commander and all his Lieutenants and Sergeants, to the detective supervisors and all his bosses. Then you've got all those victims always calling. Can't forget them. But I've cried about all this before. The more I think about it, the more I realize it doesn't really matter so I may as well stay and go through the motions.

WHEN I GET BACK to the office, Tommy's still at his desk plugging away at the computer's keyboard. I get his attention and toss him the keys with a "thanks." He nods without a word and goes back to what he's doing. I check up on Mather but he's not around, so I go back to my borrowed cubicle and find the motivation to box up Scanns' belongings. It doesn't take long, three boxes in all. I find some packing tape lying around, the kind our Crime Scene Tech guys use, and I seal the boxes. With a permanent ink marker I write PROPERTY OF SCANNS, and I slide the boxes under his workspace. I'll have to remember to put them in the car and take them to Celeste's. Not now, though. I think she's still got family staying with her. I can probably get away with postponing it for a couple of days at least.

I review the Evelyn Jackson file again. It is almost committed to memory. I make a note to myself to have whatever flammable device used on her compared with the one used on Amy Noyes. I also write a note to myself to visit the M.E. in the morning.

I call that Bergine guy to set up an interview for tomorrow afternoon. I want a chance to review the videotaped interview before I meet with him, though. I grab the videotape and slip it into my briefcase so I won't forget. I'll watch it at home. Bergine's phone rings about four times before I'm transferred to voice mail. I leave a message with my office number and cell just in case I'm out. Mather shows up and I fill him in, "I was watching the interview between Scanns and the decedent's boyfriend on the monitor when they had him here," Mather tells me having noticed the videotape in the pouch of my brief case. "He's sketchy."

"How do you mean?"

"I don't know, just the way he talked about her, saying she was his baby and all, but they'd only been going out for a couple of months. It was odd the way he talked about her."

"You don't think a couple of months warrant the expression?"

"Just the way he talked about her. Over the top, you know? He was on the top of Scanns' list as a suspect. I know that. You seen that videotape yet?"

"No. Plan on it tonight."

"It's amusing stuff. Let me know what you think?"

"Sure."

"Well, man, I'm rolling out. Snap-page me if anything comes up."

"See you tomorrow," I say.

"That's right." And he leaves.

The day ends quickly. That's a nice feeling. On the drive home, I try to stay out of the foggy haze.

I POUR MYSELF A shot of Scotch. I think about food but can't decide what to eat. The refrigerator's pretty sparse and I'm too tired to go to the store. There's my decision. I slip the video into the VCR, light one of the cigars I bought and sit back on the sofa with the remote on my lap and the notebook and pen beside me. It opens with him, the Bergine character, sitting in a chair in the corner of the interview room, white walls to each side of him. He looks up a couple of times toward the lens, probably sees the little red light and knows he's on. A few moments later, Scanns enters, introduces himself for the sake of the videotape, including date and time, sits down. He looks different from when I last saw him. I turn away from the television for a second after thinking that, because I meant, 'when I last saw him alive'. But my mind recovers the image of him from the viewing and it throws me. I get an achy feeling that sickens me like after a sudden rush of vertigo. It is his mannequin-like face I see now. I have a hard time turning back to the life captured on the video.

He thanks Bergine for being there, calls him

William, then goes through all the general questioning like name, DOB, Address, "How long you lived here?", his background, and so on. Scanns thanks him again for voluntarily being there for the interview, advises him that he's free to leave at any time.

Bergine looks like he's about ten years older than the date of birth he gave, like he's in his early forties. He looks about 5'10, 140, wears khaki pants, white dress shirt buttoned down with sleeves folded precisely even on both arms. His face is thin and long with sunken cheeks and a well-groomed goatee. He asks if he can smoke. Scanns tells him maybe later, when the officials leave. I smile when I hear that. It is against regulations, but most of us allow it, including the officials. It just sounds like you're breaking rules for your guest when you say it. Bergine reminds me of an Off Broadway producer type and I'm surprised when I learn that he's an Associate Professor at UDC, Computer Science or something like that. Not that being an Associate Professor at UDC is some great accomplishment. I just would have pegged him for some wannabe struggling creative type like maybe a poet, a novelist, or God forbid, a screenwriter. He is very well-spoken, and minutes into the conversation it's obvious that he enjoys hearing himself talk and playing to the camera.

It is odd how he's so loose and amiable so soon after her death. She was his "baby," after all.

"How did the two of you meet?" Scanns asks.

"We met at the university. A course I was teaching

on Wednesday evenings."

"She was one of your students?"

"Yes. It was a six week course. We spoke one evening toward the end of it. She was intelligent, around my age. Attractive. We went out."

"How many times you go out?"

"We were seeing each other for about three months, maybe two, three times a week. Not at first, though. Had to work up to it."

"And you said that the last time you saw her was a couple of evenings before she was found?"

"Yes."

"What did you talk about?"

"Oh, my gosh, let me think. Maybe getting together that weekend, how the day'd been going. Things like that."

"Did she tell you what she did for a living?"

"You know, that never came up. That's odd isn't it?"

"She knew what you did though, right?

"Obviously. We did meet at a course I was teaching, after all."

"And the two of you were dating for about three months, and you never asked what she did for a living?"

"Never thought to. That wasn't important to me." He smiles in what looks like an attempt to be sincere. "Are you suggesting that her job had something to do with her getting murdered?"

"I'm not suggesting anything, William. I just find it strange that you see someone for a few months and don't know what she does for a living. That's usually something you find out on the first date."

"Yes, I see that that would seem odd to you."

During the course of the interview, Bergine never inquires about her job, even though he's got to know Scanns has the information. Scanns holds onto that info. After listening for a few more minutes and noting a couple of things, like his lack of interest in what she does and answers that seem to have been rehearsed, I stop the tape. It doesn't take me long to realize what Mather meant. *Guilty man* is what I think. All the signs are there. He's put at the top of my "things to do" list.

I fall asleep early and sleep soundly. When I wake up, I take a look out the window. It's snowing. Looks like about an inch on the ground already. I dress appropriately and leave. A blanket of fresh snow on the streets, Public Works having failed to do their jobs once again. I am the first to tread on much of it. I miss the ease that comes with taking Metro, but I can live without the human cluster that comes with it. The early morning darkness is beginning to give in to the light. As much as I might complain about being up and out at this unthinkable hour, there is something about it that's, well, you know, magical.

FROM THE MOMENT YOU enter, you're surrounded by that unmistakable, unnatural lingering odor of death. The thin membranes in my nostrils start to burn, and the closer I come to the source the more my living body tries to prevent me from continuing. I am all too familiar with the stairwell that leads down to the freezer and the autopsy room. Fortunately, that's not where we're going today. The smell is everywhere, though. Dr. Goshen isn't available, so we talk to one of the investigators, a boyish looking woman with bleached blonde hair. She finds the report but only confirms what I already know. I give her the report number for the Evelyn Jackson case and ask if she could dig up that report for me. Mather shoots me a quizzical look. I tell him I like the similarities, and I just want to rule it out is all. He shrugs. Big waste of time's probably what the rookie's thinking. It probably is, but my mind's set on checking it out, so that's what I'm going to do. The boyish girl returns a few minutes later and hands me a thin case jacket.

"Mind if I use your copy machine?" I ask and she shows me the way. It doesn't take more than a minute to copy the autopsy report, and then we're out of there. The short time we spent in that place wasn't short enough as far as I'm concerned. Homicide. This place is gonna be my second home. Wonderful.

On the way back to the office I review the autopsy report. A sex kit was executed and a small amount of semen found. I remember reading that in the Cold Case file, the anus area. Maggot infestation was observed inside the vagina as well as third-degree burns and third- and second- degree burns to the inner thigh areas. There appeared to be no injury to the skull. Her Hyoid bone was fractured. The cause of death was manual strangulation. The doctor noted on the bottom of the report that marked bruising on the neck is consistent with the use of latex-type gloves by the suspect.

I turn to Mather, "You got time to make a stop at Mobile before the office? I need a report."

"Yeah, I can give ya a little bit of that."

Mobile Crime's located in a refurbished warehouse in the Northeast section of the District. The wonder of DC is that, if you're blessed with good traffic, you can get anywhere you want to go within fifteen minutes or so. Nowadays, though, with all the construction going on and the potholes, you're lucky to get three blocks in that amount of time. And that's without the snow. When it comes to inclement weather the citizens in this city should just park their cars and call it a day. Drives me crazy, more so when I'm in the passenger seat. It takes us about half an hour to get there from where we are and another ten minutes before Mather is too frustrated to find a parking place. He double parks, and says he'll just wait in the car.

"I won't be long," I say.

"Take your time."

After about five buzzes on the intercom system someone finally shows up to allow me in. The officer sees the badge hanging around my neck and I turn it over to show him the photo ID. He would've let me pass with just the badge. I find my way to the cubicles where the overworked Techs rest their heads.

I make my way through the maze, passing a couple of familiar faces, until I find the spot where my boy lives. Davinci Cheeks is the name he's been blessed with. Some warm greetings, concerns and just a few complaints and it's down to business. I'm actually surprised to find him there, but I'm lucky that he's on stand-by at court and trying to do a little catch-up on the paperwork.

"Man, why'd you want to get yourself put in homicide?"

"What choice I got?" I say.

"I hear ya."

I show him the autopsy report on Evelyn Jackson. "Can you dig up the Evidence Report for this one?"

"As long as it's got the MCL number on it, I can." He takes a look, spots it and, "Old case. They got you working this one?"

"Naw, I've been blessed with the Adam's Morgan Escort. I just want to get something submitted for a comparison."

"The Escort, huh? Ain't that a load. Relax for a minute, and I'll dig this one up."

I lean against a cubicle. Displayed along these walls like trophies are the collections of gruesome crime scene photographs. Bodies with half their faces blown off, jumpers, floaters, swingers, every manner of death imaginable. It's depressing, but they keep them like they're proud of the images they captured. This is the kind of stuff they showed us in the academy and made more than one stomach turn.

I'm leaning there for about fifteen minutes before Davinci returns. He hands me a copy of the report.

"Copy machine was tied up."

"Appreciate it," I say. "By the way, who processed the Escort scene?"

"Johnson, I think, if I'm not mistaken."

"What's he working?"

"Evenings."

"How long you think it'd take to get results on a comparison?"

"Homicide case, if you're lucky, few weeks. You talking DNA?"

"Yeah, DNA and the paper used as an incendiary device."

"If they got somethin' to compare the DNA to, like I said, weeks. Combustible material, about the same. We're takin' the back burner with FBI on most submissions because of all that world events mumbo jumbo. But homicide, rape they can't really justify puttin' that on the back burner you know."

"All right. I gotta go.'Preciate the help, Davinci."

"Anytime buckaroo. Take care of yourself. Remember, the job ain't worth losing your health over."

"You got that." I say.

Yeah, *you got that.* I'm the poster child for that cause.

"Oh, and Happy Thanksgiving!" he yells as I exit.

❄

MATHER'S RECLINED IN THE driver's side, one foot on

the dash. I get in the car and he's got some lousy talk show guy like Stern on the radio. I can't stand that guy, but I'm just a visitor so I don't say anything.

"You feel like some breakfast?" he asks.

I've got to think about it for a second because I don't usually eat breakfast. "Sure," I say after I remember that it's the most important meal of the day. Maybe that's what I need to do, have a healthy breakfast every morning. Take that energy level up a few notches. That's what I need. More energy, that is. Feel like I'm among the living. When was it I started feeling this way? Most of the time I feel like the walking dead, and for the life of me I can't remember a time when I felt different. I know there was a time because I've got people like Clem who tell me so, and pictures that prove it. But I face the past like a bug faces the windshield of an oncoming car. I don't really have the time to reflect before I'm hit hard with the realization that my past is either fiction or belongs to someone else. That's how I feel. The pictures don't even mean much. They just capture the image of some guy who looks a lot like the guy I see in the mirror every morning, but with a full smile.

I'll never forget the monster staring back at me in the mirror so many months ago. I dragged myself out of bed. I had an ear ache. I had not slept well, but that's not unusual. I went to the bathroom to brush my teeth, looking down at the sink. I noticed that the toothpaste mixed with saliva was pouring out of my mouth as if from an open spout. It was the oddest thing. It would not stay in my mouth. I had no control. I looked up at the mirror, stunned myself, and slipped on a couple of drops of water, almost fell to the floor. A sudden reaction to what I saw staring back at me. It was a distortion. The mirror was cracked. No, it wasn't. Was I caught in a dream state, like the last time I took Ambien? No, I was definitely awake.

There was the left side of my face, the lip completely fallen in a frozen state. I scared myself, and I don't scare easily. I've seen things. A stroke was my first thought, but I felt normal. I tried to swish water and rid my mouth of what toothpaste remained inside. It just spilled out, and I bit my lip in the process. It bled.

I dabbed my face dry and called my Sergeant. I would not be coming in that day. I slurred my words. He knew me well enough to know I wasn't drunk and so he was concerned. The second call was to my doctor.

I had never heard of Bell's Palsy. I learned that my seventh cranial nerve was inflamed. It is one of those conditions where there is no comfort in the knowledge of a cause. I like to know things like that, but my doctor gave me hope that a full recovery was in my future.

"More than eighty percent of those diagnosed with Bell's Palsy fully recover," I remember he said. It was usually a matter of a few weeks. "Just take the medication, and massage your face."

I did not fall into that eighty percent

category. I am going on four months with only minimal improvement.

Mather and I decide on the hotel at 15th and Rhode Island. Good breakfast buffet and fifty percent off for police. I haven't been there for a couple of years. Last time was with a guy I used to work with at the district, retired now. A few uniforms are sitting at tables when we enter the lounge area. I don't recognize any of them but Mather does. They all do the knocking knuckle thing and about a thirty-second catch-up and then we find an open table by a window and a television. They got the news on. Waiter comes and drops us a couple menus, but we tell him just the buffet and a pot of coffee.

I grab a plate and stack it with French toast and a couple of links of turkey sausage. Mather piles his plate with scrambled eggs, bacon, sausage, country potatoes and grits. I think to myself that that's maybe how it starts, walking with the dead, I mean. He adds about half a stick of butter for the grits. He's got to have a high metabolism to eat like that and maintain his girlish figure. I don't tell him that, though.

The local news highlights my case. They show a photograph they found of her, like one they got from the model agency, something I'm sure the family appreciates. After a brief report of the negative status of the case so far, they interview a girl who calls herself a prostitute's advocate. Another term I'm sure the family appreciates. She looks like she just came off the front line of some IMF protest at the World Bank and her commentary makes my stomach regret the breakfast I'm having. According to the advocate, we aren't taking this case seriously because she was an escort, "sweeping it under the carpet" kind of thing. I'd like to know where that information comes from. Mather looks at me like "I'm glad I'm not in your shoes," and all I do is smile, because, for all I know, he's their police source. My pager sounds. The text message reads: CALL ME IN THE OFFICE, ASAP. RUCKER.

"That didn't take long," Mather says.

I unclip my cell from my belt and call. Rucker answers and asks about the status of the case. I fill him in with what I've been doing; tell him he should set that police source straight because I've been devoting all my time to this one.

He asks me about this Bergine character and I tell him I left a message with him and'll try him back if I don't hear from him this morning. The conversation doesn't take long and afterwards I sort of miss the independence that came with being a simple robbery investigator.

"What do you got?"

"Just Rucker. Saw what we just saw. Covering his butt is all so he knows what to say when all the chiefs call him. But my question is, when did prostitutes get an advocate?"

"This city breeds all kinds. Next thing'll be the corner drug thug advocate. Every time one gets killed or locked up they'll get one of their reps on the news. Talk about how the System's responsible."

"I don't know about this world we live in."

"You need help on this?"

"No. I need to get that boyfriend of hers in the box, follow up on some of the evidence is all."

"You think there's a connection between this one and some old crack head case?"

"Naw, I don't think there's a connection." I say just in case.

"I thought you said before you like the similarities?"

"Sure, but that doesn't mean I think it's the same guy."

"The term's Serial Killer."

"Yeah, right. Start spreading that one around."

"Personally, I think the boyfriend did it. He found out what she did for a living, she didn't want to give it up like he wanted so he takes it like he's paying for it."

"Tape sure doesn't make him look good. You know what assistant's assigned to this?"

"Not sure. Call Pank, he'll know. He might even be handling it 'till he assigns it out. You know Pank, right?"

"Yeah, I know Pank. I've known Pankhurst since he was a Misdemeanor Assistant. Most all my old robbery cases went through the office he's head of now."

He stabs a couple of country potatoes with his fork, shoves them in his mouth.

"I've got to tell you, though. You know I don't want this assignment? I wanted it the first time I put in for it years ago, but my command wouldn't let me go."

"Blamed it on something like shortage of manpower,

of course," Mather adds.

"You got it. And now that I'm settled, they push me in."

"Rucker's your boy, isn't he? Just tell him you want out."

"Maybe I will. I don't know."

Mather's uniform buddies stroll out, and so do we a few minutes after. We head back to the office.

I start thinking about what I said. *"Settled."* I've never felt settled, and certainly not at Cold Case. I was counting the days until the end of the detail. Getting assigned to VCU was my original goal when I was promoted to detective. In my experience, it's every aspiring detective's original goal. I knew I'd have to do my time in the district, but if I worked really hard, maybe get noticed, I'd make it here. It was something I romanticized, investigating the ultimate act. The dead do tell tales. There's always a story, even though the language is veiled at times. That's what I used to think. The reality set in, after watching so many homicide detectives over the years, with puffy dark clouds under their eyes, living at work, and then Scanns, who slowly withered to nothing more than a vacant stare. Where's the romance in that?

TOMMY'S SLEEPING AT HIS cubicle as we pass. Mather chuckles. I head back to my spot and Mather says, "Catch ya later. Let me know if you need anything."

I look at my watch and decide I've given this guy

Bergine more than enough time, so I give him another call. The recorded voice answers again and I say, "This is the second message I've left for you. I will expect to hear from you by early this afternoon or I will be forced to take other measures." Polite but commanding and we'll see if he calls.

Two hours later, I get a call in the office. It's Bergine. The "other measures" part usually works, especially if someone has something to hide. If he doesn't, he'll be angry at my having left a message like that.

"I've been very busy with classes," he says apologetically. And then, "I thought a Detective Scanns was on this case?"

"He was. Detective Scanns isn't here anymore, so I've been assigned the case."

"I see, so how can I be of further assistance?"

"I'd like to talk with you. Today, if possible."

"Whatever I can do to help, but today's a bad day."

"It won't take long. I just need some more information. I think you can really help us on this one."

He hesitates with a couple of 'uhmms' and 'ahhs' and then, "Of course I want to help in any way I can. She was...very close to me."

"What time is good for you this afternoon?"

"Maybe two o'clock, or so."

"That would be good. You remember how to get here?"

"Yes, but couldn't we meet somewhere else? Get a coffee or something?"

"It would be best if we talked here, Mr. Bergine. It's

a lot easier than lugging all this paperwork around, you understand?"

"Yes, I do. Why don't we say around two o'clock then?"

"Good. I'll expect you then."

"Sure thing, Detective,"

After that I go to Rucker's office. He's in, typing madly at the keyboard.

"Got a second, Rucker?" I say.

"Take a seat."

"I'm good," I tell him. "I've got the interview set up with William Bergine. He'll be here at around two."

"Excellent. You want someone in there with you?"

"I'd rather not. I'll videotape it."

He stops typing. "Scanns said he's a good suspect?"

"The video I saw would suggest that but I've been fooled before. I'll have a go at him, see what happens. I need to get with Johnson at Mobile, too, see what he got off the scene. I'm going to see if Bergine'll voluntarily give hair and DNA samples; if not, I'll see if I got enough for a warrant."

"I'm getting ready for the morning meeting with the chiefs, and you know I'm going to get hammered on this one."

"That's why you got the bars."

"Here, you want them, you go for me?"

"That's all right. I'll stay with the little hammer you got over me."

"Just give me someone who can close a case around here. That's all I ask."

"You got some good guys. You just take a couple of aspirins before the hammering and let your boys do their job. You're the one that wanted the rank, remember?"

"Just be on your text pager if I need you."

"Sure."

"And get a confession out of that guy," he says as I'm walking away but I don't answer.

I log into the computer and run a Triple I on Bergine. An FBI number pops on the screen, and I get excited for a second until I run it and find it's just a couple of possession marijuana charges he picked up years ago out of some Po-Dunk sheriff's office somewhere in Florida. Other than that, he's clean. I run him for complainant status and find that he's been a victim of a couple of crimes. But then, I can run nine out of ten citizens who live in this city and find the same thing. One report he made was lost property and the other two, burglaries at his residence. He lives in the lower end of the Third District, off 9th Street, Northwest, so that kind of thing's common. Crack heads in the neighborhood finding an easy target. One guy's usually responsible for a dozen or more burglaries, so you can imagine how that area gets torn up. Probably bought the place fifteen years ago, when he could get it for around 80k. I'm familiar with the block Bergine's on. All politically active members of the ANC. I don't think he's one of those upwardly mobile types—probably just all he could afford way back then with what he got paid as an Associate Professor at UDC.

Right around the corner you've got one of the biggest crack and heroin dealerships in Northwest. They've been selling dope there since the 1950s. Some of the old-timer junkies who managed to survive by who knows what means are still hanging in that area. They're the ones you see with the dark eyes and the fat fingers. Then a couple of blocks on the other side, just off 7th Street, you got that one block where you can buy any kind of contraband you want, everything from cartons of cigarettes, counterfeit movie DVDs and music CDs to Pampers. Used to be a pool hall right on the corner, known hang-out for all the great pickpockets in the DC area. That's where the grapevine started, the spot to buy all the stolen credit cards and IDs, and get the latest info on what big business conference was coming to the shiny new glass Convention Center, maybe share some of the trade secrets. That's a bit of Bergine's backyard. I can get into it in more detail but I don't want to. The less you know, the happier you are. That's why I'm so miserable. Let's see just how happy Bergine is.

I'M THINKING ABOUT WHAT I read in the book I'm having a hard time finishing, about how our life can be like a tangle of unfinished tales. That's how I feel as I drive along traffic-infested streets through all the squalor to that narrow side street where William Bergine lives.

Bergine never showed for the interview.

I left him two messages and never got a call back. It's no surprise. I've had Complainants do the same thing. But he's not a complainant and he's looking more and more like a good suspect. I can't take the chance that he is good for the murder and that he thinks I might have something on him, when I don't. Maybe that's why he didn't show. Maybe he'll have a good excuse for not returning my calls, but maybe he just hit the road.

That's why I decided to take a drive—a surprise visit.

I turn onto his street and find a parking spot a couple of houses down from his. I scan the area for his car, but don't see it. It might be parked in a space in back but from what I remember about these homes, most of them have cracker-box back yards and narrow alleys with barely enough room for the trash cans.

As I get out of the car I notice two kids sitting on a stoop across from where Bergine lives. They give me that sideways stare as I walk up to the door and ring his doorbell, then knock through the security gate with a couple of hard raps. Nothing. I try to open the security gate, but it's locked. I grab a business card out of my wallet and stick it between the door frame and the edge of the door, so when he gets home he'll know I dropped by.

I decide to hang in the cruiser parked along the curb, to keep an eye on his house for a bit. Maybe he'll return. It's one of those three-story red brick row houses. All the houses are connected together but some of them are painted different colors. The house right across the street from Bergine's, where those two young thugs are sitting, looks like a thorn in the side of an otherwise clean block. They're probably thinking I'm here because of them. They smile at each another like, "Yeah we see you sitting there, trying to be sly."

These things never go as planned. I know this all too well. It could've been easy. Bergine shows, confesses. Case closed. But, instead, I'm sitting here thinking things might go better and he'll show. I sink back into the seat and close my eye, but just for a second. I hold my bad eyelid down. It burns a little from the nippy air. I think about my empty humidor and how I should fix it up and get it set for some nice cigars for when Clem gets here in case I feel inspired to smoke around her. I think about carefully placing the cigars inside to moisten and age like wine. I like the way moist cigars feel between the fingers when they first come out of a good humidor.

My attention's diverted, though, by a couple who look like one of those upwardly mobile types. They pop out of their blue-brick attached row house, neighboring the sunflower-colored one. The female's armed with a large plastic garbage bag and they're working together to clean the litter from the dirty snow on a tree box and the gutter in front of what is probably their first investment. They're a young, attractive couple and probably frequent places like Old

Marvin's or Sunday brunch at the Corcoran. *What do they think?* That their presence, like white blood cells, will destroy the affliction a couple of doors down? They probably don't plan on growing old in the house they've spent so much time fixing up, so why bother? The investment isn't worth all that. That's my opinion, anyway. Their house sits on the tiny lot, tightly wedged between a white-washed row house and the neighboring sunflower yellow brick one. There are angled rows of bricks under a second-story window ledge, just above the stoop where the mopes sit snickering, buckle slightly, giving the structure an appearance of having a defiant smile, just like theirs. The basement stairwell's riddled with rusted bike parts, weather-beaten children's toys, 40s, and crumpled Doritos bags. It looks like the only place on the block where snow hasn't been shoveled off the sidewalk. It stands alone, rebellious, a statement to those unwanted neighbors trying to push them out.

Examine that building's documents and you'll probably find that the grandparents of those kids, who bought it some fifty years ago still live in a room on the second floor behind the structure's defiant smile. They're content with the fifty-inch flat-panel HDTV with surround sound and DVD player that one or both of the boys bought for them by slingin' on the stoop. I've executed dozens of search warrants in homes like that one. Run it through the system and I'd find that vice or some other unit's already executed a search warrant there. One more and grandpa's home will be on the market and selling for 500K to some upwardly mobile type.

Probe their minds and you'll discover that they're good, clueless people, trapped within a room on the second floor, bewitched by families possessed by digital spirits.

I just know the two young ones on the stoop are waiting for me to leave, so they can conduct their little transactions while their grandparents are in their room, watching a rerun of the "Cosby" show. And people like the young attractive couple down the street with their large garbage bag; well, they'll just keep coming, along with all the other white blood cells, and fight the good fight and go to those little ANC meetings and write those little letters. It's not going to change a thing. This I know. What I don't know is why they make me so mad. I can just look at them and read their lives. It's a curse. I've been wrong a couple of times in the past, but that's rare. And I like my story better, so I'll stick with it. I think too much anyway, another weakness of mine.

My pager rings. It's the Sergeant's number at VCU. I obey and make the call.

"Sergeant Barnes," He answers.

"What's up, Sarge?"

"Where are you?"

"Sitting on Bergine's house, hopin' he'll show."

"He won't," Barnes tells me and before I can ask what he means he says, "Just got a call from Park and they just found him swingin' from a limb off the GW

Parkway."

"You got to be kidding?"

"Ask anybody. I don't kid. You ready to copy this number. They're waiting for you."

I grab the pen out of my shirt pocket. "Go ahead," I say. He gives me the number and I write it in my notebook. After I disconnect with the Sarge my bad eye tears a long steady stream. I take my sunglasses off and wipe it with the back of my hand. I slip the sunglasses back on.

"Sonofa gun," I say to myself.

FOUR

PROBE BERGINE'S MIND AND all you'll find are dark musty rooms, like this home he kept in life.

It's Friday—my Saturday.

I just left Bergine's hole-in-the-wall office at the university. Not much there, except a desktop computer, scanner and a couple of files that I'll go through later. In about four hours Clem will be at the Mayflower. If I'm lucky, I'll get out of here in time for a quick shower and change of clothing—wash away the timeworn decay lingering within these walls, and now on me. At least I won't carry the stench of his death with me. The body was found within hours of his last breath, and even if it had been discovered days later, this cold weather would have preserved him.

I find it hard to believe, having been to Amy Noyes' apartment and knowing what little I know about her personal life, that she would have had anything to do with this guy, if she had ever seen this place. Maybe that's how it happened? Why not? It's as good a motive as Boo Boo shooting Shorty 'cause Shorty looked at him too hard at a club one night. Probably better.

The Mobile Crime Tech is trailing behind me like an unwilling bodyguard. I want to tell him maybe the officer posted outside needs help holding up the front stoop, but I know that's unkind, so I let it go. We both know there won't be much to recover from this scene. Mather should be here soon though, having called moments ago from court.

I replace the latex glove on my right hand after I tear the palm on a bent-out staple attached to a medical document found on a desk with piles of other documents, unpaid bills and junk mail. I find the doctor's name on one of the documents and notebook it. No suicide note yet, but that's not uncommon. The ones that want to go just go. No need to tell a story. Those are for the ones that want to be found. Hope is waiting for the knock on the door that never comes. Self-pity's stronger than hope, and so they fall. I've seen their faces; that fatal moment cast in a milky-eyed mortal stare. I can always imagine those final seconds. Bergine, he didn't have that look. His mind was made up before the drop. No look of surprise on his face, just a shell left hanging on a limb.

I scan his bedroom before I begin. The air is thick and smells of sweat and semen.

The nightstand in his bedroom is riddled with prescription containers of anti-depressants and pain killers, like misplaced chess pieces, and an unfinished glass of red wine that chased down the pills. A small crystal ashtray is piled high with ash and cigarette butts, and his bed sheets are rumpled and clumped at the foot of the mattress—*must've been a restless sleeper.*

"Take the sheets," I tell the Tech. A couple of grunts, a slight moan, but he obeys, folding them over on the mattress then stuffing them in a large paper bag marked EVIDENCE.

"This supposed to be a suicide, right?" the Tech asks.

"Swinger's a suspect in a homicide. You think I'd be wastin' your time otherwise?"

He grunts again, marks something on the bag, and sets it aside.

I open the nightstand drawer and find old receipts, phone bills, a layer of pennies and nickels scattered underneath. I take the receipts and bills and slip them in a plastic evidence bag, set them next to the Tech's evidence kit.

I take the portable phone, punch in *69 and get a number and notebook it. I tap the redial button and the same number appears on the caller ID, but I disconnect before it dials. I check the ID for all the incoming calls, and that same number appears several times. I notebook the other numbers, none of them I recognize. No calls from Amy Noyes. *That's odd.*

I take the laptop on a dresser, tag it, and set it beside the other items. I lift the mattress to check underneath. Nothing. I check the other side, and still nothing. Under the bed, I see one shoe, several unmatched socks, and underwear. I pull them out, one at a time. I take the stained underwear.

"These, too," I mutter.

I hear shuffling from the other room and turn as Mather enters. "You find a note yet?" he says, then notices the Tech dropping the underwear in a paper bag.

Mather's wearing a navy blue suit with delicate line patterns, a crisp white shirt, and what looks like a Thomas Pink tie. *A little bold for that suit.* But I don't say anything, because I still don't know him well enough.

Instead I ask, "You going to search this mess wearing that suit?"

"That's what the dry cleaner's for. Got an extra pair of gloves?"

I pull a couple of latex gloves out of my front pant pocket and toss them to Mather. He turns to the pudgy Crime Scene guy, slipping the gloves on and says, "What's up with you, Slappy? You ready to get dirty?"

"This is your world, not mine. You find it. I bag it."

"Won't be bagging much here," I say, "'Cause what I got is a primary suspect who committed suicide, had a relationship with the decedent, and even if I find his DNA on her, what use is it?"

"But you're still getting a blood order, right?"

"Because that's what I'm supposed to do."

"Naw, 'cause you need to cover your ass," Pudgy

says.

"Well, I say this is the season of hope, brother. Maybe he left his confession secured on the fridge with a magnet, so that's where I'll start," Mather replies.

"Let that hope carry you through, but only for the next two hours, because that's when I'm rollin' out," I tell him.

"You mean you have a life?" Mather chuckles.

"Just through tomorrow."

"Won't take long to clear this place," Mather says with confidence, then turns to strut out of the room.

"See if you can find a cell phone for this guy. He had to have a cell phone."

He gives me the thumbs up sign like he's thanking the coach for starting him on varsity, and then walks out of the room.

I've been in worse places, executed search warrants in such holes that I'd have to bag and toss my own shoes and clothing after. I'd walk out, feeling like things were crawling around my scalp. Nothing was ever there, but I'd still have to scrub my body, wash my hair three or four times before I was comfortable again. Bergine's place is nothing compared to some of the spots I've been in. Just as we're preparing to leave, Hattie shows up. He looks surprised when I tell him there isn't a note, disappointed when I advise him this doesn't look like it'll be a quick closure.

FIVE

I'VE GOT FORTY-FIVE MINUTES before I have to meet Clem. It's only a ten-minute walk to the Mayflower so I spend a little more time in the hot shower, holding my left eye shut and letting the strong surge of water massage my crippled face. Maybe the seventh cranial nerve will settle, and it'll fall back into place. That's what I think, but still manage to lapse back into that familiar melancholy state. That's when I try to think of the excuse I'll come up with after not showing up tonight. I got good ones—three open homicides. That's a pretty good excuse. Also, getting stuck on the search warrant all night is another one, but that would be a lie.

I choose my favorite charcoal gray patterned shirt, un-tucked over baggy blue jeans, old Doc Martin leather jacket and a scarf wrapped around my neck. I've won the battle over self-pity and decided that I could not lie to Clem. After the hot shower, the wind is unwelcome against my face, so I cab it.

Not many people at the Mayflower bar, mostly

hotel guests and what look like old regulars. Clem's lounging in one of the comfortable sofas toward the back, near a window and off to the side of the piano. *Piano man must be on a break.*

She looks like she hasn't changed a bit, still keeps her hair the same, still dresses simply and wears makeup sensibly. I actually get an achy feeling in my gut when I see her. I give myself a couple of mental kicks to make the feelings go away, then wave when she quickly stands after noticing me.

"Love the look," she says, and we hug. She grabs my chin between her fingers, moves my face to a profile like she wants a better angle. "It gives you character."

"I felt like a change," I shrug. She smells like figs, like something grown out of good soil.

"What's this?" she asks, patting my right side, where my gun is holstered and hidden under the shirt. She knows what it is and doesn't expect an answer. She kisses me on the lips. "It's good to see you, Ezra."

"Good to see you." I take off my jacket, set it over the arm of the sofa and then we sit. "How was the trip?"

"All right, but glad to be settled, even if it's only for a couple of days."

Clem already has a drink on the table, looks like a dirty martini. I half smile. "What's with the martini?"

"Something different. Stronger."

"You look good, Clem."

"You too, actually."

"Actually?"

"Yeah, I really did expect to see Two Face the way you talked. You look tired, though."

"Working on two hours sleep, but I'll be all right, as long as the waitress finds us."

She does, as if on cue. Clem was about to respond with some note of concern. It makes me uncomfortable when she shows concern, genuine though it is. I order what I always order, Lagavulin, neat with a water back.

The Piano Man returns to the bench.

"There he is," I say.

"He looks just like he did the last time we were here."

"What, about three years, and it feels like yesterday?"

"You're so right. I wonder what that is," Clem says.

I want to say, "It's because we're so connected," but I know it's just age. It throws time into warp drive. He starts on some old song that was way before both our times, but listening to it in a place like this, with Clem, is comforting, nonetheless. I look at some of those old timers at the bar and wonder if it feels like yesterday for them.

What I like about Clem is that she's so relaxed in these silent moments. But it's only in times of loneliness, like now, that I think of her as more than just an old friend. The thought makes me quiver.

Clem breaks my reverie. "Hey, I'll understand if you're too tired to hang."

If only she knew.

"I'm good," I say, straightening up. "You see me

fading off, just give me a nudge."

The waitress returns with my order. I take a long sip. "I've been looking forward to tonight, something social. I needed it. You came at a good time," I say changing the subject.

"I feel the same," she says and lifts her drink. I lift mine, and our glasses meet with a light 'clink.'

"You haven't been a social creature for a while," I scold with a slight smile.

"Work can do that to you. At least you're in a place you can relax a little. What's that called? That TV series?"

"*Cold Case,* and it's nothing like TV. Besides, I'm not there anymore. I got my sorry self transferred to homicide."

"Great! That's where you wanted to go, right? I mean, it's a better show, after all. Detective Ezra Simeon, Homicide."

"Right," I say, like I know the real story. "But naw, that's how I felt a few years back. I'm tired now, burnt out, bored. Whatever you want to call it. I was fine where I was. You remember my buddy Scanns?"

"Sure, how is he?"

"Dead."

She raises her eyebrows and puts her drink down. "Dead? When? What happened?"

"Not too long ago, before we last spoke."

"Why didn't you tell me?"

"I really wasn't ready to talk about it. Don't mean to be so callous, but the more I think about it, the angrier I get. In a nutshell—he had a bad heart, in both the literal and the figurative sense. And they found his dead body on a sofa in the home of this girl he was keeping on the side."

"Oh my, his poor wife."

"Yes, but she was never told where he was found, so as far as we know, she didn't know about the girl."

"How long was he seeing her?"

"I don't know for sure. A while, I guess."

"Oh, she probably knew."

"You mean that woman's intuition thing?"

"Just that human sensitive knowledge thing between two people who should know each other."

That makes me nervous, I think, then say, "Maybe she did. Maybe she didn't. What's important is she didn't know where he was found." I take a sip of my drink and continue. "So, shortly after the funeral, I get notified that I'm detailed to homicide to take over his case load."

"Why didn't you just tell them no if you didn't want to go? Stick up for yourself?"

"You're such a civilian."

"Something you were once, and still are more than you think."

"Don't ever compare me to your kind. I'm a new breed—evolved."

"Sorry to shatter your new world, but to me, you're still the same person, just a lowly English teacher, with a slightly dark nature. You should just go back to teaching."

"As much as I find myself complaining, I can't imagine doing anything else right now."

She accepts it at face value. "Cheers to that, then." She lifts her glass. "And sorry about your friend."

"Then here's to Scanns, despite his choices." I lift my glass. Another clink.

The Piano Man goes off into *White Christmas* and I find myself falling back into the sofa, cradling the swirling scotch in my hand. I feel snug sitting beside Clem, the thought of Christmas right around the corner and maybe more snow. That happy sad season, where even the coldness of winter is made warm.

"I miss the seasons," Clem murmurs, gazing out the window, and I realize she was right about that human sensitive thing. I'll be more careful about what I think around her.

"Move to New York then. They got offices there, right?"

"Yes, but California's where the real action is."

I almost laugh, but realize she is serious. Her definition of action is not the same as mine.

Before I know it, I've nursed through my second drink, and the Piano Man's closing with a final song. I realize there's a third thing that will hasten time, besides reading and sleeping—good company. I don't want this night to end, but I'm tired and actually looking forward to a sound sleep. We have the whole day together tomorrow, and I'd rather not be tired. So we pay our tab, leave the waitress a healthy tip, and I walk Clem to the lobby. We hug. She smiles like she just remembered something and says, "One whole evening and you haven't mentioned Priscilla once. I'm impressed."

"I didn't, did I? That's odd."

I give her a peck on the cheek and we wish each other a good night. Funny thing is, Clem's presence would always trigger Priscilla moments, but not tonight. Maybe things are improving. I think about this on the walk home, but not too much, for fear I'll bring her back.

❄

I SLIP THE PATCH on my eye. My friend, the wind, is less frequent now. It's not long before I fall asleep, though, even without its chant.

And I wake up, not knowing if I have dreamt.

It's 8:30.

I roll to my side, away from the clock, and close my eye again. *Clem's a late sleeper.* Plus, she's on California time.

I try to lose myself, but can't. I've already looked at the clock, so now it's too late. The sleep won't take me back. I pull the patch off and set it on the nightstand. I get up and walk into the living room where I lie on the sofa, pick up the Dickens bio. I start the final chapter, "The Alleged Optimism of Dickens." I get through a couple of pages where I read, "He knew well that the greatest happiness that has been known since Eden is the happiness of the unhappy."

I like that. I think I've said something like that before.

I place the marker back in the book and set it down on the coffee table. *Happiness of the unhappy.* It sounds like Christmas to me. But it's too early to muse and definitely too early to consider anything extraordinary, so I just lie there and stare at the ceiling, thinking about where I'll take Clem today.

Forty-five minutes of mental preparation.

I decide to straighten up this place, let in a little bit of light. Clem might want to stop by. She's always thought of this place as the "cozy dungeon," too. It doesn't take long to clean up. It's not like I have the kind of hang-time here that would create a real mess. Everything else is just comfortable clutter, and adds to that cozy factor. After I'm satisfied I've done enough, I shower, have my regular two cups of coffee and a little bit of the anxiety channel.

No news day, so the producers focus on the likelihood of more terrorism on the home front. If they can't get you one way they'll get you another. That's their job. I put the mute on and wait for the weather.

Today's forecast, chilly but sunny, mid-forties. For me that means the leather jacket, scarf, sweater, sunglasses, and my comfortable brown jeans.

I meet Clem in her hotel room at the Mayflower. The room is surprisingly messy for only a one-night stay. Bathroom towels tossed in a pile at the foot of the unmade king sized bed, opened soda cans on the nightstand beside it, along with a haphazard stack of papers. She has two small carry-on pieces of luggage, rummaged through like she had a hard time finding something.

"Looks like you've been here a week."

"I wish. Sit down or something. You're making me nervous."

I sit on the edge of the bed.

She slips on her shoes, looks up at me. "What's it like out there?"

"Chilly," I say. "But not so bad for someone who's used to it. You got a good jacket, right?"

"I'm prepared. Don't you worry about me."

After the shoes are on, she goes to the bathroom, checks herself out in front of the mirror. She pulls her thick, dark hair back with an elastic cloth strap and slides the band so it covers a portion of her ears. The harsh light against the glossy white tiles might reveal too much for most of us to bear, highlighting those unwanted lines and blemishes. Not Clem, though. The sun was always her friend. Her skin is smooth, like a pearl. That pearl skin, along with her dark hair and green eyes, makes her stand out from the typical California girl. Surprisingly, she was born and raised there, but her parents left after they retired, replacing the beach for the mountains. They grew tired of the constant threat of a sinking land.

"I'm ready," she decides. She grabs a coat out of the closet, looks like a vintage pea coat, then a long purple scarf that wraps around her neck a few times. She turns, arms spread out, like I should be proud the way she looks. "Ta Da!"

"You look great, Clem." And then out the door we

go.

Outside the hotel, we grab a cab and head to Georgetown for brunch at the Bistro Français, on M Street. I only go there when Clem's visiting. I'm thankful when I learn she just wants to grab some brunch and maybe walk around a bit and take it easy. I start evenings tomorrow. Roll call's at 2 p.m., but my body still feels like it's on day work. I'm dragging a bit.

Clem calls the waiter "Garçon" when she orders. "That's what they call them in Paris, so they expect it here," she tells me. She called one of the waiters Garcon on her last visit here. He didn't take it well, thought she was serious and the title beneath him. This waiter says we can pretend to be in Paris if we want.

Clem orders something with crêpes, and I get the Eggs Benedict, same thing I ordered last time. The restaurant fills up quickly. All the talking and laughter in this room mix together, like a loud bad dream. I can isolate each conversation if I focus, but I'm pulled back when the waiter returns with coffee.

"Thank you, Garçon," says Clem and the waiter exits with a slight bow. "I didn't have coffee this morning," she tells me.

"I appreciate the fact you like real coffee. Just want you to know that."

"Real coffee? You mean black, straight up, grinds in your teeth coffee?"

"Smile. I'll let you know when to pick 'em out."

She smiles like the Cheshire cat. "Thanks."

"So what time you flying out tomorrow?" I ask.

"Ten in the morning."

"I'll give you a ride."

"No, I'll take a cab."

"I'll give you a ride," I insist. "You never let me give you a ride."

"Because I've got a per diem for that sort of thing, so why bother you? Besides, I have to get there two hours early, and I know you have to work."

"It's no bother."

"Then what will I do with the per diem?"

"I don't know. Buy another scarf," I suggest.

She grabs the end of her purple scarf hanging over her chair, "What's wrong with this one?"

"Looks like they used grape juice for dye."

"It's a nice shade of purple," she says, dangling the end over her fingers. "It's expensive."

"I'm sure it is."

"Listen, it's Prada," she says.

"And that makes it a better color?"

"What do you know about high fashion?"

"I know a lot of things."

"I'm sure you think you do, coming from the guy whose idea of good color combinations are shades of gray and black."

"I like to call them earth tones."

"You need to brighten up your wardrobe with some color. Let me help you."

"Listen, California, last thing I need in my wardrobe is anything *Vogue* says is in. Anyway, I got some color in my closet."

"I get *Vogue* for the articles, not the fashion."

"Okay, okay. So I'm taking you to the airport, right?"

"You can take me to the airport," she decides before the coffee cup touches her lips.

"You make it sound like I should thank you now."

"Yes, because the per diem's paying for brunch."

"Thank you."

Washington is a city designed for walking. All these vehicles occupied by high-strung irritable people, honking their horns, edging up on each other like bullies ready to kick sand, don't belong on these narrow streets. Too much anxiety out there. It's Saturday, and it looks like rush hour. I am thankful for Clem. Her presence is like a sedative.

We walk until we find ourselves at the Potomac, leaning on a rail and gazing over the river to the Virginia side, where it's thicker with trees and snow. The river's freezing up in places, working its way toward the middle, where the ice is at its thinnest. The wind is calm, with only a mild bite. I gaze at Clem, with her grape juice scarf wrapped around her neck and chin, with a restful, slight smile and accommodating eyes. I want to gently lean against her. I want to kiss her. I look away before she notices my admiration, but keep her in the corner of my eye for comfort. I don't know what it is about this time around, as opposed to all her other visits. Am I just lonely right now, or are these unexpected feelings I'm having for Clem, real? Maybe it was that "pushing forty" baby talk we had at the Mayflower. Whatever the case, I'll never let her know how I'm feeling. We've been friends for too long for me to go and mess it up with something more than a friendship, or to even approach her with the idea.

Work has left me for the moment. I try to find the place she's at, in that distance, over the trees, the buildings, where we can see for miles.

If I try real, hard I can smell the ocean.

If I try real hard, this moment will stay with me.

THE AIRPORT WASN'T BUSY. I left Clem after she walked through security toward her gate. Now driving along the Parkway back to DC, I notice a plane angling upward over the river, having just departed National, and I wonder if she's on it. I don't even know if it's pointed toward Los Angeles. I like to think that it's her plane, though, and that she's looking out one of those little windows down to the river and the Parkway that stretches along it, just to see my car. I almost roll down the window and wave, but it's too cold and too corny.

Memorial Bridge is ahead, stretching across the river from Virginia to DC. There's a desirable loneliness about the city in the winter, especially on Sunday.

I think about my time with Clem. After our Georgetown walk, we ended up at my place, where we stayed until late that night. We talked about nothing in particular, mostly listened to the music that got us both through the eighties, now contained within sleeves of a thick canvas CD case. Those CDs used to be stacked one against another in milk crates. My quick LA departure left so much behind. All remnants of a past life, probably buried somewhere in some dark California closet. *I did not mention her name.* And as I listened to those familiar songs with Clem, no bad thoughts came to mind. They've only arrived now, because the calm has left, after yet another brief visit.

Day crew's still working when I get to VCU. I notice one of them. Anderson, I think. He's got some time on and a belly that grew with it.

"How's it been?" I ask.

"Slow day," he says thankfully.

I nod and give him a look like I'm happy for him.

"You're here early."

"Things to catch up on, you know?"

"Pace yourself," he advises.

"I learned that one a long time ago, but thanks anyway."

The sleeping detective with a familiar face is at it again and looks like he's been in the same position for days. I move quietly, because I'm still on his time, setting the coffee on the desk beside the CPU and my briefcase under the cubicle.

I log in to the computer. That's the first thing I usually do because, by the time you get done with everything else, it's usually booted up. The Windows startup sound echoes out of the speakers as the machine comes to life. The familiar face stirs, but that's all. He quickly falls back to his original position and condition. I turn the volume off.

I pull out the three case jackets from my briefcase and notice the boxes I packed with Scanns' personal items, still where I left them. I'll have to take those to Celeste at some point, but not today. It's Sunday. Sunday's not a good day for something like that. I'll call tomorrow.

I set the case jackets on the uncluttered desktop and then sit back and watch the monitor while all my files download. By the time the icons pop up on the screen, about five minutes has gone by.

I check my departmental e-mail, only to find the latest newsletter from the Mayor's office. I delete it.

I sit for a moment, starting to lose myself again, shake out of it, and then look around to make sure no one saw.

I open up my case management file that contains my running resumés, type in the file number for the Noyes case, and then click the mouse for search.

I grab my notebook, flip through the pages to find the number I recovered from Bergine's phone. I want to see if I can find a name or anything else it might be linked to before I call it. I hate cold calls. It's better to have something beforehand so you don't stumble around the conversation. I find the number, click on the Inquiry field with the mouse and then again for Telephone Numbers. I type in the number. No results. That means a report hasn't been affiliated with the number yet. I pull myself off the chair, find Anderson playing Mahjong on the Internet. "We got a Hanes Directory somewhere around here?" I ask.

Anderson turns from his screen, "Should be in the Sergeant's office where the Log Book is."

"Thanks."

The day work official's not in, so I scan the area until I see the Log Book. The directory's on a shelf underneath. I shuffle through the pages in an attempt to find the prefix, but no luck. It has to be a cell phone or a new listing.

I call Dispatch to check reverse call, and they tell me the prefix comes back to a cell phone. That usually means subpoena, unless you have a good contact at the service provider. I don't, so the next step before I think subpoena is cold call.

I go back to the desk, look at the number on the notebook until I'm staring so hard I lose focus.

I make the call.

Four rings and a male voice on the other end that almost sounds live, "This is Daniel. Sorry I'm not here to take your call but please leave a message so I can get back to you. Ciao."

Ciao?

I hang up without leaving a message.

Who says "Ciao" anymore, anyway? Clem doesn't even have the guts to say that. Or maybe she does, but not in my presence. She knows better than that. I remember a cop when I was in patrol, he used to say "Ciao, baby!"—Two words you don't use together in my book. He said it like he wanted to be sophisticated and street smart at the same time. But he just looked silly, and I was embarrassed for him because most of the guys laughed behind his back.

Ciao. That's right, baby. I'll enjoy meeting this guy.

SIX

NOT MUCH TO DO on Sunday except catch up on paperwork, make sure your to-do list's in order, and talk to witnesses if you're lucky enough to have any. I decide I'll use some of this idle time and go through one of the Boo Boo cases I chose to neglect when I first got to VCU.

The portion of Scanns' Case Resumé that describes the scene indicates that nine expended 9mm shell casings were recovered from the kitchen floor and that a large area of the kitchen wall and ceiling was spattered with blood. Four of the nine slugs were recovered.

I find the pictures secured in an evidence envelope, shuffle through them. One of the eight-by-ten photographs reveals the decedent on his back laying over a sheet of his own glossy blood, his right arm in a stretched-out position, as if reaching up toward the shooter. *A futile attempt at mercy.* His face—a bewildered look, like he couldn't believe what was happening, like he wondered why the world suddenly fell beneath his feet.

He was thrown out of one shoe, maybe during a struggle. His sock has some cartoon character design on it, something a little kid would wear, but this guy's in his thirties. I look closer. *Bugs Bunny.* I envision him picking those socks out and sliding them on his big feet after he got out of bed, never realizing the end he'd meet wearing them. I think about his sister and her little boy finding him like that.

I find the autopsy report.

He's 38 years old, weighs 242 pounds and is 5 feet 11 inches in height.

Gunshot wound number one has an entrance located over the forehead 4 inches below the top of the head, half an inch left of the anterior surface of the body. It penetrated the skull traveling through the right cerebral hemisphere and was recovered in the right occipital lobe of the brain. The track of the wound is from front to back, slightly left to right and downward.

Gunshot wound number two entered over the right earlobe traveling through the right and the left cerebral hemisphere, exiting the skull. The track of the wound is from right to left and slightly upward.

I quickly read through gunshot wounds four, five and six and then the rest of the pages, including the dissection of the body. I search the case jacket for the canvass information and it's the usual stuff—no one saw anything. Scanns interviewed the sister. But she doesn't know how this could have happened. He was a "churchgoer," she said. "Never been locked up." I look for decedent history. Nothing. It doesn't look like Scanns had gotten to that.

I do a couple of criminal checks on the decedent, Tomlinson, running him through our local system, but only find DC permit info that has his license as expiring in two more years. I log into NCIC, the FBI's national database so I can do a Triple I. He's never been locked up. Anywhere. That's a surprise. He just might be a decent guy. I run a check on complaints he may have reported, and a few things pop on the screen, mostly miscellaneous incident reports and then one Simple Assault which occurred four months ago, almost to the day. I note the criminal complaint number.

I dig through the file, find the sister's information. I check her out. Nothing there either.

I think I'll take a drive today, visit his neighborhood, then stop by the Third District, where I need to find that Simple Assault report.

MATHER AND I DRIVE down the steep ramp of the Third District's upper level parking, take a left on to U Street. I read the 251 on the Simple Assault while we drive.

According to the report, a suspect identified as "Peanut" punched the complainant, Scott Tomlinson, knocking him to the ground. The narrative suggests that the assault was unprovoked. Based on my experience, that's probably not the case. With what little intuition I have left and all those miscellaneous incident reports I found in the system, I'm willing to bet Tomlinson didn't care for the likes of Peanut in his neighborhood. Confronted him maybe, and got smacked down for it. A Third District detective tells me their records don't indicate an arrest was made or that "Peanut" was ever identified. As usual, not much was put into closing this case, as easy as it would have been. Still, it's a good lead and something I can follow up on. You never know. I've been lucky like that before.

Tomlinson's neighborhood is typical of so many of the Northwest neighborhoods nowadays—tear them down so you can build them up. But some things will never change, like the five boys I see hanging at the corner ahead. It's thirty something degrees out there, and they don't have anything better to do than stand at that corner and act like they're doing something other than slinging drugs. That'll never change. Doesn't matter how high they make the rent.

Mather pulls to the curb ahead of the small public housing unit Tomlinson used to call home.

"Mind if we just hang here for a second?" I ask.

"Sure. You think one of them is Peanut?"

"Chances are one of them knows Peanut."

"I think there's Peanuts in every crew in DC."

"Probably right," I say.

He keeps the car idling with the heater on. The social club starts to break up, just like I knew it would. Our presence has that effect on DC outdoor social clubs. Two of them walk away in opposite directions, looking our way just so we know they're tough little boys. I got my eye on the chubby one. I open the car door. Mather turns the engine off and follows. I shut the door, walk toward the short, chubby one. He's trying to gain a little distance, but his baggy low rider pants and the slippery sidewalk prevent him from getting too far.

"Hold up there, little man," I say, but he keeps walking. "You think I'm going to ask twice? Come on, now."

He stops because he knows better. If he hadn't been through this before, he would've kept going, learned for the next time.

"Why aren't you all in watching the game?"

"It's half time."

"You know I could care less about what you all are doing on the corner out there. I got bigger business."

He shrugs. My business doesn't mean anything to this guy unless he's the one who's cuffed.

"They call you Peanut, don't they?"

"I ain't Peanut."

"Come on now. I know Peanut when I see him," I tell him.

"Man, I ain't Peanut."

"What do they call you then?"

"Dread."

"I don't see no dreadlocks on you."

"I cut 'em off."

"Well, you better grow 'em back if they gonna call

you Dread. What's your real name? I want a first and last."

"Calvin McKorkle," he tells me like he's not even used to saying it himself.

"Well Calvin, you telling me they call you Dread but you don't got dreadlocks? I say you look like a Peanut."

"Naw man, I'm tellin' you I ain't Peanut. Peanut's over there." He points toward the corner where Mather's talking to three other members.

"Which one?"

"Over there."

"I can see you're pointing, and I know you don't mean my partner. So which of the three, unless it is you?"

"One with the twists."

"Where do you live?"

He points down the street. "Over there."

"Well, before you go over there, I need you to step back over here for a minute. All right, Calvin?"

He shakes his head like I'm wasting his time.

We walk over to Mather and the rest of the crew.

I grab my notebook from my back pocket.

"I know it's a silly question, but anyone got ID?" I ask.

No one answers.

I notebook their names and vitals when they give them to me, then run them through dispatch and they come back with no wants. A little hard to believe, but they're still young. The one with the twists in his hair tells me his name's Michael Puller but they call him Peanut.

SEVEN

TAMMY MCPHERSON TOOK OVER her brother's small two-bedroom apartment after he was killed. She used to share the bigger bedroom with her little boy when he was alive but after his death, she convinced herself to move into the other room so her son could have his own space. She had just gotten back from church a few minutes before we arrived, and the apartment still smells of the fresh-baked brownies she made for the people there. She apologizes for not having any left to offer. Mather looks disappointed. She asks her son to go in his room while we talk.

She looks like she's in her early thirties, heavyset with a thin face lined with the stress of too much grieving. I'm sitting beside her at the end of the sofa. Mather is sitting on the matching love seat angled beside it. It's clean and uncluttered in here, unlike this neighborhood. A King James Bible is on the coffee table in front of the sofa. A notebook is beside it with doodles of abstract images and crosses and some writing; looks like quotes from the Bible.

At the bottom of the notebook, "FOR NOW WE SEE THROUGH A GLASS, DARKLY; BUT THEN FACE TO FACE: NOW I KNOW IN PART; BUT THEN SHALL I KNOW EVEN AS ALSO I AM KNOWN," is handwritten in large letters and "see through a glass, darkly" is underlined several times. There's a little smiley face drawn at the end of the sentence.

I place my own notebook on my lap and ready my pen. During our preliminary conversation I notice that her attention is drawn to the bad side of my face more than once. I explain my condition to her. She's heard of it before. Someone at the church had it.

"I know it must be painful, Ms. McPherson, but there are just a few questions I need to ask you. I'm sure some of them have been asked before, by Detective Scanns, so please bear with me."

"Okay," She nods with a forced smile.

"Did your brother have any problems with anyone, maybe someone from the neighborhood?"

"He had problems like we all had problems—with those little criminals always at the corner there, with their drugs and gambling on the streets."

"He make a lot of complaints to the police about that?"

"Always. Sometimes they'd drive by and move them on but then they'd be right back there after the police left."

"Did he ever go down there himself?"

"I don't know. He never told. I wouldn't put it past him, though. He was brave like that sometimes."

"You ever see him get in a fight with anyone?"

"No, Scott was a nice man. He opened up this place to me and my son when his father left."

"When your son's father left?" I ask.

"Yes."

"Where's your son's father now?"

"Prison, for all I know and care."

"Scott ever have problems with him?"

"No. The only thing that man cared about was drugs. He could care less about his own son, let alone my brother."

"What's his name?"

"Ronald McPherson."

"So you're married, then?"

"If you want to call it that."

"The police ever come by here about problems you all were having with the boys out there?"

"No. They called once though. Some detective left a message for him on the phone."

"What was the message?"

"Just to call him. I don't remember his name."

"How long ago he call?"

"Over a month ago, I think. I don't remember."

"Any of those boys out there ever say anything to you?"

"No. I never talk to them and they never talk to me."

"What about after, I mean after he was killed, anyone come up to you, say anything?"

"Just people from church and good neighbors."

"What did they say?"

"Nothing I can really remember. Just well-wishing, that's all."

"Do you know your neighbors around here?"

"Some. I haven't really been here that long to get to know anyone like that."

"There's still some good people in this neighborhood," I say as if that's supposed to be comforting.

"Yes," is her quiet reply.

The 119, Witness Statement, covered a lot of questions, some of which I asked again just in case there was something else she remembered. It happens like that sometimes. I've had victims, weeks after, suddenly recall something crucial, something you wouldn't think they'd ever forget.

I look at Mather, see if he has anything. He shakes his head. I spend a few more minutes talking to her, but not about anything worth noting, just general background stuff.

"God is my strength," she says for no apparent reason as we walk toward the door.

I look back at her and try to smile, but my face tightens up with a sudden twitch of my left lip. It probably comes out looking like a sneer. Now I got a new image of myself to lighten the state I'm in—Johnny Rotten.

When we get back to the office I make a note to myself to call Pank on Monday, ask him about the Simple Assault Tomlinson reported. I'd like to see if there's anything we can do with it. Then I write a follow-up report to the Tomlinson case resumé. It includes the interview with his sister and identifying the suspect in connection with the Simple Assault on Tomlinson.

We manage to get through the rest of the day without catching a case. Before I leave, I give Daniel another call. The last thing I want or need is to bring this home with me. I don't want to do that anymore, especially the kind of cases you pick up here. And if I don't give this guy another try, that's exactly what I'll do. It rings like before and then clicks over to the message again. This time I leave him one, ask him to call me at his earliest convenience regarding William Bergine.

❄

MY HEAD WAKES UP before the rest of my body. I slip the patch off. My eye is dry. I reach over and grab the tube of gel and let three drops fall on my eye. My body jerks a little on the first drop, as it always does. Gel rolls down my cheek like a tear, so I wipe it away with my bed sheet. I lie there for a while, until I become restless with thought. I push up, toward another day.

I call the day work Sergeant before I leave, let him know I won't make roll call because I'm getting with Pankhurst about the Noyes homicide. I force down some coffee that has cooled to an undrinkable state, grab my briefcase by the strap and head out.

The days are getting colder. I wrap the scarf around my neck and make my way to the car.

While the engine warms, I call Pank on the cell,

but it kicks into his message service. I leave one, telling him I'm on my way there and hope he'll be around to talk.

I find a nice parking spot on F Street near the Police Memorial. I place the "Official Business" MPD placard on the dashboard, secure the car and make my way to 555, meeting and greeting familiar faces along the way. I get through security and up the elevator to the 9th floor without losing too much time. But as I step out, I almost walk right in to Salty Dog, one of those familiar faces you'd rather avoid. It looks like he hasn't shaved in a couple of days. His tie's loosened and the top shirt button is undone. I'm actually surprised to see him here. Maybe things have changed at the district since I've been gone. Salty had this uncanny ability to stay under the radar—the great disappearing act when something broke. His presence here suggests he picked up a case he couldn't get out from under.

"What's up, Salty?" I say as I step out of the elevator.

He sticks his hand in to prevent the sliding door from closing.

"Same old crap, different day," he says like all his kind say.

If ever I say that, shoot me. It'll be my time to go.

Salty stands there, looks at me like he wants to say something else. Instead he steps in and the doors slide together, and we stand in awkward silence. I look at my reflection in the metal mirrored elevator and realize Salty had the same kind of faraway gaze

Scanns had in the metro tunnel. I look at my image and hope something's not going around.

It's only a few steps to the receptionist who is sitting in a secured booth surrounded by thick glass. I show her my badge and identification and she buzzes me through.

The floor is busy. It's always busy here. The small offices I pass bear the names of the assistants that occupy them. Officers and detectives inside, telling their stories, pitching their cases, or just wrapping things up so that everything fits nice and tight inside accordion folders.

There are eleven floors in this building, and the floor you find yourself on depends on the kind of case you have. The assistants on this floor get the case after it's been approved by supervisors like Pank. He's the one who usually hears the story first.

Pank's sitting behind his oak desk in a large corner office with a view of the building museum and part of the Police Memorial. At the right angle, you can see the Monument poking between buildings. His back's facing the door as he types away on the keyboard attached to the laptop. I tap on the open door. He turns, sees me and smiles.

"He's back!" he says.

I enter, step up to his desk, and he stands so that we can shake hands properly. He sits, smiles this sincere smile that I'm sure influenced jurors when he used to work the court rooms.

"How are things, Sim? I heard you got a spot at

homicide. Congratulations."

"Yeah, right."

"That's what you wanted, no?"

I'm about to get into it but an image of Salty stops me. All I say is, "Yeah, better late than never. How is everything?"

"Crazy, like always. You're looking better."

"Thanks. You got some new faces up here, I see."

"Rotation time. I got your message. So what's up?"

"You know I picked up that Escort case from Adam's Morgan?"

"No. Your guys don't tell me anything anymore."

"Well, everyone's a little crazy right now. Too much work. So who do you got assigned to it?"

"Patricia Morgan, she's to the left down the hall—one of the new faces on this floor."

"I think I know her from when she was in Grand Jury. I'll get with her. I'm actually here on another matter. The Tomlinson shooting."

"The one on Clifton?"

"Yes. Who'd you give that one to?"

"No one yet. I'll handle it for now. What do you have?"

"Possible suspect. Here's the story; the decedent's an active member of the community, never been locked up, appears he was a decent man, pretty vocal about the corner drug thugs just outside his apartment. Complained about them all the time. I find this report he made a couple of months before he was shot, for a Simple Assault. The suspect was identified as Peanut."

"And Peanut is one of the corner drug boys?"

"Yes. I'm pretty sure I got him ID'd. And what I want to know is what I got to do to get him locked up on that Simple Assault charge."

"There any witnesses?"

"None identified on the report. No."

"The complainant's dead, no witnesses. Unless there's someone we can take to the Grand Jury, I'm afraid there's not much we can do."

"That's what I figured. So I have to find a witness."

"You find a witness, I'll sign the warrant."

"I'll be knocking on some doors, then."

"Sounds like it, buddy."

"Nothing's easy anymore," I say, partly in jest.

"The right way rarely is."

"True that," I half smile. "So, everything good with you?"

"Dandy. Come up later this week, and we'll have lunch."

"I'll be around. See ya then."

"Take care," he says. "Oh, and do me a favor, and let Morgan know you're on the Noyes case."

"All right," I tell him.

I RECOGNIZE MORGAN WHEN I see her. She hasn't changed much—still looks like she might be in her mid-thirties, but then again, maybe younger, depending on how she handles the stress. From what I remember, she's aggressive but fairly easy to work with. We had a couple of cases a while back when she was on the second floor in Grand Jury.

She's on the phone and smiles when she sees me, then motions for me to have a seat in one of the two chairs in front of her desk. I set my briefcase on the floor beside my feet as I sit. She gives me the "just a second" signal with her left hand. During the course of her conversation, I hear words like "your client," "debriefing," and "status hearing," so it's safe to assume she's talking to a defense attorney. I occupy myself with nosiness and scan the office.

Six boxes are stacked along a wall next to two filing cabinets to my right. Blown-up photographs affixed to a large Styrofoam board reveal violent crime scenes. Books and thick binders have been placed on shelves in no particular order, mostly law-related stuff like Black's Law Dictionary, DC Code and Rules of Evidence. The kind of stuff you get when you join the club. Framed photos of a dog sitting on a sofa and Morgan posing with friends line the top of the bookshelf.

After a couple of minutes, she hangs up. We shake hands, then reminisce briefly about one of those cases we worked a few years back involving an eighteen-year-old defendant with a BB gun and a stolen car. Things have changed a little since then. Nowadays, all you have to do is change eighteen to twelve or thirteen and BB gun to 9mm.

"Pankhurst wanted me to stop by, let you know I'm working the Noyes homicide," I tell her.

"Yes, your Lieutenant told me you were on that. I'm sorry to hear about Detective Scanns."

"Me too."

"So where are we with it?"

"Well, as you probably already know, we have a primary suspect who just committed suicide, no evidence to speak of to tie him to the murder, but still waiting for DNA. We searched his home and managed to recover a couple of things that I'll follow-up on—phone numbers, things like that."

"Is there anyone we can bring in for an interview, maybe put in the Grand Jury?"

"Might be, but like I said, I need to follow-up on all that, see what we got. I'm coming into this thing fresh." I mention the similarities with the crack head cold case. "Can you get me a blood order for Bergine. Shouldn't be that hard, since he's laid up at the Morgue."

"I'll have it for you by tomorrow. Give me a call in the afternoon. I don't want this to look like some fishing expedition, so keep that cold case to yourself for now."

"All right." I stand, grab the briefcase strap. "I've got to roll, head back to the office. I just wanted to let you know I'm on it. You still got all my info, right?" I ask.

"I'm sure I do, but just in case, give it to me again."

"I got an extra business card," I say, then pull my wallet out of my back pocket and slide out a card. I write my new office number on the back. "Here. My cell and pager's on the front." I offer the card and she reaches across her desk and takes it.

"I'd like to go over everything you recovered from Bergine's home, maybe later this week. I'm prepping for a trial that starts next Monday, but I'll find some time somewhere."

"I'm on evenings. Just hit me up." I shoulder my briefcase.

"See you later then," she says. "Don't forget to call tomorrow for the blood order."

"Thanks."

I walk out.

At the elevator, I suddenly realize I don't miss this place.

VCU's empty when I arrive, and I wonder if we caught a case. But then, I'd have gotten a page if that happened. On the other hand, I've been feeling a little like the red-headed step child around here. I walk to the Sergeant's office. The Admin Sergeant's the only one there. He's sitting with his back to me, working on the computer.

"What's up, Sarge," I say.

He turns, looks at me for a second, remembers I'm the red-headed step child. "Same ol' same ol'," he exhales. Maybe I startled him. He swings back in his chair to face the monitor and whatever work seems to be overwhelming him.

"Sergeant Barnes around?" I ask.

"Him and Hattie went to some meeting downtown," he says dismissively, his back to me. I'm thinking I did startle him before.

"What about everyone else, they working something?"

"Most of them're in court. Don't know where everyone else is."

I leave and feel better that I wasn't excluded from anything, even though the last thing I want right now is the burden of a crime scene and the sight of another unseasonable death.

Peanut's on my mind, so I find the Live scan, type in his name, see if I'm lucky enough to find an arrest photo in the system. I am. His image pops up. It was taken over a year ago, but he hasn't changed, still has that same smug "You ain't got nothin' on me" look that he had when Mather and I stopped him the other day. I click print for a copy of the photo. After that, I print eight additional photos of subjects with similar characteristics, for a photo spread, just in case I find a witness to the assault. All this takes me about forty-five minutes.

It's early in the tour. I'd like to hit Tomlinson's neighborhood again, knock on some doors, but I'm afraid to ask the admin sergeant for an available cruiser. I get the feeling the last thing he needs is more questions. Instead, I open the Noyes case jacket, find Daniel's cell number and grab the phone and call.

Two rings.

"Hello?"

THE DAY FALLS TO rest and the evening settles into

semi-darkness as most of the squad returns from court, or working the streets.

Mather finds me. I let him know I finally got in touch with a friend of Bergine, Daniel Emmerich, and we're scheduled to meet tomorrow at his office on Connecticut Avenue, at around three. Mather says he's got to be in court, but if I drop him off, I can take the cruiser to the meeting and pick him up later. I agree, then ask if he's got some time to canvass Tomlinson's neighborhood again, see if I can find a witness.

I log off the computer, finding nothing on this guy Daniel. At least when you have Peanuts and Boo Boos, you know who you're dealing with. Just type in a few numbers and press enter and there it is: a life history.

The block's clean when we get there. Maybe these boys have regular working hours? Or maybe they know the corner's hot now that we've made our presence known. More than likely, it's neither and they just had something better to do, like increase the district's crime rate. I make a mental note to give the Third District's Vice Unit a call, see what they have on these players. That's what I should have done to begin with, but my mind's been a little crowded lately.

Mather takes the east side, where Tomlinson's building stands, and I take the west. It doesn't take a lot of knocking before I realize the failure of expectation. All these people have to do is think of Tomlinson's fate before they consider stepping out. But then, who am I kidding? Most people here have settled comfortably into this mess they call a neighborhood. I have a hard time figuring if they're reluctant to move out of fear or just plain lack of caring. I'm pretending they even consider such things. But here I am assuming again. Tomlinson was killed because he was an activist for this place and pissed off one of those little boys on the corner. For all I know, the shooter's his sister's little boy—his nephew. Nowadays, what else would you expect? I notebook the information as I go, including the addresses of the homes where there was no answer. I'll come back to those some other time, if I have to. Mather hits me on the direct connect before I get to the next door, tells me to come to an apartment on the second floor of Tomlinson's building.

I walk a short flight of stairs and open the stairwell door leading to the second-floor hallway. I see Mather at the west end of the hallway. I walk into the apartment. It smells like roses and old cedar, like something worn into the walls and fabrics with age, not sudden and store-bought. Mather introduces me to Viola Paget. She's eighty two and she tells me she saw the kid who smacked down Scott Tomlinson.

I MAKE IT TO the office about an hour before roll call, because I want to write up the affidavit for the arrest of Michael Puller, aka Peanut. I'll have Mather leave it with Pank when I drop him off at court—pick it up after my meeting with Daniel Ciao. It's a piece of cake affidavit, though. Basic stuff and only takes three paragraphs to show probable cause that Michael Puller assaulted Tomlinson. If I didn't have that rose-scented old lady as a witness, it wouldn't be so easy, and I'd still be pounding the pavement. I get the draft done well before roll call and bring it to Hattie for review.

Hattie's sitting in his office talking on the cell when I tap on his door. He motions me in and then to sit. I do.

"Okay Sweetie," he says, then, "I got to go now, sweetie," and he disconnects, sets it on his desk. He smiles uncertainly like he was uncomfortable having me hear him talk that way. The way he said sweetie was like he was talking to a child, but for all I know he doesn't have any kids and that was his wife he was sweet-talking. That'd embarrass me, too.

I hand him the affidavit, "This is the Puller thing I was telling you about. I wanted to get it signed first thing Monday. You got a second to look it over?"

He takes it. "That's your day off."

"I'm not sweatin' it. I'll just put in for comp time." He takes the affidavit, sets it flat on his clutter-free desk. It doesn't take him long to finish reading.

"Good job," he says as he initials and dates the bottom right corner of the page and hands it back to me.

"Not much to a Simple Assault narrative," I say.

"But he won't know that's what he's being arrested for, right,

"No, if he's the shooter, hopefully he'll think I got him on the homicide," I say.

"Mather going with you on this?"

"Of course. It's all he's got."

"Okay." He looks at me briefly as if waiting for me to say something. "This guy Bergine, he's good for it though, am I right?"

It takes me a second to gather my thoughts. "Quite honestly, we don't have much in the way of evidence, and I certainly don't think some judge is going to consider inconsistent statements and suicide probable cause. I don't know what to tell you, Lu."

"I'm not talking about a warrant here."

"Unless you know something I don't know. I'd have to say no."

He nods, obviously disappointed.

On the way to my desk I wonder if I misunderstood him. It doesn't take me long to realize I didn't, but I still give him the benefit of the doubt because Bergine looks pretty guilty, and maybe Hattie had some false sense of hope based on that. I don't know. All I know is, based on what we got, which is next to nothing, the worst thing that could have happened to this case is the suicide of our prime suspect. At least alive, we'd have had a chance of breaking him. At least alive, we'd have had a better chance of catching him screwing up on something. It takes a pretty sick character to take his own life and leave us with nothing—taking that knowledge with him like that. He didn't even bother to smile before he took the drop. At least that would have given me some idea of where he stood.

When I get back to the detectives' room, Tommy tells me I got someone on the line. "Been on hold for a few minutes," he says.

I pick up the phone at the desk. It's Tammy McPherson, Tomlinson's sister. After I apologize for keeping her waiting, I tell her what I can about the case.

"I've been praying for you," she says with purpose. "That the Lord would grant you great wisdom."

"Thank you," is all I can think to say, and I realize it comes out sounding like thanking someone who says "God bless you" after you sneeze.

So I thank her twice.

WHEN MATHER SHOWS UP, I give him the affidavit and he says he'll drop it off at Pank's for me. After that, we hunt down the cruiser and I drive him to court. Then I head over to Daniel's office. It is an annoying fifteen minute drive, complete with potholes, pedestrians and mindless drivers. I get there without taking a life, though.

Daniel works out of an eight-story building, a couple of blocks south of Dupont Circle. His offices take up most of the fifth floor. He greets me in the lobby area with a soft handshake and a loud smile, dressed casually—tan, pressed khakis, white unwrinkled designer long-sleeved shirt rolled up evenly at the sleeves. His face is long with thin shiny skin and eyes that are set close together. Wavy light brown hair is designed to fall in calculated strands over his angled forehead. The handshake does fit the man. There is money in everything about him, and for the life of me, I can't imagine this guy hanging out with the likes of William Bergine. *Not meant to be a compliment.* In their differences, they are equally disagreeable characters. We move to his office and sit in well-worn leather chairs under a large window with wooden blinds and a view overlooking Connecticut Avenue. This office he keeps is equally smooth in character and like him, laden with the consequence of financial gain.

After a brief introduction, I learn that he is the chief software architect for a once-small company that designs, manages and maintains websites for other companies. He tells me that the company's success is the result of his efforts. He is well-spoken and mostly speaks well of himself. I learn this in a short period of time. Not a good sign.

"Would you like something to drink? Coffee? Soda? Water?"

"No, thanks," I say tersely. He smiles and probably assumes my abrupt character is typical for my job. I open the reporter-style notebook to a blank page, jot down the date. "I need a little information for my records, before we get started, if that's all right."

"No problem," he says.

I start by asking his full name. "Daniel Adrian Emmerich," he replies confidently. He then slowly spells out the last name, "E M M E R I C H."

I then gather some basic information like date of

birth, current address, and phone numbers. I am surprised to learn he is forty-six years old. But then that shiny face does suggest some unnatural means of countering all those problems associated with aging. That might have something to do with it. Or, it might just be genetics. I almost want to ask what his secret is, but I'm afraid I might want to try it later in life, Clem's Botox jokes notwithstanding. I probably couldn't afford it.

"I'm a DC native," he tells me proudly. "Raised right here in the Dupont Circle area."

I am surprised again when I learn that he does not come from a family of wealth. His father was a *Washington Post* music critic and his mother was a clerk at the Library of Congress. Both retired and living outside of Flagstaff, Arizona. "Had their fill of this climate," he tells me, then adds that they left him the three-story red brick home with an English basement, mortgage paid. Chances are it's worth substantially more than what his parents paid for it. That's the address he still carries. His modest family background does not change my opinion of him, though. There is something about his character that I find irritating. Maybe it's the dispassionately loud smile of his or his equally nonchalant attitude, despite my presence. After all, a friend of his was found stretched on a rope and hanging from a sturdy limb off the George Washington Parkway. That would be reason enough, in my opinion at least, to appear at least somewhat subdued.

"How did you and William meet?"
"Our mothers worked together at the Library of Congress."
"So you've known him for quite a while?"
"Yes."
"Best friends?"
"More the burden of friendship tied together by the length of time."
"Almost like family, then?"
"Yes, you could say that," he smiles, liking the comparison.
"When did you last see William?"
"Had to be at least two weeks ago. I'll contract work out to him sometimes—simple programming stuff. I believe that's why we got together that day."
"Did he have a desk here?"
"No. He would use whatever desk was available or just work out of his home."
"You ever meet his girlfriend?"
"I was wondering when you would get around to asking that. Yes. We met once, when the three of us got together for lunch in Adam's Morgan."
"You were wondering when I'd get to that?" I ask, attempting a shrewd half smile.
"Yes, isn't that why you're here?"
"That and the death of your friend, William."
"It was suicide, right?"
"Yes, it looks that way," I say, suggesting the possibility it might not be, a door I would not have opened if he hadn't asked if Bergine killed himself. He didn't

have unwanted help. Faking a suicide by hanging is a very hard thing to do. Good evidence has a way of revealing itself post mortem or by other means. "Is there anything you might be able to offer that'll help me with the investigation?" I continue.

"Detective, if there was anything I could offer, don't you think I would have called right away?"

"Maybe," I smile again. "When did you all have lunch?"

"Let's see," he says, looking toward the ceiling, "It had to be over a month ago but I'm really not sure."

"When did you learn of her death?"

"Actually, I found out about it on the news, and then I called William."

"What did he say?"

"He was pretty out of it, couldn't talk. I think he was on medication or maybe drunk. I don't recall him saying anything worth remembering, really. Like I said, if there was anything, anything of importance, I would have called the police."

"He didn't mention the police talking to him? Anything like that?"

"No. My impression was that he was incredibly distraught over the whole thing and wanted to be left alone. You see, William kept very much to himself. He never shared his personal life with me. More and more, our relationship had become business-oriented, anyway. The only time I really ever talked to him was when I had work for him, and even then, it was all so superficial." He looks at me with gravity and then says, "Do you suspect him of killing her?" He says this like he had rehearsed it, like it was a line read out of one of those bad scripts Clem and I used to enjoy so much. I am so taken by the way he said it that I almost forget to answer.

"The boyfriend is always the first one we look at. Do you think he's capable of something like that?"

"I'm sure you know this already, but William was on all kinds of medication. He was a manic depressive and for that reason very difficult to be around. But he was never violent, at least that I have ever seen. But then, you never know someone as well as you think you do."

"That's true," I allow.

"Whether he was capable of something like murder? I would like to say no."

"You would *like* to say no," I return with emphasis.

"I don't think he's capable of something like that. He was a very vulnerable, needy sort of person, and my impression would be far too scared to follow through with something like taking someone's life."

"I've seen passion turn the mild-mannered into monsters."

"I imagine in your job you've seen just about everything. I haven't. I am just telling you what I think, based on my personal knowledge and the years I have known him. Nothing more."

"And that's why I'm here, because you were friends. And please don't misunderstand some of my questions. They are necessary."

"I appreciate your job. Believe me, I do."

"But then you did say you never know someone as well as you think you do."

"True. You don't."

"So that time the three of you had lunch was the only time you had seen her?"

"Yes."

"Do you know what she did for a living?"

"Yes, I believe she worked for a dating service," he laughs a bit, suddenly embarrassed.

"Why is that funny?"

"Well, you know, escort. But quite honestly, it could have been legitimate for all I know. But I've never known one to be legitimate."

"Is that how the two of them met? The dating service?"

"No, I believe William told me that they met through a class he taught. She was attending it."

"So obviously, he knew what she did for a living."

"Of course. Maybe old William was a refreshing change compared to some of the men she'd had to put up with. He may have been a hard person to deal with, even slightly worn and ragged, but he was intelligent and sometimes a fun person to be with."

"And he didn't mind what she did?"

"Again, he didn't talk much about his personal life, but from what little we did talk about, it didn't seem to bother him. He's not like most people you meet. Things that might bother you or me would not bother him."

"How did it come up that she was an escort?"

"I don't really remember. I may have asked what she did for a living. In fact, I believe I did, and he said something like, 'Oh, she goes out with other men for a living.' I thought he was joking at first because he said it so dryly and had such an odd sense of humor to begin with, often saying certain things just to get a reaction out of people. I inquired further and learned what she did."

"Why do you think William killed himself?" I ask him.

"My opinion, if that's worth anything—William was already a mess to begin with. This girl was the first girl that seemed to take an interest in him for a long while. I think after she was killed he felt his life was hopeless. I'm just assuming this, of course, based on my years of experience with the man. He was always so morbid and fixated on death anyway, but I never thought he was capable of taking his own life. Her murder must have really screwed him up to make him take his own life like that." He crosses his legs and leans back in the chair like he's contemplating something. "You know, I do remember him saying something very strange, now that I think about it." He straightens in the chair.

"What is that?"

"When we spoke over the phone once, before I saw the news story about her death, he told me he hadn't heard from her and she wasn't returning his calls. He said he was very concerned and wanted me to go over to her apartment with him to see if she was all right. Odd how I just remembered that."

It is odd, I think, but don't mention it. I do say, "It's common, don't worry about it. Us sitting here talking like this might trigger a memory."

"Yes, that must be it," he says with conviction.

"I find it strange that he needed you to go with him, though. Why do you think that is?"

"Quite honestly, I just thought she was giving him the brush off. I didn't really think about why he needed me to go there with him. But now, I just think that it's very odd that he would ask that of me. So is that important? Something you can use?"

"It's interesting. I'll say that much. When did you have this conversation with him?"

"I think it was a Thursday, and based on what I learned from the news, it had to be a couple of days before the police found her murdered. I'm sorry, I don't remember the exact date."

"So that wasn't something you thought the police should know?"

"I don't know what I was thinking. Obviously, I didn't give it much thought."

"You have any ideas about all this?"

"I don't know what more I could offer you than I've already said." He takes a deliberate breath. "William was very messed up. That is all that I can really tell you."

"That is all you can really tell me? As in there might be something else that you don't want to tell me?"

Emmerich smiles and says, "Detective, you're reading too much into what I say. But I know that's your job. The fact is, William was very messed up. Plain and simple."

"Help me out here, Mr. Emmerich. I have the impression that you can help me more than you are." I say this with the sense he's being a little more calculating than he wants me to know. "I mean, on the one hand, you tell me you don't think he would be capable of murder, but then you tell me how messed up he was, and it's like you're insinuating that he might have been capable. So, if there's something you know, just tell me. I'm here because I need your help. Did he tell you anything?"

"No, of course not."

"So give me your theory."

"Maybe in one of his manic states, I don't know. Maybe he could be capable of murder! But I just could not say for sure. He was more comfortable on the Internet than with real women. That I do know. And he seemed into her. But maybe she was like the Internet for him. I imagine you have his computers?"

"Why would you ask that?"

"William was the type to keep his life on the computer." He pauses to eye his expensive watch. "I'm sorry, if you have any more questions, could we make it another time? I have meetings now."

"Yes. I appreciate the time you've given. And I would like to talk again."

"Of course," he says.

We end the conversation there. I thank him again. In his very cordial but nonchalant manner he shakes my hand and shows me out. As I walk to the car, I decide that this guy is full of himself and just a little too charming for my taste.

I make my way back to the U.S. Attorney's Office to meet with Pank and get with Mather. The bothersome drive doesn't affect me because my mind is preoccupied with his statement.

There are certain things that we can suddenly remember, and others we can suddenly decide to remember. One is involuntary, and one is calculated. I'm pretty confident that everything about Daniel Emmerich is calculated.

I PICK UP THE Affidavit from Pank then get a warrant typed up and get everything signed by the Judge in Chambers.

I find Mather, standing at the curb in front of the U.S. Attorney's Office, or what those of us in the trade refer to as The Triple Nickel, because the address is 555 4th Street.

"You want to try to snatch the kid up now?" he asks after shutting the passenger side door.

"Now's as good a time as any," I reply. "I appreciate the help," I add.

"No problemo."

On the drive to find Peanut, I fill Mather in on the informative interview I had with the cool Mr. Daniel Emmerich.

"I feel for you, brother," is all he says and I suddenly appreciate the simplicity involved in working a case where Boo Boo shoots Shorty.

As we pull up the block, I notice four of our friends from before hanging on the same corner. One of them looks like Peanut, aka Michael Puller. That'd make my life easier, picking him up here rather than having to hunt him down later. I want to take care of this thing while I still feel the motivation. A warrant in hand does that to me—stirs the blood a little. It's like the power that charges a comic book Super Hero with magical strength.

We park.

"It looks like snow," I say, gazing out the front windshield.

Mather agrees and then we step out.

We walk to the crew on the corner.

"We're lucky," I say to Mather after spotting our boy amongst the crew.

"Imagine that," Mather says.

Before we get there Peanut, Puller tries to slowly walk away. Mather gets to him before he gets too far. "Hold up for a second," Mather tells him. Puller reluctantly stops.

I tell the rest of the crew to roll on, that we got some business with their boy Peanut. They comply.

"What you want with me?" Puller asks.

"Turn around," I tell him. I pat his waist area and pockets and squeeze the areas around the puffy winter jacket he's wearing to make sure he's not holding anything. I feel something like keys in his right front pants pocket and what might be a wad of money in the other, but that's about it.

"Man, what's with this?" he huffs.

"You gotta go," I tell him.

"For what? I ain't do nothin'!" He insists.

"We'll explain everything," I say. "Let's just wait 'til we get outta here, all right. Don't want your boys knowing too much."

I notice Mather keeping an eye on Puller's boys, who have their eyes on us from about a half a block up. I motion for him to pass me the handcuffs while I got Puller against a wall. He does and then I ask Puller to put his hands behind his back.

"What you gotta do that for?"

I cuff him.

"It's the way we got to do things."

I don't want to wait around here for a transport so I say to Mather, "Let's do this the old-fashioned way, so we can get out of here."

We walk the grumbling Peanut to the car, do a quick search of his person just to make sure, and then sit him in the back seat. Mather secures the seat belt for him then steps around to the other side and slides in to sit beside him. I step in the car and we head back to the office.

Puller is silent in the back seat for the whole drive there. That's a good sign. Usually means he's either contemplating or adrenalin has stirred him up so much his body's starting to shut down. Either one works for me.

When we get to VCU we secure Puller in one of the interview rooms. I take his personal property, including shoe laces and belt.

"You don't have nothin' hidden in your underwear somewhere, do you?" I ask.

"Naw, I ain't got nothin'."

"Don't want to find anything dropping from between your butt cheeks later, so tell me now if you have something, and we can work it out."

"There ain't nothin' gonna drop from nowhere."

I nod and exit, closing the door behind me. I make sure it's locked.

I thank Mather again for the help and tell him I got it from here if he's got something else to do. He tells me he's going to sit in the monitor room and watch a bit of the interview. I want to let our boy sit for a while, let that adrenalin stir up his bodily juices some more.

"I'll be kicking back in the monitor room," Mather says.

I PUT PULLER'S PROPERTY on the book, fill out a couple of forms and then, about twenty or so minutes later, I check the monitor room. Mather's still sitting there, arms folded and reclining in the chair with his feet propped up on one of the metal brackets for the thirteen-inch monitors. One of the monitors reveals Puller, cradling his head with crossed arms on the table. His oversized black puffy winter coat is now crumpled on the floor beside his chair.

Watching him sitting like that takes me back to my school days as a teacher in California and some of the students, just like Peanut there, with that same 'last chance for attendance' look. It was a chore, a charge, and something like doing time. That system in so many ways is just as frustrating to me as the one I find myself in now. Is it just me or is there actually something to it? Michael Puller, aka, Peanut. Just look at him.

"Sleeping like a baby," Mather says, derailing my thought.

Another good sign, seeing Puller like that. That means he's ready.

"Don't want him to feel too comfortable," I say lightly. "You mind sliding in a DVD for me? I'll let you know when to record."

"I can do that," he says.

I open the door to the interview room. Puller doesn't move, still cradling his head on the table.

"Sit up for me," I tell him politely.

He slowly complies, raising himself up to a sitting position. He's wearing an equally oversized official Cowboys jersey. I know that'd piss off some of the detectives around here.

"It could be dangerous wearing that jersey 'round here," I say in jest.

He just snickers like he knows I'm playing, but even if I weren't he thinks he's tough enough to laugh.

"You get shot in the head, or somefin'?" he asks,

looking at the usual side of my face.

"Yeah, somethin' like that," I say, because that's easier to explain.

"Man, that messed you up—musta hurt."

"No, not really," I tell him. "Straight to the seventh cranial nerve, didn't feel a thing."

He nods like he understands.

"You want something to drink? Soda? Juice or somethin'?" I offer.

"You got Pepsi?"

"Yeah, I think so. Sit tight. I'll be right back."

I close the door, ask Mather to hit the record as I pass him toward the soda machines. I hear him laugh a bit and mutter something about me getting shot in the head.

When I open the door, I find him cradling his head again.

"You not getting enough sleep at home?" I ask him.

"Yeah, man, I'm all right," he says sitting up.

"I got you the Pepsi you wanted."

"Thanks." He grabs it, twists the top off, lets it fizz for a second, then takes a stiff gulp and sets it on the table. He has a round young face with nice eyes that don't fit that apathetic attitude of his. I've seen it countless times before. The apathy, I mean. Nothing different here. He sips the Pepsi like he's sitting in a living room with his buddies watching a football game.

I grab my notebook out of my back pocket and sit down in a chair in front of him, but in a position where the table doesn't come between us. I introduce myself, then, for the benefit of the video, I announce the date and time and ask him his name.

"Michael Puller," he says looking toward the lens of the camera like he was talking to a judge.

"I just need to get a little background information from you before we get started, all right?"

"Yeah."

"You're what, nineteen?" I ask him.

"Yeah."

"What grade you get through in school?"

"Tenth."

"What high school?"

"Balou."

"What was your favorite subject?"

"Math."

"Math, no kidding? I was pretty bad at math myself. You still live with your parents?"

"Naw, man, my aunt."

"That the address on Robinson Place, right?"

He nods.

"Your parents still around?"

"My mom stays in Maryland, somewhere."

"What about your dad?"

"He in New York, at Ray Brook."

"How long he been in there?"

"Goin' on eight years."

"What's he in for?"

"Robbery."

"You talk to him?"

"Naw, not much."

"What about your mom?"

"Naw, she ain't locked up. She's a hard worker."

"No, I mean you talk to her often?"

"Yeah, we talk sometimes."

"Why you stay with your aunt and not your mom?"

"There ain't nothin' to do in Maryland where she lives."

"You got a job?"

"Naw."

After jotting some of this down along with some other basic notes like height and clothing description, I set my notebook on the table and slide my pen back into my shirt pocket.

"Here's the thing, Michael," I say, taking out a rights card from the same shirt pocket. "You got a story I want to hear and I'm sure you got questions you want me to answer. Am I right?"

He nods again.

"I need you to answer yes or no for me."

"Yes."

"You got rights, and in order for us to talk with one another I got to read you your rights. But I want you to understand the most important thing, and that is if you agree to talk and you sign this card, you still have the right to stop talking at any time. Just 'cause you sign this card doesn't mean you have to talk. It doesn't force you into anything. You understand that?"

"Yes."

"You want to talk to me?"

"Yeah, I guess."

"You guess? I mean, you don't want to talk, I'll just get up and go and that'll be that. You want me to go?"

"Naw, I want to talk."

"All right."

I tell him he's under arrest and then slowly read his rights and he agrees and then signs the waiver. I slip the card back into my shirt pocket, sit back a little in the chair.

"Another thing I need you to understand, and it's probably the most important thing for you to remember during our talk here."

He rests his elbow on the table and stretches his feet out a bit.

"I want you to understand that some of the questions I'm going to ask you I might already know the answers to. I'm just telling you that 'cause I don't want you to jam yourself up and get caught lying on videotape, all right? 'Cause that won't look good. I might ask you somethin' I already know the answer to because I'm testing your truthfulness."

He nods, looks up at the camera lens again then remembers and says, "Yes."

"I've been doing this for a lot of years. I'm not gonna sit here and waste my time if I start catchin' you on a bunch of lies. Is that good?"

"Yeah, I hear ya."

"You live on Robinson Place but you hang all the way up here in Northwest. Why's that?"

"Thems my friends here. I grew up with most of them."

"Oh, you lived in that neighborhood before you moved in with your aunt?"

"Yeah, before my dad got locked up."

"I see. Where'd you live, there?"

"Clifton Terrace," he says.

"Used to be a rough spot a few years back."

"Yeah, I guess."

He leans back a little in his uncomfortable chair, but still rests his arm on the table.

"Have some more Pepsi before it gets warm."

He obeys and takes himself a couple more gulps, then burps.

"Excuse me," he says.

I let out a bit of a huff. "That's why I can't drink that stuff," I say. "Messes my stomach up."

"Yeah man, that escaped me."

"You play sports in high school?"

"Played some football." And a little belch this time.

"What position?"

"Running back."

"I can see that. You gotta be fast then, right?"

"Yeah, I guess."

"And you were good at math. What happened, man? Why'd you drop out?"

"I don't know. Money, I guess."

"But you said you don't have a job?"

He snickers like he just realized I found him out on the drugs and how he really makes his money.

"That's all right," I assure him. "We're not here for that. But you know that already, right?" I don't give him time to answer. "So you grew up in that neighborhood, huh?"

"Yeah. Yes."

"I didn't see much of a record on you as an adult, most of it petty stuff like possession of weed. But you caught yourself a couple of gun charges as a Juvie."

"That was when I was fourteen, fifteen."

"Right. That was a ways back." I lean forward a bit like I want to speak confidentially. "I take it the reason you haven't asked me why you're here is because you already know why. Am I right, Michael? And remember, don't get caught in a lie for that videotape up there."

"Yeah, I guess."

This time his eyes roll up to look at the lens, like he doesn't want the camera to know. *Guilt churning inside him like acid indigestion.* It could be the simple assault working him like that, or it could be the homicide. My bet is he's the shooter. He'd have given up the assault right away. That's no big deal to a kid like this.

"Go ahead and tell me."

"What?"

"Tell me why it is you're here."

"About that man that was shot." He straightens in his chair, obviously feeling a little more uneasy.

"What about the man that was shot?"

"I guess you saying I did it."

"I want to hear your side."

He snickers, leans back in the chair and then forward again, finally straightens up.

"Have some more of your Pepsi," I suggest.

He does, sets it on the table after.

"Go on man, tell me. And remember the videotape."

He shakes his head.

"I know the truth already, but this is your opportunity. But if you wanna leave it like this I'm telling you it won't look good for you. The truth is the most important thing, and it might be the most important thing you ever say. So tell me what happened."

"What I got to tell you for if you already know?"

"Because that's the way it works here. And I'm also trying to give you a chance. You see, the tape will go to a judge along with what we have and know. The judge is gonna see the way you're just sitting there, all carefree and everything, not taking this seriously, and then he'll see what you did to that man in your old neighborhood—it's not gonna be good. The best thing you can do for yourself is to tell me your side of the story, and let it be known how sorry you are. I don't really need you to say anything, I got everything I need. I want you to help yourself, because I know things haven't been easy for you. A judge might have more leniency on someone who is repentant and cooperative."

He sits up straight, looking like that Peanut brain is working harder than it's ever worked his whole life. I look at him sitting still in that uncomfortable chair, his left foot tapping unconsciously to an irregular beat. *That guilt thing again.* And for a while it looks like my bluff is going to work, but now he's contemplating a little too hard. You either get them right away or you spend the next several hours hoping you'll get them any way you can. I don't want that to happen. I pull my chair up so I'm closer to him, our knees almost touching.

"Michael, we got you man. You don't got a choice. Be a man. Tell me what happened?"

"How'd you get me?"

"It was easy."

He smiles, bites his lower lip. Thinking. Then he says, "It was like, you know, like he would always mess with us, like he owned that whole block or somefin'," he begins suddenly. "One time when we was all hangin' together, me and some friends, he comes up and gets in my face, and I'm like 'what to do, what to do' and my friends are laughin', an he was pushin' at me, an I had no choice, so I hit him."

"Go on," I say.

"He gets up and says how I really messed up and he was going to call the police. I told him he best go on his way and he did. Me and my friends was like blah, blah, blah, and how I'm going to get picked up now, so I got out of there and went back to my Aunt's. After a few days I saw that nothin' happened so I goes back to my old neighborhood, and my friends are like 'You messed up, man' 'cause now the Po Po were jumpin' out on them all the time and they were tellin' me how it was because of what I did." He sips his Pepsi, shakes his head.

"So what did you do?"

"Man, I didn't do nofin'. I stayed there in my old neighborhood. I figure he didn't call the police because they never came after me. One time we was just hangin' around on the stoop of the building—"

"Which building?"

"The one on the corner, where that man lives. We's just hangin' there mindin' our own when he comes by and tells me I got a warrant on me for assaultin' him and that I'd better go on and get off of his stoop. I say it ain't his block and this ain't his stoop and he says he's gonna call the police to come pick me up, said it's like a 'second sighting' or somefin'. He goes in and I'm like 'what to do, what to do' so I follow him in just so we can talk. It was like he panics, just like that, attacks me with some big knife, so I had to defend myself."

"Defend yourself, how?"

"Man, you already know that. Why I gotta say what you already know."

"So you defended yourself."

"Yeah, it was like that."

"And you used a gun to defend yourself. If I had a guy run at me with a knife, I'd shoot him. In a second. Where were you when you shot him?"

"In the hallway at that building."

"Now you know that's not the truth. Unless you moved the body. You do that?"

He considers this, grinds his teeth, "Naw man, we was in his apartment."

"All right, that's the truth. What kind of gun was it?"

"Some nine, I don't know."

"Where'd you get it?"

"It belonged to my Dad."

"Where's the gun now?"

"I don't know. Maybe at my aunt's."

"You said he attacked you with a knife?"

"Yeah. Some big knife from his kitchen."

"What did you do with the knife?"

"I didn't do nofin' with it. It must still be there."

"We never found one."

"Well, I don't know what to tell you about that," he says.

"You're mixing some of the truth with lies, Michael. I told you I know the answers to some of the questions I'm asking. He didn't attack you with no knife, and you know it."

"Man, I'm tellin you he did! And I had to defend myself!"

"Someone as fast as you had to defend himself using a gun, against an old guy like that. Why didn't you just turn and run?"

"Man, I couldn't run. I was trapped."

"How?"

"Man, I just was. I'm tellin' you it was self defense. I ain't got nothin' else to say."

"Where were you? How were you trapped?"

"I just was. My back musta'been against a wall."

"All right. What wall?"

"I don't know man, just a regular wall."

"What room were you in?"

"The kitchen."

"So your back was flat up against a plain wall?"

"Yeah."

"And he was in front of you with a knife."

"Yeah."

"And you want to stick with that story."

"Yeah. That's what happened."

"Why'd you go in his apartment?"

"I told you, to talk."

"Did he invite you in?"

"C'mon, man."

"That's a simple question, Michael. Did he invite you in? You wanted to talk, right? So, did he invite you in or not?"

"I guess he had to 'cause I was in there."

"I mean you just got done assaultin' the man so I'm a little curious why he'd invite you into his apartment."

He doesn't answer.

"You want to stick with that story all right. But you'd be better off with what really happened because that one's got a lot of holes in it and it sure don't look good for you."

"That's what happened," he says adamantly.

"All right, all right. So if we go into your aunt's house we gonna find that gun?"

"Yeah, probably."

"Where?"

"In the basement, on some pipes over the washer."

"Were any of your buddies with you when you shot him?"

"Naw, man, just me."

"What'd you do after you shot him?"

"I went back to my aunt's, stayed in my room."

"And? What, you just stayed there?"

"Naw, I played some X-Box."

"So the X-Box was somewhere else, then?"

"Huh?" he questions.

"I asked if you just stayed at your place after you shot him and you said no, you played some X-Box."

"Naw man, I wasn't thinking."

"So the X-Box is in your room?"

He nods.

"But I understand. It's like the X-Box takes you to another place, huh? That's what you were thinking?" I ask half joking.

"C'mon."

"You sure you want to stick with that self-defense story, despite everything we know?"

"That's what happened."

"Because I'm tellin' you, it ain't gonna fly. You need to tell the truth, show some remorse. Let everyone see how bad you feel. That pit you dug for yourself is getting pretty deep."

I push my chair back again, grab my notebook and cross my legs.

"Anything else you want to say?"

"Yeah, I'm sorry that man had to die," he says like it means nothing at all.

You can only spend so much time on something like this. I spend a couple more hours trying to get the real story, but stupid wants to stick with the one he's got. He's shut down. He's jammed himself up pretty bad with all those inconsistencies, anyway. The most important thing was his admitting he shot Tomlinson. Even if there was a big knife, self-defense wouldn't fly, because Peanut was young and fast and all he had to do was turn and run away. His back wasn't against a wall. Tomlinson's kitchen had three walls and they were all jammed with cabinets and appliances. The kitchen has a wide arched opening to the living area. And this guy, he sits here, like this is nothing. Like it's a game. Guys like him are easy because they're not afraid of anything, because they're too stupid to realize they should be afraid.

I had a sense he'd give it up one way or another, though. Honestly, I thought he'd take a little more work, but then I'm not surprised. He probably really does think he's going to beat this thing on self defense, as silly as that is. But you never know, with a DC jury, he just might.

THE ALARM SOUNDS A constant high-pitched shrill, and my body snaps up like a thousand volts just shot through me.

6:30 a.m.

The alarm never sounded like that before. I must have

slept hard for the three hours I was allowed. Now I have to paper this case with the U.S. Attorney's Office. I realize if I don't hop out of bed now, I never will. My whole body aches, and I think I wrenched my back jumping up like that. I hear the reminder beep on my pager sounding. I must have slept right through its awful call. *That's odd.* I check it. According to the time, the page came through about an hour ago, from Rucker. What's he thinking? He had to know I was asleep. I check it. It reads:

> GOOD JOB*!* CLOSURE*!!* NOW GET THE OTHER ONE OFF MY BACK*!!!*

Wonderful, is all I think. Good friend.

A chill runs through my body when I step out of the shower. I feel good when I dry off. I actually feel good in general despite the achy body, lack of sleep, and the obnoxious message Rucker sent me on the pager.

I pick out my charcoal gray suit, light blue shirt and favorite burgundy tie with the little black square patterns. I pour myself a cup of stale coffee and remember I never called Tomlinson's sister. I should have called her last night, but paperwork and gloating got the best of me.

I knew it felt like snow the other day. I step out to discover the city fresh again, having a new blanket of powder draped over the lawns and sidewalks. The early morning commuters have already made their paths clear along the sidewalks and streets. I breathe in, and I am suddenly overwhelmed with an odd sense of hope. Odd because it is not a desire I have for anything in particular, sort of like the smell in the air with the coming snow. Something you can't see yet.

Pank assigns the Puller case to Morgan. It's a closed case with a confession, so more than likely he'll plead out, and it shouldn't be that much extra work for her. At least that's what Pank thinks. I hope that's the case. I hate going to trial. I give her everything I've got, including the original videotapes and all the reports Scanns generated.

It's about two hours before my tour begins, and I remember Tomlinson's sister, Tammy. I decide that I shouldn't phone. I should tell her in person. So I do. I find her at work, after calling first.

When I tell her, she cries, with a thankfulness that I know is not meant for me. She lifts her hands to the air, in front of all her co-workers and yells, "Praise God!"

She hugs me, taking hold of me suddenly and unexpectedly. But I embrace her and pat her lightly on the back with my right hand. I don't know what to say, so I just let her hug me until she's done. And then I leave.

In all my years, I have never told someone that the person responsible for the murder of their loved one was arrested. I can't count how many live victims I have advised that the person responsible for committing the crime against them was arrested, but that's entirely different. I am not trying to diminish the crime against the victim, because they need the closure. They need to regain that feeling of safety that was torn away from them along with their belongings. Some were even physically hurt, but they survived. For most, losing the comfort of safety in your own environment is worse than stolen possessions. But this is different.

I hit Hattie on his cell phone and request leave for the rest of the day. I want some time to myself, rest this achy body on the sofa and sink into oblivion. Do Nothing. Maybe read. Tomorrow is Thursday and the beginning of my three days off. The judge granted Morgan a five-day hold on Michael Puller, so I have to call Court Liaison first thing in the morning to get a hearing date on Puller. It'll probably be Friday morning, and I'll be sitting in that court all day waiting for the case to be called.

I have to admit, but only to myself, that I got lucky in solving the Tomlinson Murder. Although luck is that one thing you'll never find in any investigator's handbook or taught at any Academy course, it is the one thing that most investigators, in my experience anyway, are thankful for. It's been on my side on more than one occasion. It's the best partner you'll ever have most of the time. That's the way it happens. No technique. No skill. Just luck. Well, slow-minded defendants might have something to do with it. But usually, the way it comes together, is all about luck. *And I'm hoping it finds me again, soon, before those loud voices threatening Rucker's complacent way of life find their way to my cozy dungeon.*

Realizing Christmas Day is closing in, I spend most of this day shopping for gifts. Clem and I have an understanding, maybe a call or a card. I'll buy her something, though. I always do. Then there's my mother, and younger sister. Jewelry is usually a good call. And phone calls are always necessary. Definitely phone calls, as much as I hate them. Clem is the exception. I think it's a family thing. I have to mentally prepare for those moments, and sometimes that takes hours. Mothers are such a strange breed. Their presence or the lack thereof can have the same damaging impact on a young life. For me, the bulk of the relationship with my mother was one that was developed over the phone. I did not have that standardized notion one assumed a son should have for a mother, or vice versa. Although, she tried and sometimes I even tried. Those were awkward moments, like the feeling you get from someone who was a bit too needy.

COURT.

From a distance, 500 Indiana Avenue looks like a large tomb set against a landscape of monuments. Only once inside do you acknowledge life, that conglomeration of humanity, gathered in all its halls and courtrooms, like living organisms in a hungry body, working to keep the system alive. Here is pressing motion, restless stillness, emphatic loudness and intense silence all at once.

The judge has not taken the bench yet. I scan the courtroom but don't see Morgan. The seasoned courtroom clerk is positioned in an enclosed well to the side of the judge's bench, which is respectively positioned in its lofty place, so that all heads tilt upward. It appears as though the clerk is organizing stacks of case jackets in what will probably be the order in which they are called. Then some of those eager defense lawyers enter through a side door to the right of the clerk's area. This is the holding area where they meet with the defendants who were detained at Arraignment, or held pending trial. That is where Michael Puller should be, and I wonder if one of those young eager types who just walked through those doors is Puller's appointed counsel. A Deputy U.S. Marshall steps into the courtroom from inside the same side door, drops some handcuffs on a chair beside the clerk's work area, then walks back through the door.

It does look like the beginning of a very busy day. The seats are filling up with officers, defense attorneys, family members, friends, and what look like other defendants, the ones who were not held. It's easy to spot them in this environment. The defendants, I mean. They're the ones with skittish eyes, uncertain smiles, or bowed heads. They're smart enough to realize, most of them anyway, that they have no control here. I do notice one of Puller's boys, one of the guys Mather and I stopped on the corner the other day. He's sitting toward the middle with two girls dressed like they should be stepping out to a Go Go.

I see Tammy McPherson swing open the door and walk in, holding her son's hand. She notices me immediately and so I stand.

"Hello, Ms. McPherson," I say as I extend my hand.

She takes it softly, smiles just as softly as she greets me. I extend my hand to her son and he offers his little hand.

"Say hello to the detective," she tells him.

"Hello," he says shyly.

"Hey there," I return.

I tell her she should sit toward the front so that the judge can see her. Fact is, the judge won't have a clue as to who she is, but I say that anyway because it gives her the impression that the process is more than it really is.

Morgan pushes through the double doors just as Ms. McPherson sits in the second row with her son. She's holding several Prosecution case jackets, including Michael Puller's, the one that I helped put together during the papering process the morning after Puller's arrest. She's wearing a simple, dark blue tailored jacket and matching skirt that hits right below the knees. The collar of her white blouse sticks out on one side, as if she quickly threw her jacket on as she was running out of the office. The suit is conservative. Her shoes reflect more of her true personality—three-inch pumps with pointy toes from one of those designer places only women know about and a style I don't really care for, but women can only understand. It's like Clem with her Prada scarf.

Morgan seems stressed, probably having rushed in from another court room. She motions for me to follow her out to one of the witness rooms. I notice through the corner of my good eye, Puller's boy turning his head and watching me as I exit with Morgan.

"I tried to get here sooner," she says, walking into the small witness room with three soiled chairs angled every which way against a wall. She fumbles with several case jackets and finds Michael Puller's.

"You get with his defense attorney yet?" I ask.

"I left a message, but you know how they are."

We quickly go over the case and whatever I might have to say in the event I take the stand because Puller decides not to waive. It's like she forgot who she's dealing with, and I'm someone who needs coaching. But that's how they all get during crunch time. She's no different and so there's no offense taken.

When we enter, the judge is on the bench and the first case is called, some guy arrested in 7D for carrying a pistol. I take a back seat again as Morgan moves to the front row, finds a seat beside some other Prosecutor.

The court room clerk announces the next matter of the United States verses Melvin Whoever. The Deputy Marshal escorts the 7D defendant into the court from the side door. He is wearing an orange jumpsuit and his hands are clenched together in front of him with his head bowed as he is directed to the table to the left of the podium beside the Prosecutor. He stands beside his defense attorney and the hearing begins.

And it goes like this for about another two hours, one case right after the other. One defendant after another escorted through that side door by a marshal or called up by the Court clerk. And I'm sitting here listening to all those familiar stories, some of the same stuff I used to get into when I was back in patrol and as a district detective. Nothing new here. And I see Ms. McPherson sitting there solemnly beside her little boy, who, it seems, judging by his stillness and fixed eyes, has already learned how to escape into distant places.

I notice an old stubby man in a wrinkled gray suit with a red tie and uneven hair, like he took fashion advice from a client instead of a hair stylist, walk quietly into the courtroom. I recognize him. He's an old-time public defender, who's been around probably since this tomb was built, maybe even before. He looks around, moves toward the front like he spotted his prey. Fortunately for me, it's Morgan. Or unfortunately, depending on how you want to look at it. Right now, I'm looking at going home. She turns her head up after he taps her gently on the shoulder, smiles politely, stands and follows him back out the double doors.

A couple of minutes later, I walk out to see what's up.

They're talking in the foyer area. I stand beside Morgan. The old guy stops talking for a moment, looks at me then looks at the badge hanging around my neck by a long chain and continues.

His pale, ghostly scalp is visible through his poorly cut and thinning hair on his oblong head. He has bits of dry flaky skin clinging to whiskers just under his ragged sideburns, and the tip of his nose has pores you could probably pick lint out of. He speaks gently but is very expressive in his speech, and I sense that he can manage to be pretty eloquent before a judge if he has to, despite the appearance. Or maybe the appearance is his act—the "run down but not out of commission yet" look. Some judges might respect that. You'd think this guy's been around long enough to have some kind of respect.

"I haven't had a chance to talk to my client yet," he advises Morgan. He turns to me with a shrewd smile, like he recognizes me, then, "Let me go back talk to him and see where we stand on this. You know I'd like to dispose of this as much as you would," he tells her, dropping his head a bit like he's frustrated. He turns to me again. "So you arrest him on a warrant for Simple Assault and he confesses to murder? That's something," he says, not expecting an answer, like he doesn't believe it happened that way. He walks away, shaking his head and swings open the door leading to the courtroom to talk to Puller in the holding area. I can see him through the glass panel on the door, still shaking his head.

I think Morgan sees by the look on my face, I'm a little worried about this guy. She says, "I'm going to wait inside."

"I'll be in the hall. Just let me know."

"Don't disappear," she orders with concern.

"What do I look like?" I ask like I've been insulted.

Rows of uncomfortable chairs line each wall, which extends the length of the hallway between the entrances to each courtroom. I find a clean chair close by and sit. The halls are busy and loud.

I see a rail of a girl with a world globe for a stomach yelling at two tiny obnoxious kids dragging and spinning themselves along the floor. Some people step over them as they pass, others just a quick step to the right or to the left and then regain their stride. The mother's no older than seventeen, and it looks like she'll be popping another one out of that little body any minute now. I'm surprised she didn't break in two with the last one.

I see a defense attorney talking to his young thug client. The hearing obviously went well, because I hear the counselor say, "All you got to do is mind the curfew and stay away from the block and you'll be okay."

The young thug who can't keep his pants up nods accordingly.

"You get caught up on that block again, they'll lock you up for contempt of court. You understand that, right? All you have to do is stay clean for the trial."

The young thug nods in the same manner.

I'm sure he understands.

Other conversations drift by, but they're all similar. Nothing really new here, either.

And so this is how it goes.

I sit back and try to lose myself in my own head for a while, shove these people out of my space.

Morgan calls for me just as it starts to happen.

And the next thing I know, I have to take the stand, because knucklehead wants to go to trial despite the confession. He wants to take his chance on a jury.

The judge finds probable cause and holds Puller without bond. That means we have a hundred days to get him indicted and go to trial.

With a little luck comes a little misfortune. Can't have one without the other. At least I have a hundred days.

I hit the Metro and head home.

When I get there I find a message from Clem on my voice mail, so I call her.

She apologizes for not calling sooner and tells me about the grueling plane ride back to LA and the three-hour delay because of what was thought to be a security breach at the gate.

"I had a nice time in DC. Maybe next time I'll stay a little longer. Or maybe you come to LA."

"Unlikely," I inform her.

That's about the extent of the conversation, and then we wish each another a Merry Christmas, Happy New Year and end with how we'll talk soon. And that could be a year, but then it could be a month.

Depends on our moods and our schedules. But like I've said, the length of time doesn't really matter because it'll feel like no time at all the next time we talk.

There's not much to the days off when you're in my position in life. Most of the hours in a day consists of what has already been established through the course of years, as routines. Most of the time spent in between those routines consists of what I like to call cerebral laundry. I find myself undergoing this cleansing process more and more these days. *More so since this detail.* I have a tendency to bring things home with me, and I don't like people like Emmerich or Bergine cluttering my space.

I FEEL RESTED, HAVING slept over twelve hours.

I get to the office, and the detective with the beach ball in his stomach and whose name I can never remember tells me I must have an admirer. When I try to inquire, he just points in the direction of the desk I occupy.

On it I find a large round Tupperware dish tied with a bow, and a thick rectangular item wrapped in nice Christmas paper with designs of candy canes and bells and sleighs. An envelope is wedged between. I open it. It is a Christmas card of some scenic small Christmassy town. I open the card and written in handwriting is:

> *For all your hard work. Always in my prayers.*
> *You don't have to wait for Christmas to open.*

In Christ, Tammy

I open the Tupperware to discover freshly made chocolate chip cookies. I smell them, and they smell like her home did the day we interviewed her. I open the other item and see that it's an old leather-back Bible, and I'm thrown a bit at the discovery. It's an odd thing to send someone, but then she is a churchgoer. I remember what that was like. It hasn't completely faded away. Regardless, it's a nice gesture and one that I hope did not come with lofty intervention. There's a piece of torn paper as a marker between the beginning pages so I open it. I read that it was presented to Scott Tomlinson from his mother, and then the date, August 5, 1967. Scott's mother signed it with love and then beneath that is another handwritten note from Tammy McPherson that reads:

> *This is an old Book given many years ago to my brother by my departed mother. It brought him much comfort in life and now it is my desire that it should bring you much comfort in life.*

She signs it like she signed the card. I smile uncomfortably, and I don't know why, because no one's around to see. I close the Bible and carefully wrap it in the paper as if to conceal it, then I slide it to the corner of my desk. I'll remember to take it home, I start thinking about how this Bible is an item that's been in her family for many years, and I suddenly don't feel comfortable accepting it. I've received gifts from victims before. This is nothing new. Well, this one is, as personal as it was to the giver. Most of the gifts I've received in the past were flowers or chocolates or things like that. I realize how much it must have meant to her to give it up, though, and I convince myself to thank her instead.

The big tummy detective looking over my shoulder surprises me with, "Look like good homemade cookies."

And I wonder how long he's been there. "Grab a couple," I say. "They're for the office."

He takes three of them with his thick-fingered hands. "That's what I like about Homicide, those thankful loved ones," he says. And then he's suddenly gone, like that big stomach, full of helium, carried him over the cubicles somewhere.

I have a couple of cookies myself. They are good. Some of the chomped up cookie gets stuck between my teeth and my cheek, on the bad side of my face, so I have to scoop it out with my finger. I hate having to do that. I grab a paper towel from a neighboring desk and wipe my hand.

EIGHT

MATHER CALLED IN FOR eight hours leave. I've got quite a bit of leave myself that I'll have to burn eventually. I'll figure something out. I don't want to lose that vacation time. Maybe a road trip. Maybe just stay at home and read and sleep. Right now, all I can do is sit at this cubicle, void of anything representative of myself, and think about the Amy Noyes case.

I go through the evidence recovered by Scanns and what I seized out of Bergine's home and office. I list all the phone numbers from each location and compare them. The only number I find in common is Bergine's cell, but nothing else. Nothing that would link Emmerich to her.

Maybe I'll find luck somewhere down the line. Hopefully, it still wants to be my partner.

By the time I'm done sorting through all the evidence again and itemizing everything again, I look at my pager and see that there's only two more hours to go on this tour. Most of the midnight crew is already here, the schedule having been set up so we overlap for the last two. I feel like I've accomplished something. And for some reason I start thinking about how we haven't caught any cases in a while. That's when I hear a pager sound somewhere in the office, and then mine suddenly sounds while it's still in my hand and then more pagers sounding, like banshee echoes all around me.

I can tell it's not going to be a good scene when I see the yellow crime scene tape sectioning off what appears to be a two block radius.

I'm riding with Tommy and Yvonne. We park along a curb at the intersection, where crime scene tape is secured to a stop sign. A marked cruiser with flashing emergency lights is parked in the middle of the intersection. A couple of uniformed officers stand on the outside perimeter of the tape that stretches across the road. News crews are already here, with the cameras on tripods directed toward the action. I recognize one of the high anxiety reporters. He's a tall slender guy who always wears nicely pressed shirts tucked into tan cargo pants. Might be going for that urban war zone look, I don't know. He's on a cell phone, probably calling in for a live feed, or talking to his police source. Tommy reminds us not to be caught on camera with smiley faces, but that makes me smile. Fortunately, the only side of my face that can smile is the one facing away from the camera. My Palsy side's the serious side.

The Cameraman shifts his camera in our direction, to catch us walking onto the crime scene. I hate cameras, because they have such power. It can make you suddenly conscious of even the most common bodily task. An officer with a sullen face lifts the tape for us as we bend down slightly to enter. I realize the look is probably due to the falling temperature and the post he's been assigned. About a dozen other officers and officials, both uniform and plain clothes, are in the area. *This has to be bad.* We pass through them to a smaller secondary area that's sectioned off by tape.

Hattie's already on the scene. He sees us coming, and, judging by the look on his face, we're now sure this is something we're not going to like. Hattie pulls up the tape to allow us in. A couple of our guys, Beaumont and Fletcher, are hovering over a fallen body—a male, on his stomach, half on the sidewalk and half in the gutter. His right leg crosses over the posterior of the left leg, like he tripped over himself. He is fallen between two parked vehicles. I notice that one of the parked vehicles looks like a detective's cruiser. And before I can put too much thought into it—

"It's one of our own," Hattie says with a grim look. "Detective Untermeyer," he finishes.

Detective Untermeyer?

For the life of me, I don't recognize the name.

With great reluctance, I move toward the fallen body. His left cheek is pressed against the icy sidewalk. A large amount of blood, more shiny than the surrounding ice, is frozen on the sidewalk around the area of the neck and upper body. The flow toward the gutter was halted by a clump of dirty snow. I step over his legs but don't have to bend down to realize who it is.

And my heart sinks for Salty Dog.

"We're all on this one," Hattie says standing behind me.

That means we work it through, as long as it takes. Beaumont and Fletcher are up, so they're catching this one. Even Mather calls in to come off his leave and assist.

IN THE MOMENTS AND the hours that follow, this is what we learn: Salty was working evenings and following up on a case involving some neighborhood crack head female who stabbed a complaining witness in the face. Salty was in the area attempting to track down the suspect. Witnesses on the scene put Salty with a female who matches the description of his suspect and now our suspect. The witnesses say he stepped out of his car to talk to her, she argued with him, and the next thing they saw was her making swinging motions toward his face and head with an object. Shortly thereafter, Salty stumbled forward like he was drunk and then collapsed. According to Beaumont, it appeared as though the fatal stab wound was a thrust into the neck, probably cutting through the carotid, judging by the radius of the spurts and the amount of blood. He was losing so much so fast that he probably tripped over himself. If the blow to his head from the fall didn't kill him first, he would have soon bled out, long before the ambulance arrived. Didn't look like he had much of a chance to react. His weapon is still holstered and secured with a snap lock.

I've been on the scene of homicides and accidents involving officers on more occasions than I care to remember. It never matters whether you know them, hate them, or never heard of them. When you're on the scene of a fallen officer, it's like a part of you fell with them. I can only liken it to a bond created by fraternity, years and years of sodality engrafted in us through the installation of some magical oath. It is an awful feeling, and made more awful, after I remember seeing him last, standing in an elevator, with that odd faraway look. It is yet another image that I am forced to keep.

Beaumont and Fletcher take the witnesses back to VCU. By that time we're pretty sure who the suspect is. We had a lot working for us on this one. Patrol responded quickly, managed to secure the scene properly and locate a few witnesses. We had a ready-made suspect who already had a history of cutting men up. Her name is Josie Ragsdale, a local crack head with no fixed address. Beaumont gets a definite confirmation after he puts together a photo array and shows it to each of the witnesses.

TWENTY HOURS.

No sense in going home. I'll just end up sleeping

through the next tour, which is only four hours away. Rucker offers me the sofa in his office, but I respectfully decline. So I find a nice quiet spot, against a wall at the last row of cubicles where I am now reclining in one of the chairs with my feet resting on another chair. My jacket's blanketed over me, mostly covering my face to protect my eye and shield it from the light. I begin to nod toward sleep when I experience that familiar dozing off drop, like my head's on a spring and suddenly disconnected from my shoulders, only to snap quickly back. The jacket has slid down my face. I look around, see if anyone noticed.

No one.

Those who haven't already found slumber are probably still out searching for the suspect. Most of the crew on my tour are somewhere around here, at their own private spot, trying to get a couple of hours. We'll be at it soon enough, unless the others find her first.

I cover myself up again, lean back, and try to find that comfortable position, and it's not long before I feel that deep falling sensation. But this time I allow the full drop.

When I wake up, three hours have gone by. My body aches, and it takes me a while to come around. When I do, I kick my chair and sit up. I put my shoes on, then take my shirt off the wire hanger hooked on the edge of one of the cubicles, button it up and tuck it in. *This shirt's got one more day of life in it.* I grab my tie and walk toward the bathroom.

Beaumont is at his station typing away.

"You find her?" I ask hopefully.

"No. We got the warrant signed, though. We'll get her." He smiles like he's sure about what he said.

"You get rest?" I ask.

"Couple hours. You?"

"Same," I say, then throw him a wave and head toward the bathroom.

My face in the bathroom mirror is a frightening sight. *To me, anyway.* And I hope I don't look this way through the eyes of others. I splash cold water on this tired skin and pat it dry with a few of the cheap paper towels from the dispenser affixed to a wall, which end up tearing off and sticking to my wet skin and whiskers like Velcro. I pull the torn shreds off. Not much I can do about brushing, so I gargle water a couple of times and spit.

I find Mather sitting in his chair with his feet propped up on his desk. He's playing solitaire on the computer, dressed in a clean shirt and slacks. He looks fresh. Too fresh. It has to be the same genes that allow him to eat the way he does, but then I realize it's probably just his age. I only got about ten on him, which isn't so bad, but I've abused myself throughout the years, and it makes that ten like twenty.

"You feel like some coffee?" I ask him after he sees me.

"That's what I was about to ask you."

Mather drives, heading toward another spot he

discovered at 17th and Q Streets, Northwest. I crack the window a bit, let some of that crisp wintry wind slide through to wake this body up.

"What do you got working on that Escort case?" Mather asks.

I look at him briefly, then turn back, let some of that snappy air hit my face again. "I got a decedent who saw possibly hundreds of clients, all of whom are potential suspects. And so many of whom I'll never find. On the other hand, I got two good suspects, two guys, one who can and one who could lie with an ease that I can only assume comes from experience. And the one who could had the gall to kill himself and leave me with nothing." I shake my head.

"They always leave something."

"Yeah, that's what the textbooks say, so it must be true," I return.

"I'm next up. I hope I catch something good to work like you."

I don't say anything, because that's the first time I've heard him say something simple. If I had my choice, we'd never catch a homicide.

The coffee I buy is of little use. This body is too far gone. My mind is racing, though, coming nearer to an anxious state. A muscle on the bad side of my face, between my upper lip and nostril, twitches involuntarily and then tightens sharply. I massage it until it relaxes. The twitch stays for a while. I count to fifteen before it stops. The record's thirty so far.

We get back to the office in time for roll call.

The rest of the tour is spent trying to locate Josie Ragsdale. All available resources and manpower are devoted to it. Teletypes have been sent, posters made and shared with the districts and other jurisdictions, new areas canvassed, people interviewed and the media alerted. It is only a matter of time for her. She'll eventually make her way out of one of the hundreds of abandoned buildings she's secreted herself in, because she'll soon need the one thing that can feed life back into her rapidly decaying body.

I check my 'To Do' list on the computer and find a few things I have to get done. I call the FBI lab with the hope of finding something out about the DNA I submitted for comparison. One of the techs advises me that the results will not be ready any time soon. That's typical, and so I'm not terribly bothered by it. Sometimes it takes months. Nothing new, and so I move on.

Mather said he'd be in court for most of the day. I get with the Sarge and ask for an available key to a cruiser so I can take care of a couple of other things on the list. He obliges, and I find myself inside one of the more neglected vehicles—coffee stains on the seat and a piercing smell.

I make my way to DMV, to meet up with a contact I have there and see if he can pull a driver's license photograph of Bergine for me. I get a good color printout of a current photograph. It's a picture of him with a ridiculous smile, like the kind you probably think you have when the dentist wedges those uncomfortable blocks in your mouth for an X-ray. I also have him print out a photograph of Daniel Emmerich. I put the two of them together, look at them side by side, and wonder what an odd friendship they must have had. Sitting in the idling cruiser, I stare at their photos some more. I pull out my cell to call Aletheia Wynn.

I hurry over to her place. She answers her door promptly again, but this time she is fully clothed and even looks normal. Maybe even preppy, and I wonder if she's going to school, but I don't ask. She is wearing fitted jeans, a blue Georgetown Hoyas sweatshirt and white tennis shoes. Her hair is pulled back in a pony tail.

"This will just take a minute," I say.

She invites me in.

"I just want you to take a look at these pictures, tell me if you know any of these guys."

"Okay,"

I take the photos of Daniel Emmerich and William Bergine out and hand them to her. She looks at the two photos briefly, seems to hesitate for a moment then holds up Emmerich's photo to show me.

"Yes, of course. This is that William guy Amy was dating."

I look at her blankly and for a quick second I think she held the wrong picture.

I take it and turn it for her to see again. "You're telling me that this is William Bergine, the man Amy was dating?"

"Yes, that's him."

"What about him?" I ask indicating the other photo of Bergine she is holding. "You seen him before?"

"No, I don't know who this is. He looks scary, though."

She hands the photo back to me and I slip it into the case jacket. All I can think is that I somehow fell into one of those bad screenplays Clem and I used to read.

NINE

WHAT WAS EMMERICH THINKING when he chose to lie? That I'd never find out? That during the course of this investigation, he could keep his relationship with Amy Noyes a secret? He can't be that stupid. I am limited, or hindered, rather, by the restrictions found in actual existence. Lying about his relationship and even using William's name is not enough to get me into his home or office, let alone lock him up.

That little thing called probable cause.

There are dozens of reasons he'd lie. I can think of two real good ones right off the bat. He has a girlfriend or wife and he plays around a lot, uses William's name and info so it won't get back to her, so he lies out of fear. He's a local business man, a *pillar* of the community, who is having a kinky relationship with an escort, uses William's name in an effort to remain discreet; so he lies to the police out of fear. Maybe it's both reasons. Maybe it's neither, but I can go on and on, think of at least a dozen more times. There are probably several, and most of them based on fear and most of them a good reason for lying—but equally, a good reason for killing.

Now William, there's a character. Why would he lie like that? Act like he had a relationship with Amy Noyes? Put himself in a position of being the prime suspect? It's one thing covering up for a friend when it comes to protecting his personal life, but quite another when it comes to murder. And he did it with such ease, and on camera no less. But equally, there are several reasons I can think of on his behalf; money, loyalty, both. Or maybe fear is his motivation too. *Something hidden*. People lie for much less. People kill for much less. It's nothing new under this sun.

And for these reasons, I have elevated Daniel Emmerich to the undesirable position of suspect, alongside his friend William. He knows something, or had something to do with her murder. That's what I'm thinking, and I'm looking forward to the next time we talk.

THE COMPUTER FORENSICS UNIT. The name suggests something bigger than it really is: Three guys crammed into a dismal corner office on the third floor of Headquarters with one window that provides a view befitting this somber environment. Old metal desks and tall new work benches with tall swivel stools and angling directional work lights and computers and computer guts and tall computer towers, all crammed together.

Detective Marvell is there to greet me when I enter.

He gives me a CD and about thirty pages of the accompanying printouts from what he has recovered from Amy Noyes' computer. I slip them into my shouldered leather briefcase and clasp it shut.

"You guys have a chance to look at the other laptop and CPU yet?" I ask.

His body shrinks when he shrugs, "I'm so backed up you're lucky you got this one."

"I'd appreciate whatever you can do. The guy's a suspect."

"Yeah, a dead suspect from what I remember, so it's not like you have to worry about his doing it again, right?"

"Give me a break, Marv. I can't let this one sit like that."

He gives it a few seconds for effect then straightens himself up and says, "I'll see what I can do. Check back with me in a couple days."

"I'm on midnights next week. Any chance before then?"

"Man, you are pushing it, aren't you?"

"I just know what you guys mean when you say 'a couple of days'."

"Like I said, I'll see what I can do."

"I'll see you in a *real* couple of days then."

He shakes his head.

"Thanks," I say as I open the door to leave.

He just waves like he's glad he's rid of me.

So out of Headquarters I go. Nods, waves and mock salutes shared along the way with a few of those familiar court faces. And a few minutes later, it's up the elevator to the ninth floor.

Morgan's not in her office, but the door's open, so I grab the one seat that's not already occupied by stacks of documents or paperwork stuffed within accordion files. I pull out the pages Marv gave me. They are copies recovered from the hard drive of all the text that might contain personal information such as e-mails, address books, letters and documents and so on. I've reviewed stuff like this before. Lines of text are found between what looks like nonsense to me, and it's a little like trying to find Waldo, as far as the strain on the eyes is concerned. I snag one of Morgan's yellow highlighters from her desk, just in case I see something I like.

I don't find anything. What I am able to gather as I flip through the pages is that she used her computer as a simple word processor and nothing more. She had an e-mail address, but there are no e-mails. Even if she had deleted them we could get them. I find just the beginning of what looks like a resumé for a local TV station as a Community Reporter; some downloaded material related to other job searches. It looks like she was hoping to get out of the business she was in, just like her friend Aletheia. And then I remember what Aletheia Wynn said concerning their business, that most of it was referral-based and came over cell phones. As Aletheia Wynn said, the Internet attracted creeps. It also can attract law enforcement. Maybe that's why I'm not finding much on this computer. Amy Noyes was either computer illiterate or smart enough to keep anything related to her business off it. I don't find anything that would suggest she was taking any kind of computer class. There are no documents, no papers, nothing related to homework or attending classes of any kind. In fact, I can't remember any documents recovered from her apartment suggesting that either. Sometimes it's not about what you find, but what you don't find. But I'll have to double check. I pull the notebook out of my briefcase and make a note to myself.

> CHECK BERGINE'S CLASS ROSTER AT THE UNIVERSITY!

Morgan shows up after about thirty minutes and prints out some subpoenas.

I hand one of the subpoenas to the Records Clerk at UDC about twenty minutes later. She returns with copies of the roster, revealing the names of Bergine's students over the past couple of semesters. In an effort to be thorough, I ask if she can go back a couple of years, just in case.

After another fifteen or twenty minutes, the young Records Clerk returns with additional pages, which I place alongside the others in my briefcase. I shoulder it after I thank her and then make my way back to Morgan's office.

Morgan's back is facing the door as I enter, and she's typing madly on the computer. I knock lightly on the door a couple of times. She turns.

"Be done in a minute," she says.

I sit, pull the printouts from my briefcase and review them. When Morgan finishes, she turns in her swivel chair to face me.

"You have plans for Christmas?" she asks.

"New kid on the block. I'm working it."

"You?" I ask as a matter of politeness.

"Pittsburgh, where my family is. You find anything good?" she asks, referring to the documents I retrieved.

"According to these records, Amy Noyes never attended any classes there. But, so far, I've only checked the last year."

"Didn't he say in the videotaped statement that they had met a couple of months prior to her death? In one of the classes he taught?"

"I seem to remember that. Yes."

"Then why would he make that up?"

"Because he's protecting Emmerich. That's what I think."

"Okay, we've established that Emmerich's lying. So we need to start at the beginning again, but this time, see if there's any evidence that can connect Emmerich to her murder. Maybe he'll agree to come in for an interview."

"I'd like to hold off on talking to him right now—see if I can find something on him first." And before she can reply, I say, "I'll copy these papers for you, then I'm heading back to the office, look through all these names again."

"What about her computer?"

"I'll copy those documents, too."

"Okay. I'll subpoena her phone records for both her cell and land line. I've got a couple of contacts."

"Thanks. You got a good contact at the FBI Lab, too? See if we can speed up the DNA."

"I know someone. I'll get the number and call you," she says.

I leave the Nickel feeling a bit frustrated. I don't know why. I've been feeling that way a lot lately. In the short time I've been at homicide, I've already closed a case. That's a good thing. So I should feel motivated, feel like I've accomplished something worthwhile. But then I think about "Ciao Baby" Emmerich, sitting in his three thousand dollar ergonomic desk chair and loving how untouchable he thinks he is. And maybe he is untouchable. Maybe I'm just barking up the wrong tree, and the real suspect is one of the Johns she's been seeing. Maybe all these circumstances that point to Bergine and Emmerich are nothing more than what has already been suggested. For all I know, the Amy Noyes case jacket will end up being filed, and stacked up along with all those other unsettled spirits at Cold Case.

The office is empty. They're all satisfied in their ways. I haven't quite found mine yet. You'd think I would have after all these years, but I haven't. I feel as though my whole career has been one big detail, never having the time to settle in someplace. Even at the district, everyone coming and going, like Union Station most of the time. And I'm like the guy sitting on the bench waiting for the train.

As I look through the rest of the names of the students who have attended Bergine's classes, one catches my attention: Evelyn Jackson.

The Cold Case?

Before I get too excited, because it's a common name, I note the social security number which is also provided. I check the Cold Case file.

It's the same girl.

Just like that. What do you know.

Evelyn Jackson. A common name.

She attended one semester at UDC, almost a year before she was found dead in a gutted abandoned building. I called her Parole Officer. She had successfully served one hundred and twenty days in an inpatient drug treatment program and was given the opportunity to attend classes at UDC through a grant. *Trying to better her life.*

William Bergine, now connected to two women, killed in the same manner. Daniel Emmerich, now connected to these same two women. Still circumstantial, but getting stronger.

I update everything on my case resumé.

I call Morgan, fill her in.

"So we have a Cold Case involving a prostitute who was murdered in a strikingly similar manner to this Amy Noyes, and who *was* a student of our suspect, and we have this Amy Noyes, whom the suspect claimed was one of his students, but we can't find any information that says she was."

"The plot thickens, huh?" I chuckle.

"Like a real mystery."

"I submitted Bergine's blood for comparison in both cases. But you know how that is. You get me a number yet?"

She asks me to hold for a second, then comes back with a name and number.

"She's helped me out in the past," Morgan says.

I make the call right after I hang up with Morgan. An operator at the FBI's Washington Field Office answers, and I ask for Mary Cruden.

I'm transferred to her extension. A young-sounding voice answers. I introduce myself and drop Morgan's name, and then give her the short version. She asks for the Lab number and the information related to both decedents and the suspect. She tells me she'll see what she can do and to give her a call back in a couple of days. And I wonder if she means this literally. I'd like to believe she does, so that's how I leave it. I hang up the phone and hope for the best.

SALTY'S VIEWING IS SCHEDULED for tomorrow. Everyone's going. There'll be a departmental procession for the funeral, the following day—Tuesday. He was killed in the line of duty. Officers will attend from all over the place, like one large family. I dread these things. Rucker's made arrangements for everyone to meet outside VCU for the procession. We'll take the cruisers, join up with the procession on Constitution and 6th, near Headquarters on

Tuesday morning.

Beaumont and Fletcher are the only guys not around when evenings roll out after we relieve them. The Sarge said they're working this thing through and out following up on some leads somewhere in Maryland. The floating detective with the helium tummy is out sick, so it's a light crew for the first night. Just me, Mather, Tommy and Yvonne. And the first night is always the toughest to get through, especially during that time in the wee hours, when the steady calm falls over the city and your body wants to follow with it.

I pass Mather on the way back to my desk, but he's talking on the phone so I don't bother him. I find a note on my desk to call Robert Noyes. Apparently, he called expecting an update on his daughter's case. I feel like kicking myself. That's something you don't want to forget to do, and I'm surprised I haven't heard from Hattie about this one. When I commit something to my notebook as a reminder it's usually like an internal alarm clock. It must be out of order. I tape the note on the side of my monitor, so I'll be sure to see it and make the call tomorrow.

Surprisingly, Hattie does appear over my shoulder as if he were monitoring my thoughts, or had been waiting for my arrival in order to jump down my throat about failing to communicate with the family. The note from Robert Noyes is in plain view.

"You're looking tired," he tells me.

"I always look tired, Lu," I advise him.

"I'm going to need an update from you on the Noyes case by morning for the Captain. He's got the morning meeting tomorrow."

"I'll have it on your desk in a few."

"Good. Good. If I'm not in the office, just drop it in the in-box. Everything all right, then?" He asks like there should be something wrong, or I should confess or something.

"All good, Lu. Unless you've heard something I haven't?"

"No. No," he says like chuckles. "Good job."

"Thank you," I say, and he turns and walks back toward the hall that leads to his office. The family hasn't complained, so I skated through that one.

It takes a little creative writing to put the narrative together, especially with Evelyn Jackson in the picture. I don't put too much into the discovery of her name, but even the mention of a decedent in a Cold Case now associated with an open case will raise a brow or two. Next thing I know, they'll be screaming I'm trying to make him into some kind of serial murderer. I decide to keep it in, despite the possible repercussions. So it begins with the initial information provided by Scanns' Initial Case Resumé and then goes on from there. I write it up like an affidavit, which is a chronological order of events, like I'm building a solid circumstantial case against Bergine. But the real creative writing comes in when I have to introduce another person of interest, Emmerich. Probably something they don't want to hear, either, but I'm not here to please, or am I?

I finish in about an hour. Hattie's not in his office, so I drop it in his in-box. I fully expect my pager to sound before the end of this tour.

Mather and I roll around the Adam's Morgan area through most of the midnight hours, listening to the busy police chatter over the Third District air and searching for late-night spots serving decent coffee.

A couple of coffees later we find a parking spot and keep the car idling.

"I hate midnights," I say for no particular reason.

"You get used to it."

"You get used to it if it's your permanent tour. It's this rotating crap that's gonna kill me," I respond.

"I had permanent mids when I was in the Section."

"When you first came on?" I ask.

"Yeah. I liked it. You're left to do your own thing. You don't get messed with for all those details like IMF, some Presidential or whatever special event this city's got going on."

"I hated details, too," I say. "It's not natural, though—midnights. The body's not meant to operate on that tour. It has to mess you up somehow."

"I turned out all right," Mather says.

"We'll see," I return.

He smiles, slurps that latte.

"You going to get this guy in for another interview?"

"I'm thinking I will, soon."

"Father Confessor."

"You keep saying that."

"I just heard you have this way about you in the box, and suspects open up to you."

"Where'd you hear that?"

"Tommy said something when you had that kid in the other day, maybe Captain Rucker, too. Heard you were good for hundreds of closures back at the District."

"Corner thugs and crack heads are a piece of cake. Most of those guys don't care or don't know any better. Just got to find something you can relate to them about and, they open up. People like Emmerich and Bergine—they don't work that way. At least in my experience."

"I agree with that," he says.

My pager sounds with that awful, EEEE!! EEEE!! EEEE!!! And I almost toss my coffee.

Mather laughs.

"I hate this thing," I say.

It's a message from Hattie, just as I thought—asking me to call him in the office.

"Something up?" Mather asks.

"Hattie wants me to give him a call." I pull out my cell and punch in the number. He answers after one ring, asks what I'm working and then whether I can break away and get back to the office.

TEN

"SO, THIS COLD CASE, how did you find that?" Hattie asks, sitting behind his desk.

"When I was detailed there, I reviewed it. Actually brought it up to Scanns when I saw him in court one day."

"Yes," Hattie says with a slight compassionate nod. "And according to your write-up, you've submitted samples from Bergine for DNA comparison in both cases?"

"Yes."

"Maybe we should take all this information concerning the cold case out then, at least until you get the results back."

"You don't agree, even without DNA, that it's unusual we got her attending one of his classes a year before she's found murdered in the same manner as Amy Noyes?"

"I agree with you one hundred percent. I just don't want one of my guys put in a position where the chiefs are going to think a cold case is about to get closed when it won't."

"I appreciate that, Lu, but like I said, even if the DNA comes back negative, this is still going to have to come out. It's pretty good circumstantial stuff. But I thought I made that clear in the write-up?"

"You did. You did," he says scanning the write-up. He looks up and nods, like he suddenly agrees with me. "Good enough then. We'll keep it like this," he says.

"All right," I say. "Anything else?"

"No. No. Thank you."

I make my exit then.

Morning appears, like it never left. Relief's almost up. My body feels like it's kicked into overdrive and I'm good for a few more hours at least.

I'm thinking I don't want to go to the viewing—for selfish reasons. The funeral is the most important thing, anyway. While deliberating this, my pager sounds.

It's Marvell.

I call him, and he tells me I should come down right away because he's probably got something I want. He won't give me any info over the phone, acting like it would be giving up the contents of a wrapped Christmas present if he did, so I hurry down.

I'm early enough so that parking is not an issue. I actually find a spot right in front.

Extremely windy day, though. The flags on the poles in front of Headquarters snap violently, and sudden gusts shove me forward.

The door to the Computer Unit is slightly ajar, so I push it open and walk in. Another detective is working at one of those tall work tables. I haven't seen him around before. Looks like some new blood recently assigned.

"Marv around?" I ask him.

"In here!" I hear Marv yell from the other room before the new blood can answer.

I find him in another work area, bent over some documents he's flipping through. When I walk in, he turns and hands me one of them.

"That, my friend, is probably what you would refer to as a memento," he says with raised brows like he's proud.

I look at it. And frankly, I'm stunned at what I see.

It's a print out of a picture of Amy Noyes. It appears to have been taken post mortem, as it reveals her fallen in the same position in which she was discovered, the mud like a memory foam pillow under her head. Thick flames are caught in the still life, having engulfed the magazine that was rolled and inserted in her vagina, now curling and wrapping over her thighs.

I get a sick feeling in my stomach.

"Pretty freaky," Marv says. "Found it in the laptop recovered from your suspect's home. He changed the JPEG file extension so it doesn't appear as a JPEG anymore, then he renamed it and hid it in the System 32 folder. But it's all in the write-up. Actually, pretty basic stuff for a guy you said teaches computer science."

I barely hear what Marv is saying. I can't get over the photograph and actually having this copy in my hands. It doesn't look real, almost like some sick doctored photo you might find on the Internet. I suddenly remember what Emmerich said about Bergine's relationship with the Internet and the comparison to his relationship with Amy Noyes. *Why am I not surprised?* I force myself to set it aside along with the other documents. I ask Marv to repeat what he said and he does. I'm not so computer illiterate that I don't understand it, and he's right, it does sound relatively easy to do. But it isn't such a bad way of hiding something and having it available when his sick mind needed to relive the experience.

"Incredible. Any other ones?" I ask hesitantly.

"That's the only one like that, but I got dozens of downloaded porn. There was no attempt to hide these from anyone." He picks up a stack, hands it to me. "Lot of writings that you're going to want to go through, too."

I flip through the pages and quickly realize if you were to Google "crack head prostitute sex," or "violent sex acts," this is probably what you'd get. Sick stuff.

"Can you tell if that hidden JPEG was downloaded or scanned?"

"It wasn't in the history. It looks like it was most likely taken with a digital camera and imported."

"And this other stuff was definitely downloaded?"

I ask.

"Oh, without a doubt. I included the history for you."

"All right. Good job."

"Digital cameras, scanners and the Internet are creating a whole new monster, huh?"

"Yeah on that," I say. "You know, we never did recover a digital camera from Bergine's home when we searched it."

"Well, at least you have this image," Marv says.

So out the door I go to spend an hour or so at Morgan's office, sorting through a bit of what we have. Before I go home, I leave a polite but desperate message for Mary Cruden to call either me or Morgan for a status on the DNA.

After another hard day's sleep, I head into the office and spend most of the tour going through all the files and photos. By this time, the Amy Noyes photograph has become a popular item among some of the more depraved detectives at VCU. Something like this is hard to keep to yourself. One person sees it and then it travels through our extensive and well-organized grapevine in a very short period of time. It gets to the point where I have to lie and advise everyone, including Rucker, that it is secured at the U.S. Attorney's Office, and the master image is on a hard drive at evidence.

What Marv was able to recover is pretty extensive and involves everything from chat room history, e-mails and some pretty sick Internet sites he had visited on a regular basis. There are only a handful of e-mails between Bergine and Emmerich and all of it, just as Emmerich suggested during our interview, is business-related. There is no correspondence related to Amy Noyes, or even women in general for that matter.

Other things I slog through include Bergine's attempt at poetry. In my experience, based on personal relationships and even searching the homes of so many suicide victims over the years, I have yet to find a manic depressive, suicidal person who has not found the need to express his self-indulgent emotions with poetry. Bergine's, I am not so sorry to say, is some of the worst, some of the most pitiful self-indulgence I have seen so far. It does confirm that he was obsessed with sex, death and God. But what else is new under this sun? Everyone I meet in this business is obsessed with sex and death and God.

I organize everything based on the level of importance, with the exception of the hidden photograph, which is actual evidence and would be all the way at the top of the list. Most of what is important isn't anything I would be able to use to close the case. It is mostly information that reveals his sexual motivation and affected character.

I stuff everything in the case jacket. I set it on the desk and look down on it, thicker now then when I first began, and I am bothered by that one thing that prevents a nice and neat package—Emmerich and that damned picture of him that Aletheia Wynn identified. I call Morgan about scheduling a Witness conference.

❄

SALTY DOG, AKA STANLEY Untermeyer, was buried with all the ceremony and tradition that comes with a life lost in the line of duty. When I finally get home, *at such an unreasonable time for a midnight detective*, I turn on the evening news. Not because I feel the need for more anxiety in this life of mine, but because I want to see what kind of coverage they have on the funeral. It does make the top of the hour report. And after showing footage of the processional and its long line of departmental cruisers and motorcycles from our department and surrounding jurisdictions, the reporter talks briefly about the case and the suspect still at large. A reward is offered by Crime Solvers for her capture. Ten thousand dollars. That's a lot of days of chasing the high for some crack head. And that's who'll probably give this girl up—some pipe partner friend of hers. Fortunately for me, but most fortunately for Rucker, there is no report concerning my case. So I power the television off.

I undress, slip on the eye patch and then stretch across the sofa in nothing but my boxers and t-shirt. *The unhappiness of the happy* comes into my head after I close my eye, like a distant, still voice.

❄

I THINK I MAY have had an unhealthy influence on Mather. Or maybe I just triggered something already buried deep within his psyche. Ever since I introduced him to my good coffee spot in Adam's Morgan and his palate has experienced flavors other than those offered in a Styrofoam cup, he has endeavored, with almost a chaotic passion, to seek out and experience every coffee spot in DC. He is now slurping some funky five-dollar version of a latte from a spot in Capitol Hill. I've got my regular cup, whatever the house blend is. We both came in early for a little comp time. Mather, trying to build his up, because that comp turns into money eventually, and me, because I'm expecting Emmerich at the office for a follow-up interview. He was charmingly sympathetic to my work hours and agreed on this evening, having reminded me that he wants to help in any way he can.

He actually shows up a few minutes before the scheduled time. I greet him at the front and escort him to one of our small yet inviting interview rooms.

"These are the only private rooms we have," I say.

I see him glance over to the handcuffs bolted to the table.

"That's if I find you haven't paid your parking tickets," I tell him.

He smiles oddly, like someone who just figured out he was taken at Three Card Monte.

"Have a seat. I'll be right with you. You want a soda or something? We have coffee, but I don't think you'd want to chance that."

Another smile, but not so odd and, "I'm okay for now. Thank you."

"All right, then. I'll be right back."

I join Mather in the monitor room, still sipping a coffee drink that has to have cooled to below room temperature by now.

"And you think this guy had something to do with it?" Mather asks.

"If he didn't, he knows something. You going to hang out and take in the show, or what?"

"It looks like it might be entertaining, and besides, it's the only channel we got."

I almost want to give him the thumbs up for that one.

Emmerich's resting his folded arms on the table, hands clasped, like he's waiting for the classroom teacher.

"Hey, listen," I begin, "Would you mind if I videotape this interview, just so I don't have to spend all my time writing."

"Videotape?"

"Yeah, it's just easier on me that way because I can refer back to the tape for the important stuff. Otherwise, I'll have to be taking notes and breaking up the talk. I'd much rather this be more like a conversation than that."

"I don't have a problem with recording this. Do I have to sign something for you? Is that how's it done?"

"How did you know that?" I ask with my Joker smile.

"The business part of me," he returns with one of his own. "Formalize everything."

I get a waiver, and he signs it. I go back to the monitor room and slide a VHS into the machine and press record.

"Rolling. Isn't that what you used to say?" Mather asks.

"I was an English teacher," I say.

"Whatever you say," Mather smiles

I go back to the room, sit down and cross my legs. For the sake of the video I announce the date and time, and ask Emmerich to speak his full name.

"I appreciate your agreeing to come all the way over here and talk with me," I say.

"Of course. I told you I would help in any way."

"I know. Thank you. Now, after our initial interview, you had brought up some interesting points. That's one of the reasons I wanted to talk to you again. But also, there are a few questions I need answers to, and my first choice for the answers is, unfortunately, not with us anymore."

"And you expect me to have the answers only a dead man can give?"

I pause a moment. Then, "That's sort of callous, isn't it? Especially since the dead man was a good friend of yours."

"Please don't misinterpret my response. I don't mean to sound so callous, but the more time I've had to think this whole thing through, the more anger I feel toward him and this whole situation I fear he has caused."

"Even though it might be obvious, tell me what

makes you angry?"

"Primarily, for taking the cowardly way out, especially if he had anything to do with her murder."

"So you've had time to think about things. Any new ideas?"

"Well, as I also told you before, he called me, worried about her, and needed me to go with him to check up on her," he begins, looking directly at me. "So think about it. Why would he be so afraid of going himself? He's not so scared of the opposite sex that he would need me there as some sort of buffer. Also, he hadn't been dating this woman for so long that he would even worry about having to check up on her after not hearing from her in a couple of days. How does he know that's not how she is in general? How does he know she's not just avoiding him? These were a few of the questions I was asking myself. But, most importantly, why was he so insistent on checking up on her?"

"I don't know if we talked about this before," I look at him quizzically and continue, "but some men, and women for that matter, especially if they already have emotional problems, sometimes go a little overboard in a new relationship."

"Well, this was over the top to say the least, but not in the way you are suggesting."

"So now it's your opinion that William knew something or was somehow involved?"

Without hesitation, he says, "Yes, I think he was."

Another measured pause on my part and then,

"How, exactly, was it left after he asked you to go with him?"

"I told him he was crazy and a grown man. I said she was probably out of town or with a client and for him to relax."

"So you never went with him to check up on her?"

"No, of course not. No."

"Did you hear from him later?"

"No. I told you I called him after I heard about her murder on the news."

"That's right," I correct myself. "You had also mentioned something very interesting before about William's relationship with the Internet and actually equated that to a relationship with a woman."

"Yes."

"What did you know about his life on the Internet?"

"Only that he spent most of his time on it. There were times when he was working out of one of our offices, and I'd find web addresses to these off-the-wall porn sites."

"What kind of sites?"

"Just out there, you know."

"No. I don't unless you describe them."

"Hardcore sites. Triple X. Women portrayed in such ways that would be very difficult for me to describe."

"And that's why you asked if we had his computer?"

"Yes. If I found that kind of stuff on our computer, I could imagine what you might find on his. Am I right?"

"I can't really get into what we may or may not have

right now. What's important is the information that you have."

"I fully understand," he says.

"And why didn't you give me this information about what you found on your computer when I was at your office?

"Because we had already cleaned that computer, and I had that meeting to go to. But that's why I'm here now."

"You sure you don't want a soda?."

He looks at what appears to be an expensive wrist watch.

"You all right with the time?" I ask.

"Yes. I'm fine. That's the benefit of a high position. I can show up when I want."

"I wish I had that luxury."

"I can imagine," he says with an even tone, almost like he was suddenly bored.

"When was the last time you were at William's house?"

"His house?" He repeats and after shaking his head back and forth for a couple of seconds. "I don't remember when I last visited him. It was a while ago, though."

"You don't have to be exact."

"Over a month ago."

"Do you know how to get in touch with his family?"

"William's family?"

"Yes. We haven't been able to notify anyone in his family."

"He was an only child. His mother raised him, but she passed away...oh, it had to be three years ago."

"And the father?"

"They divorced when we were in our teens. I would not be able to tell you how to get in touch with him."

"Then you're like the only family he had?"

"You could say that," he says after a bit of hesitance.

"Back to what you were saying about the Internet. If we did have William's laptop, what do you think we'd find on it?"

"Like I said, probably a lot of what I found on our work computer, maybe more."

"Maybe more like what?"

"I don't know. You'll have to tell me that after you've looked."

"You think if he had anything to do with Amy's murder, there'd be information on it?"

"I can only tell you that he kept that laptop with him like most mothers keep a baby."

"He didn't let it out of his sight, then?"

"No, not that I ever saw."

He stiffens in his chair. I don't get the impression it's a nervous thing, but more like shunning someone, probably a subconscious gesture directed at me.

I let him go on like this, and allowing him to get real comfortable with himself. Then I decide the time's about right.

"We do have another problem, Daniel," I say suddenly.

"Okay."

That's an odd reply.

"Tell me about your relationship with Amy Noyes?"

And this question does not appear to elicit any more of a reaction than any other question I've asked.

"My relationship with Amy?"

"Do me a favor. You don't have to repeat the questions I ask, because I remember what I asked."

"I told you I only met her once."

"I'm going to be honest with you now. I know you were having a relationship with her."

"You do? I would like to know how you know that, because your information is probably way off."

"I don't think so. Relationship might be the wrong choice of a word, then. Let's just say you were seeing her on a regular basis. For all I care, she was providing her services to you."

He cocks his head back. "Oh, please," he says.

"So what you're telling me right now on videotape is that you were not seeing Amy Noyes in any way?"

"That is correct, and if you have someone telling you otherwise then bring them here right now and we can settle this matter right away."

"How many times have you seen her?"

"Just that one time I told you about, in Adam's Morgan with William."

"Daniel, I don't know what it is you're thinking in that business head of yours, but if you're going to sit there and think you can get yourself out of a homicide investigation with those lies and a bit of charm, then you will soon find yourself in a messy situation."

He shakes his head like he could care less.

"Are you married?"

"I'm sure you already know that I am not."

"What about a girlfriend?"

"There are women I see, but no one I'm serious about."

"Okay, that rules that out."

He looks at me curiously.

"I mean, you don't have to hide the fact that you're getting freaky with an escort if you're not married and don't have a serious girlfriend. Then maybe it's something you have to hide from your business associates? There's no crime in that, right?"

It's almost as if he considers it, but then says, "If either of those were true, then I would agree. But neither is true because I was not getting *freaky* with that woman. You're barking up the wrong tree, detective."

"No, I'm not, but you're digging your own grave," I say, throwing him a cliché.

"So you're suggesting that I'm a suspect now?"

"I'm not suggesting it, I'll flat out say you are. And that's something you did to yourself, turning something that could be easily explained into something that's starting to look awfully suspicious."

He looks like he's considering this again, or maybe I'm just giving him a little too much time to think it through.

"You tell me what I'm supposed to think," I say.

"I'll tell you," he turns to me as if he were at the head of the table at some board meeting. "The man you want is the one you'll never be able to interview—your own words. And just because he's not alive to crucify, you focus your attention on me. That's what I think."

"Oh, I know that William was involved, but now I know you were too."

"And what makes you say that?"

"I want you to understand that I might already know the answers to some of the questions I've asked you and am going to ask you. I'm just telling you that because I don't want you to get caught in a bunch of lies. That won't look good. And Daniel, I might ask you some of those questions because I'm testing your truthfulness. The best thing you can do for yourself is to tell the truth."

He nods, looks up at the camera lens and says with calmness, "Like I said, whatever person you may think you have or whatever information you may think you have that suggests I was having a relationship with that woman is either something that is in your head, detective, or just a mistake."

"Good credible witnesses don't make things up, Daniel."

"But they can be mistaken."

"And you're comfortable with ending our conversation on this note?"

"No, let's be friends again," he says cleverly.

"I could be a good friend—you tell me the truth."

"I'm sure you could, but, on second thought, I don't think our friendship would work out. You're too mistrustful, but I think that's your job's fault more than yours."

"Here's what I think. You were involved somehow, along with William. I mean, you're a charmer, Daniel. You got good style. You live in a better neighborhood, have a better job. From what I've been able to gather, you're smarter. Better education. William? I just don't see it. I think whatever happened, poor old William was following your lead. I don't think he'd be capable otherwise."

"As wrong as it is, you're entitled to your opinion."

"That's the other thing. I'm flat-out accusing you of murder and you're still sitting there all free and easy, like this is an extension of your office or something and I'm some lower level employee, female maybe?—who you can get away with harassing like that. Maybe they take it from you because they have to, or maybe they take it because they get off on taking it as much as you get off giving it. Are those the type of women you hire? Or are those the type of women you have to go out and pay for?"

"I mean, if I were you, I'd be furious with some cop trying to say I was responsible for a murder! Instead, I truly believe you think you're some kind of tough guy and this is some kind of corporate world we're playing in. Sitting here, looking at you and listening to what you say, though more eloquent, to me you are no different than those crack babies, all grown up now and caught up in their "Grand Theft Auto" world of reality. At least I know where they're coming from. They'd flat out say they want to blow my head off. They don't have to hide the world they live in. They're actually proud of their little world. Are you proud of yours?"

"What would you like me to do? I understand this is a part of your job. I even appreciate that. What would I accomplish by getting all emotional?" he straightens up. "I'm actually starting to get a little tired."

"I thought you were a late-night person."

"Yes. Usually I am. But this conversation is not what I thought it would be."

"And what kind of conversation did you think it'd be?"

"I came here thinking I'd be able to help you with your investigation. I didn't have to come here."

"No, you didn't."

"Is there anything else I can help you with then, detective?"

"Yeah, what really happened?"

"Then I've said all I can say."

"Agree to a Voice Stress Analyzer and we can settle this mess right now?"

"Voice Stress Analyzer?"

"There you go repeating again. Same thing as a polygraph," I tell him.

"I don't trust those things."

"They're very reliable. You're telling the truth, I apologize and you're good to go."

And again, he pauses like he's considering

everything.

"No. Those things aren't reliable."

"Then something more reliable—agree to give me samples of your DNA. That's indisputable."

"Nothing is indisputable," he says with confidence.

"It's easy. I have a kit. I take samples of some of your hair, a swab for saliva. That would rule you out as a suspect. Isn't that what you want?"

"I know a little bit about the law, and I know that even if the results were found to be *negative*, as you people call it, you would never rule me out as a suspect. Also, and most importantly, I will not agree to submit anything of that nature to be used for who knows whatever purpose."

"You think the Metropolitan Police Department is into cloning on the side?"

"Please," he says. "I know how some of you operate."

"Oh, you mean planting evidence. That kind of thing. That's ridiculous, and you know it."

"Not as ridiculous as you may think."

"That's your choice, then?"

That smug lack of response is his way of saying yes.

"But being the good sport I am, you know where to find me if you need me for anything else," he says.

"We'll talk again," I say with some confidence.

He nods with tightened lips and an expression that implies, in his own mind anyway, that he's the one in control.

And that, regrettably, is the end of that.

❄

I'VE HAD COUNTLESS INDIVIDUALS in the box before and failed to get a confession plenty of times. But somehow that's not the same as this time. Maybe because the stakes are higher. Maybe because there's just something about Emmerich's character I find repulsive. Whatever it is, I don't like this feeling.

I study my face in the bathroom mirror again. I don't like what I see. The stress? The left side seems to have a life of its own, but it's the right side, the usual me, that has a sad life. I discover a few more gray hairs on the right side of my head. I pluck them, because I like my black hair black and you won't ever catch me using something like hair dye.

The Phone rings.

The caller ID reveals Clem's number. I hesitate, but decide to pick it up before it kicks into the voice message.

"Hey, Clem," I say and then sit on a chair facing my small window. *It's snowing.*

"I'm surprised you answered."

"Why wouldn't I answer?"

"I never know when you're home. Those crazy hours of yours."

"I'm on midnights through the end of the week. Actually just woke up."

"Five p.m. That's not natural."

"Shhh, my body'll here you," I say.

She snickers. "I closed on the condo the other day."

"Congratulations. Now you don't have to drive to the beach anymore."

"You got that right!"

"When are you moving in?"

"Just in time to throw a fabulous New Year's party!"

"Well, I'm happy for you."

"Happy enough to come and visit?"

"Maybe," I answer and then wonder how that came out. The familiar sound of her voice made me do it. I mean, when I said 'maybe,' that suggests I'm actually considering something I adamantly oppose. But then, I do have all that "use or lose," which I'll have to burn by the middle of January. There I go! I've just considered it further.

I pull myself back into the conversation.

"I'm sorry," I tell her. "Say that again."

"I said, what are you doing for Christmas?"

"I have to work it, but midnights. Hopefully, I'll be sleeping through Christmas day."

"You say that like it's something to look forward to."

"Sleep is always something to look forward to."

"I agree. I love to sleep. But not on Christmas day!" she says, like it's breaking some Commandment.

"I'll have pleasant Christmas dreams. What about you? Seeing your parents?"

"Of course. Lucky me."

"Watch out. There might be some snow. You gonna break out that purple thing you wear around your neck?"

"Please, please, please, you don't want to get me started. Besides I have a new scarf. It's D&G. And it's pink!"

I smile crookedly. "We haven't talked this much in years—since I left California, actually. Everything all right?"

"Yes, of course. Why does something have to be wrong because I call more often? If you'd rather, I'll wait a couple of months between calls."

"No, I like hearing from you. You know that."

I find myself on level ground again by the time we get off and have already forgotten my old state of mind.

I have some time to kill before work, so I decide on the comfort of the bed. I prop the pillows up a bit and stretch out, look toward the clock and remember the Bible Ms. McPherson gave me. For some reason I open the drawer, grab it and open to the page where she wrote:

> *This is an old Book given many years ago to my brother by my departed mother. It brought him much comfort in life and now it is my desire that it should bring you much comfort in life.*

I think how kind that is, and how much that Bible must have meant to her and her family. I've thought that before, but it has more meaning now. This is not just an ordinary book like the hundreds that occupy my shelves. Even those books are not something I can easily give up once they've found their place beside another. It's like they've become something deeply personal after you've read and enjoyed them, like friendship. I can't imagine giving away something like a family Bible, a book with words that at one time breathed for me. I can't imagine doing what Ms. McPherson did. So, taking all this into account, I open this book. I owe her that much for giving up something so meaningful. Opening it feels so familiar.

ELEVEN

MORGAN CALLS ME AFTER another thankfully uneventful tour. Mary Cruden called her moments ago and is on her way to the Triple Nickel with the lab report. I drive my personal vehicle there.

I meet Cruden and Morgan in one of the ninth floor conference rooms. The report is already displayed on the long table. Cruden is not what I imagined, based on the voice. She is larger than her voice. We shake hands, and judging by Morgan's expression, I'd say the information on the report is good.

Tomorrow is Christmas, so it looks as though I will be having Christmas dreams. This is what I think after Cruden identifies the key elements on the report. It's not what I ultimately hoped to find, but it's certainly nothing to complain about and also eliminates whatever lingering doubt I still had as to the extent of William Bergine's involvement.

"We tested a portion of the samples you gave us and found it to be a match here," Cruden says and then points to the portion of the report that indicates a

DNA match on seminal fluid recovered from both the clothing and the anal area of Evelyn Jackson.

It's one of those things you never really expect to see even though there was an original notion that led you to this place to begin with, in this case the striking similarity between both cases. Unfortunately, there was not a match with Amy Noyes.

"There wasn't enough evidence found on the scene for adequate testing,"

"You mean nothing substantial to compare with Bergine's DNA?" I ask.

"Yes," Cruden replies, then adds, "There were hairs, but they were found to belong to your decedent."

What is interesting about the cold case is that the seminal fluid recovered from Evelyn Jackson's shirt was found to be mixed with what was stated to be an "Unknown," which is an unidentified person's DNA. Then there's the flammable combustible accelerants from both cases—an identical match. It's great stuff here, and I'm ecstatic.

You put all this together; the two cases, the awful photograph, the downloads, the lies, the admitted relationship and I am more than convinced. But I am equally convinced that Emmerich was involved. That's the one thing I can't shake.

After the three of us go through everything, I make copies for Morgan, then slide the originals in my case jacket.

"It looks like you'll be closing a good cold case," Morgan says.

And it's almost as if I expect her to ask me what I'm going to do now. *I'm going to Disneyland!* But decide on home to catch a few hours.

RUCKER IS HAPPY. I get into the office early to tell him. He sits behind that desk, his legs extended and propped up on the edge of it, like he hasn't a care in the world. I try to explain that it's a good closure for the cold case, but not yet over with respect to the current one. Even though there's enough to administratively clear the Noyes case, it'll still remain active.

"This isn't some Hollywood movie with all those twists and turns and little sub-plots. This is your basic sex-related homicide that was made a little more difficult because the primary had to go and kill himself. That's all it is. You've done a good job, Ezra. Let's not make this into some wannabe Blockbuster," Rucker says. "The loud voices will cease! Close the Noyes case."

It takes a little restraint on my part, because even though I considered him a friend at one time, he's still the boss, and I can't just dive over the desk and slap him silly. I don't get into what I want to say because he already knows about Aletheia Wynn identifying Emmerich. He knows about the "unknown" in the cold case, but he easily explains it and for a minute I almost believe it. Yes, Evelyn Jackson was a prostitute, so there's a chance the unknown is another John that hooked up with her prior to William Bergine.

But there's also a chance that it's Emmerich's DNA. And yes, we all know the possible reasons for Emmerich to lie to the police. I've been through that before. But I'm not convinced, because when I think about Daniel Emmerich, I get an image in my head of a soft, rotting peach with the skin peeling off on your hand. This thought comes over me while leaning over the desk, and Rucker looks at me with an uncertain smile, but his cell phone, sitting on his desk, rings before he can reply.

As he reaches to pick it up, I notice the caller ID. I recognize the name—a local news reporter. The full name must have been stored in Rucker's cell.

He takes the cell phone, looks at the caller ID and then says, "I should get this." He answers it before I have a chance to say anything. "Whassup!" Rucker says as if to a long lost friend.

All I do is shake my head with disbelief and leave his office.

Mather's at the soda machine as I make my way toward our office area. He twists open an orange fruit drink. I shoot a nod of acknowledgement his way.

"The boss is happy, huh?"

"Yeah."

"I mean, you've been here what? Not even two months and you've got three closures."

"Two and a half closures," I say.

"How do you mean?" he asks, then chugs his drink.

"The Noyes case. The bosses closed it. Not me."

"Nothing wrong with closing it administratively."

"I know."

"Doesn't mean you have to stop looking at your boy Emmerich."

I nod in agreement.

So I call Robert Noyes and give him the news before he has to hear about it on the news. I'll keep it simple, though, no reason for him to know about anything else at this point.

After the phone call I go for a drive. I don't encounter much traffic. I remember it's Christmas Eve. That might have something to do with it. Everyone tucked away in their own cozy dungeons for the night. I think about Scanns and all his belongings under the desk and how I'll have to drive them to Celeste when she returns after the holidays. I know I won't have to write that down in my notebook to remember it.

I soon find myself around the Dupont Circle area, as if falling into that familiar haze again and allowing my subconscious mind to direct me. It's not long after that I'm driving around Emmerich's neighborhood and then on his block and then parked illegally along the curb at a crosswalk a few houses down from his address. I recline the seat a bit and adjust the rear view mirror so I can still see what's behind me. I catch a glimpse of my good side in the corner of the mirror, and for a second I feel normal.

Colorful, bright Christmas lights and decorations from neighboring homes flash in the distance. The night is still, and the clouds backlit by a full moon hover motionless over the block. I crack the window to pour out the cold dregs of an old coffee cup and notice how quiet the street is and how the wind has disappeared.

Emmerich's house sits there, as if separate from the other homes. His porch light is on, along with the yellowish glow cast by a light behind the curtain of a corner room. I wonder if that makes him feel safe. I am reminded of the one on Bergine's street, with the defiant smile. I wonder if both houses would've given me the same impression prior to accepting their current occupants. I doubt it.

And so the time passes and the darkness remains as the hour turns to Christmas Day. I sit there, not expecting anything to reveal itself to me, but instead feeling hopeful, because I realize I have time.

Eventually, daylight eases in as it always does, to obediently begin this process once again. I head back into the office for relief.

A SLOW MOVING SNOWSTORM has made its way over the city. Six inches has fallen during my Christmas slumber. It's still falling hard. Outside my window is a steady mass of whiteness backlit by street lights, caught by an undercurrent of wind moments before impact, causing pockets of frenzied flurries.

I spent the early part of the day, before sleep, on the telephone with Clem and then family.

"The presents are in the mail," my young sister said. That's typical and I'm not resentful. I'm used to it.

She tries, but years of dependence have made her very undependable.

"Hold on for a second, mom wants to talk to you," she said before I could respond. I heard the phone fumbling between hands.

"Hello, my dear son," my mother began as she always began a phone conversation with me. There was always salt in those words, 'hello, my dear son' and, for the life of me, I have never been able to figure out if she was being sincere or sarcastic.

"Merry Christmas," I said.

"I love the necklace. It looks so expensive."

"What do you and Emily have planned for today?" I asked.

"Dinner with some friends from church. Nothing exciting. Are you getting rest? You sound out of sorts. Are you massaging your face like I suggested?"

"Yes," I lied.

"I read somewhere that that is what you should do, at least twice a day. Clem stopped by and brought a fruit basket. When will you visit?" She asked as she always does, but the words sounded more sincere than usual.

"Things are pretty crazy here."

And so the conversation went on until that moment when there was a hanging pause and dead air like darkness in a stale cave. Ultimately, I was the one to sever the conversation. It ended with guilt—familiar ground.

I spoke the longest with Clem. I called her and

woke her up. I thanked her for the maroon red Hugo Boss shirt with thin mother of pearl buttons. I'll never wear it, unless I make an effort to the next time she visits. I told her it was too expensive and she should not have bought it. She countered with, "I love the necklace. I'll wear it today."

A typical Christmas day—yes, it was.

THE COLD HARD STORM had dropped over nine inches of snow by the time I left for the office. It's the worst snowstorm to hit this region in five years. Two inches alone will paralyze the city. I am thankful now for its relentless nature. It will keep everyone outside of our little homicide world busy with other concerns—keep them off our backs.

I imagine it will shut down the city for the next couple of days. It seems so peaceful and the drifts of deep unsoiled snow blanketing the VCU parking lot inviting.

I call Morgan. I'm sure the snow didn't keep her from getting to her office. She's a mover, a shaker, an up-and-comer who, I imagine, judging by all the paperwork and case jackets on her desk, is as persevering as the storm.

I need her to get me a subpoena for Emmerich. I have a feeling he won't come in otherwise. And there's so much more we need to talk about.

When noon rolls around I drive to the Nickel to get with Morgan.

"You look awful," she says handing me the

subpoena fresh off the printer.

"Thanks, I appreciate the candor," I return plainly. I slip the subpoena in the case file secured in my briefcase.

"No, really. You look like you haven't slept in days. Why don't you go home and get some rest."

"I will. It's not all that bad. Just long hours. Hasn't turned into days yet. My face droops more when I get tired. The cold doesn't help either." *I'm talking like I'm thinking.*

"Then feel free to nap here if you want. You won't bother me." She looks at me oddly, with a half sneer-like smile and furrowed brow. Maybe it's just the way her face shows concern.

"I'll take you up on it some other time."

"I'd like to have that witness conference soon. Who was the woman who identified Emmerich as Bergine?"

"Aletheia Wynn."

"Do you need another subpoena for her?"

"I don't think that'll be necessary," I say. "She's cooperative."

I shoulder the briefcase. My lower back aches as I straighten.

"Would you call me after you serve him?"

"Yes." I walk out.

"Don't forget to get some rest," she says like an order.

I take the Third Street exit out of the Nickel, in an attempt to avoid people who might want to talk or tell me how bad I look.

I forget where I parked the cruiser.

I go blank.

Seconds, maybe minutes.

And I'm facing Third Street, my mouth slightly open and my face a drooping mess.

What a sight I must be.

The only parking I find on Connecticut Avenue is the bus stop. It's a short walk and probably will be a short stay, so I take it.

Armed with the Subpoena, I make my way to Emmerich's office. The receptionist greets me with a suspicious smile.

My badge is hanging around my neck, but I turn it so she can see the picture identification on the other side.

A normal picture of me.

"I'm Detective Ezra Simeon, with DC Police. I'd like to speak with Daniel Emmerich."

"Mr. Emmerich left for the day," the receptionist says.

I have to think for a moment to remember what day this is. "He'll be in tomorrow, then?"

"Sir, I don't know. Is there someone else who can help you?"

"No. But thank you. I'll give a call tomorrow."

Her smile is more comfortable now.

I try not to make anything of his early departure, but that side of my brain is weak and it gets the best of me. If he left early, he might have gone home.

I double park the cruiser in front of his house.

It doesn't look like he's there. But then, the last couple of times I've been here it looked the same. That little light in the upstairs room appears to be off. I step out of the car and walk up to the front porch. The mail box is empty. The curtains are shut. I knock on the door.

After a minute or so, I knock again—louder this time, but still no answer. I walk back to the car, look over my shoulder before I get in, like I think I'll find him peering from behind the curtain in that room on the second floor. He's not, of course.

Because I don't want to feel like I didn't accomplish anything, I give Aletheia a call on my cell. It kicks into a voice message. I leave my numbers and tell her I'd like to set up a witness conference with the prosecutor. I drop the phone back in my inner coat pocket, and head back to the office.

MY ELBOWS ARE PROPPED on the desk and my head is cradled in my folded hands. It must look like I'm praying. I've called the numbers I had for Emmerich, but there was only that same "Ciao" voice message. I didn't leave one. I'd rather catch him live, and for now, keep him wondering as to what's going on. I tried to call Aletheia again, but still no answer. She hasn't returned any of my calls. I'm thinking I should be concerned, but then I'm thinking this isn't a Hollywood movie. It is the Holiday season, though.

I spoke with Mather. He said he managed to get a

couple of hours of hard sleep and would be back in after court.

"Overtime baby!" is what he said. I didn't have to thank him. I know now what his motivation is. But I don't hold that against him. We all need something to keep us going. I run everything I have to do through my head, try to remember if I notebooked everything. I'm sure I did. I hope I did. Did I?

"What's up, Sim." I hear behind me.

I turn. It's Tommy.

"Not much, Tommy. What time is it?" I say.

"1430," he says after looking at his wrist watch.

"What are you doing here this early? You still on midnights, right?" I ask him.

"Yeah, doing some catch up and take advantage of the OT. You even been home yet?"

"I'll leave when Mather gets here. I need to fill him in."

"Welcome to the trenches," is all he says.

The day passes, with the evening on its edge. I choose to note everything that occurred, for fear that most of this day will be forgotten otherwise.

The remainder of what was to become a sixteen-hour day was spent trying to locate Emmerich and Aletheia. I went as far as sitting in the cruiser in front of her apartment for several hours, hoping I might see her amble in. No such luck. I learned from one of Emmerich's Associates at work that he took some "well-deserved time off." It was not clear when he would return, but they would be happy to take a message. As far as Aletheia, I did track down a couple of friends and, of course, family, but no one had heard from her and, according to family, it's not uncommon for her to go missing. So why is my Spidey sense tingling?

❄

THE CAFFEINE DOES NOT take effect. I will have to make it through this day on will power alone. That may be difficult. It's a faculty I haven't needed for some time now.

Rucker calls me into his office. He's relaxed behind his desk with his feet stretched out angling to the floor.

"Brother, you look like the walking dead."

"How many people have to tell me that before I believe it?"

"You hear me say it, then you can believe it."

"I keep forgetting. Your word comes from the top of this heap."

"That's right and don't forget it. I also hear you're doing missing persons on the side, or, should I say, on the sly."

"We need her for a witness conference. How's that 'on the sly'? You got the office wired or just a couple of snitches rolling around that I should know about?"

"No, I'm just a good administrator, and I know what all my detectives are up to."

"Like Santa Claus."

"I like that. Now that's the old Simeon talking. I've been keeping up with your running résumé and I know how much you've been putting into this, but I seem to remember we administratively closed the Noyes case. So why are you hunting down an unnecessary witness?"

Who's he to tell me what's necessary to my investigation?

"So who cares if a couple of sickos get into some kinky mutual sharing? Is there anything substantial on him other than he gets under your skin?"

"I have someone I consider vital to this investigation that I need to interview further, and, frankly, I'm worried about her whereabouts."

"It's the Holiday season. I'm sure that's all it's about. I'm Santa Clause. I should know."

A dry chuckle is all that's worth. "That's what I keep telling myself, but you'd think she'd check her messages. I've left a few. Also, the decedent was her best friend. I haven't even told her about the closure."

"Has she been reported missing?" he asks.

"You know the answer to that."

"Yes, I do," Rucker says calmly. "If she shows up dead, it belongs to us. In the meantime, you have other cases that need attention."

"So the big brass is off your back?"

"It won't last."

"You're right about that, especially if everything turns bad with Aletheia Wynn's disappearance."

I shake my head and turn to leave.

"You think Emmerich was involved in some way then keep working it, but it's not your priority," Santa says and I know it's only because he's worried about the very slight possibility that she might turn up lying dead in the mud.

"Do me another favor and go home when relief comes, eat a good dinner and sleep a long sleep. I don't want to be the one pounding on your chest and giving you mouth to mouth."

"I look that bad?"

"Almost."

"Well, don't worry, my heart's strong. Just don't put me on the naughty list and I'll be okay. And take it easy on the micro management." I walk out before he can say anything, and I'm sensing my time here is short. I'm either going to snap on Rucker, and get transferred back to the district, or burn myself out again, and hope that the department has enough mercy to send me back to Cold Case. Somehow I doubt the latter.

❄

FOR SOME REASON, I remember the sound of Amy Noyes' mother weeping. It's stuck in my head. That's all right. It has found a comfortable place beside the image of my first body. They are equal in purpose, having prepared me for the mourning mothers to come, as the first body has prepared me for all the death that soon followed. But as I've mentioned before, you never get used to it. You only know what feelings to expect.

The mother gets me thinking about mothers in general. I remember the first interview with

Emmerich, the one in his office when he told me his parents retired to somewhere in Arizona. *It's funny how this mind works.* Flagstaff, Arizona. I think that's what he said.

I thank Robert and Klara Emmerich mentally for having an uncommon last name and then put everything together before the call—what it is I want to get from the conversation and the questions to ask.

Interviews with family can sometimes yield useful information. That's what I'm hoping, despite having heard a similar suggestion from a highly enlightened former friend-turned-boss. Fact is, on several cases, the family member, usually the mother, has proven beneficial. There've been times when all I've had to do is invoke the wrath of motherhood over the phone. Next thing I know they're dragging the son in by the ear. I've had some of those sons confess straight up and resign themselves to the time they know they'll have to do, rather than take more of their mother's scorn. That is the power that some mothers hold. I don't expect anything like that will happen here. I think I'm dealing with a different breed.

Klara Emmerich answers the phone on the sixth ring. I introduce myself and then provide her with a brief and rather scant synopsis of events regarding the on-going murder investigation of Amy Noyes and the subsequent suicide of William Bergine. I discover that she heard about the suicide from Daniel, but did not have any knowledge of a murder, nor has she heard of anyone by the name of Amy Noyes. I advise her that I've interviewed Daniel. "That's how I learned he was a childhood friend of William. They have been lifelong friends, correct?"

"Yes," she confirms in a tone that does not express much concern. "So you are suggesting that William murdered this Amy Noyes?"

"It's an on-going investigation, Mrs. Emmerich. I'm just looking for a little help to some unanswered questions."

"And somehow you believe that I can help answer those questions?"

"Obviously I don't know whether you can help or not until we talk," I say with a half smile, that, although unseen, I hope will lighten my tone. "This is all routine stuff, Mrs. Emmerich. I'm just covering all the bases."

"So you don't believe it was a suicide?"

I hesitate for a moment, wonder where that came from. "Not at all. I mean we have no reason to believe it wasn't a suicide. Unless you know something I don't?"

"Good, that you don't believe it was murder. And no, there is nothing I could possibly know that would suggest otherwise. I did not think it was murder, but I thought you might. That's why I asked the question. I think it is unusual that the police would call me about William's suicide and about some murder investigation I know absolutely nothing about."

"No ma'am, as I was just saying, it's really not that unusual. Especially since William did not have family to speak of and he was a childhood friend of Daniel's. You might have some very useful information. I'll never know until I ask."

"Again, I don't know what I could possibly offer other than to say I find it very difficult to fathom that William could have had anything to do with a murder. How was this woman murdered?"

"I can't really share that information with you right now, Mrs. Emmerich."

"How is Daniel involved in all of this? Is that something you can share?"

"At this point, my only interest in Daniel is his friendship with William and any background information he might be able to give me. What did Daniel tell you about the suicide?"

"He only told me that William had taken his life."

"You say that rather bluntly, if you don't mind me saying." *I should've said "with no feeling."*

"Is there another way you would like me to speak?"

"I don't mean anything by it, but I get the impression you weren't really surprised."

"Surprised by what?"

"His suicide."

"I don't know how I gave you that impression."

"Well, were you surprised?"

"That boy was fated to take his own life. There was nothing surprising about it. Was that too blunt?"

"No, but I'm a little dim. Explain it for me."

"I think what you call dim, I call crafty. I am not naïve, detective. But to explain that would take up more time than you have and I want to give. Let's just say that his mother had a history of manic depression, and, although she did not commit suicide, she gave up on her life until it gradually took her. That is as bad as suicide if you ask me. The process is the same, but slower. I am sure all those pills she managed to swallow hastened death as well. It must have been an inherited condition because dear William was just like his mother, but more obsessed with death. He was her handiwork, after all."

"What about the father?"

"The father had enough sense to leave before witnessing the end result, which was her death. I don't know what became of him."

"You were close with her?"

"We were friends, until the friendship became too much to bear."

"Because of her depression?"

"Yes, her manic behavior, an endless rollercoaster ride."

"And Daniel was William's best friend?"

"They were very close, always together. You could say our home was his home. He spent enough time there, anyway—the home in Washington, I mean."

"When was the last time you saw William?"

"I don't know, several years ago when I was in Washington settling personal matters concerning my husband's death."

"I'm sorry. I didn't know your husband passed away."

"It has been several years, and he was a sickly man.

Death was something that he eventually welcomed. He had cancer."

I develop an image of this woman, based solely on the way she talks, and I imagine she is a woman who rarely smiles. She sounds in her sixties, very tight-lipped and erect. A government Librarian. *How do they look?* I don't think I've ever met one. *But I certainly can't imagine her at my bedside awaiting my last breath.*

"So, you haven't seen William in several years. Did you speak with him at all?"

"We stayed in touch, but rarely over the phone. William liked to use e-mail. I believe I received an e-mail from him a week or so before his death."

"Did he ever write anything that would give you the impression he was really depressed, that maybe something like this was about to happen?"

"No. His messages were always short, but cordial. He has always been a very respectful and polite boy."

"He mention any women in his life—relationships?"

"The extent of our correspondence was cursory at best."

"Can you give me an example?"

"Oh, what can I say, cordial, a gardening tip he recently discovered online, or some computer advice, the weather here, the weather there—nothing as personal as a woman he was seeing."

"How often do you speak with your son?"

"He is a very busy man. He tries to call at least once every couple of weeks, maybe send an e-mail."

"What would we do without the Internet?" I say with another unseen smile.

There is no response.

"Did he ever mention any women in his life or William's?"

"No. Daniel is very much into running his little business right now. My impression is that he does not have much time for anything else. The only mention he has ever made of William is how much of a burden their friendship has become."

"How was it a burden?"

"From what I could gather, much in the same way the friendship I had with his mother was a burden. People like that are always demanding, always needing advice, attention and more time then you have to give. They can suck the life out of you if you are not careful."

"But specifically, what did Daniel say?"

"Oh, I don't remember the exact wording in the e-mail," she says beginning to sound frustrated. "He was just bothered by all of William's e-mails, phone calls and unannounced visits. That is all."

"William worked for Daniel, didn't he?"

"That is something you should ask Daniel, not his mother who lives two thousand miles away and has nothing to do with his business."

"But Daniel was bothered by all the e-mails he was getting from William?"

"That is what he said, among the other things."

"What other things?"

"What I just mentioned, detective. The unannounced visits, the overall burden of an exasperating friendship," she says with such sternness that I fear asking the next question.

"Do you still have the e-mails that either of them sent?"

"No, I always delete them after I read them."

"And Daniel never mentioned anything to you about William being involved in a murder investigation?"

"Frankly, I am surprised that he would withhold information such as a murder investigation from me."

"Maybe he didn't want you to get upset."

"Do I sound like the type of person who would easily get upset, detective?"

"No, ma'am, you don't," I say as a matter of fact. "Mrs. Emmerich, I've been having a hard time getting in touch with your son. Is he out of town?"

"Not that I am aware of."

"When was the last time you spoke to him?"

"Christmas. I found out about William's death by email. You tell me if Daniel is involved in this mess."

"I just have a couple more questions for him, that's all. I'd tell you if it were otherwise. Does he have any other friends I might be able to call?"

"I only know of his associates at work."

"Are there any questions you have for me? Or anything at all that you could offer that might help me with this investigation?"

"No."

"All right. I appreciate your time."

She hangs up without a word, leaving me with the crackling sound of dead air. Do I call her back? No. Why bother. I couldn't take any more of her than I already got in my head. And for a moment, I feel bad for Daniel Emmerich, but only for a very brief moment.

❄

I AM AMAZED AT what a simple phone conversation can reveal about a person, but then I've had a lot of practice with phone relationships in my life.

I'm tired, but more tired of complaining about being tired. My strange conversation with the bloodless Mrs. Emmerich has provoked a recollection. I grab a copy of the videotaped interview with Daniel, take it into the monitor room to review again. All that talk of e-mails and correspondence and the inconvenience of friendship starts me thinking I may have inadvertently missed a crucial step in the investigation.

A good portion of the night is spent reviewing the tape, especially the part where he talked about hiring Bergine as a programmer and discovering some of the "off the wall" porn sites on computers he was using at his office. This is what I missed and I'm excited with the possibilities. Bergine was using work computers for stuff like that and all of them were corresponding via e-mail. Even Emmerich's dear mother said her son was tired of the constant barrage of messages from Bergine. Who knows what a forensic search of some of the computers might reveal or what e-mails and documents might be found?

It was a basic next step in the investigation, and I had missed it. I'll just keep this to myself.

I outline all the facts that will go into the Affidavit and, I hope, lead to a Search Warrant for Emmerich's home and office for documents, mail matter and whatever computers they both had access to, especially the ones Bergine used. I'm sure the scope of the warrant will be limited, but even then, you never know. I might even get lucky and find the digital camera that was used to take the photo of Amy Noyes, the one that was hidden on Bergine's laptop. I need to get this past Morgan first.

After a couple of hours slaving over this seven page work of art, I call Morgan for a heads up and make my way to the Triple Nickel.

The stack of papers and prosecution folders on her desk is rising to a higher level. I have never seen stacks so high on a desk before. She scans the two warrant sheets paper-clipped to the front of the Affidavit, and then, before she reads, she looks up.

"These cases have been closed administratively, haven't they?"

"You're kidding, right? Of course they have. You know that. You're starting to sound like Rucker."

"I'm just asking," she says.

"And you know there's reason to believe that additional evidence might be found on some of the hard drives, including possible communication with a conspirator. I don't know any Judge that won't issue a warrant based on the information I have there.

Bergine's been linked to two cases. At the least, this might reveal something that will further those existing cases, or again, communication with an associate. Who cares whether the cases have been administratively closed." I realize after I've said all this that I must be sounding like someone who is taking this personally.

"And we both know why you really want to go in there?"

"Of course. There might be evidence that reveals Emmerich's involvement. How does that belief diminish the facts that already exist? What does it matter that the Jackson and Noyes cases were administratively closed on Bergine." *I already said that.* "That's not a real closure anyway, you know that. Just read, and then talk to me. Tell me what you think after."

She reads, but first gives me a look that I'll have a hard time figuring out for a while. I think it was an 'I'm a very patient person, but...' type of look. I turn away and try to occupy myself scanning all the clutter building up in this office. When my attention returns to her she has a new look—the face of a teacher who is reviewing one of her student's essays. I've been there. I know that one. I've given it, even practiced it in the mirror to perfect it. I just don't like being on this side of it.

She finishes.

"All right. It is convincing," she says as if she has resigned herself to the fact.

"Yes it is," I affirm.

"Take it to Pankhurst for approval. Call me after you leave the Judge in Chambers," she orders, always having something to say to my backside.

It doesn't take long for Pank to put his signature on it. My next stop is Superior Court and the Judge in Chambers. It's a short walk from the Nickel, made shorter by the nippy air and my long strides.

EVERYONE ON MY SQUAD is here, plus some other faces I don't recognize, all seated in the roll call room. The good officials, Hattie and Barnes, are here, too. Rucker—well, he's probably home sipping coffee, trying to find his name in the Post.

I love search warrants. They're like Christmas to me. You never know what you might find, but you hope it's what you asked for or, better yet, something you never expected.

I begin the briefing by advising everyone where we're going and that we'll hit the two locations simultaneously. After that, a brief overview of the case and what the warrant allows us to search for: notes, papers, mail matter, email communications, photographs and information contained on computer hard drives, and digital camera. I don't expect to find the suspect there. I mention that. He's on a convenient leave of absence.

I give out the assignments for the residence, such as who will force entry if we have to, search, cover the back, and so on. A smaller team will take care of the office. Members of Mobile Crime will be at both locations to seize whatever evidence we may recover. Marv and his partner are on hand for all the computers. They'll take care of the office first, then respond to the residence if needed.

We roll the vehicles out, one behind the other to 295 and then 395 South to 12th Street, where three of the vehicles at the tail break off and head to a staging area near the office on Connecticut Avenue. That's where they'll sit until we're in position and give the word for entry.

Before we make the turn on to Emmerich's block, the rear cover team for the residence breaks off, taking the alley. I lead the way to the front of Emmerich's residence. I make the call to the office crew to make their way up.

The light on the second floor is off, and so is the porch light. We quietly exit our vehicles.

I do the knock and announce, pounding on the door several times. This is a neighborhood not used to such things. When we don't get an answer, I nod to the guys on the ram and all it takes is one hit to take the door down, splintering it right off the hinges.

You treat every warrant the same, high risk, low risk, especially if you have to force entry. We make our way in, maneuvering in different directions to clear the place.

I take the stairs leading up to a short hallway. There are three doors, one's open and I glance in—*the bathroom*. The other two are closed. I nod to Mather to take the one at the other end which would be facing the alley, while I take the one facing the street—the one that has had the little light on in the past.

It's a bedroom, sparsely furnished. Nothing on the walls either, just the bed, night stand at each side, funky lime green cloth arm chair in a corner near the window, dresser drawers with a large vanity mirror against the wall behind it. It's like a motel room.

I open the closet door.

Nothing. *Nice walk-in closet.*

Under the bed, a couple of shoe boxes and a clear plastic storage container that seems to be packed with clothing.

I head back out and join Mather in the hallway. He shrugs. I holster my weapon. We go back downstairs.

Hattie hits the office team on the radio. They have walked in with no incident; secured the areas they'll be searching. No Emmerich. Just as I thought.

The search teams break off in the residence. I do a quick walk-through of the place. The well maintained antique furniture in the living room does not blend well with what looks like a brand new 42" flat screen HD TV with surround sound.

I think it's his parent's furniture, or his grandparents who left it for his parents who in turn left it with him. But nothing in this room looks lived in, even the sofa and chairs. Everything has the appearance of being well cared for over the years, like items for sale in some expensive antique shop in Georgetown on M Street. The rest of the home is much the same, even the shed in the back yard, a tidy little storage area for garden tools, a mower, snow shovel and a hedge trimmer.

It is as if this is a residence being maintained by an outside party in anticipation of the original owners' return. But they haven't returned in years.

I start upstairs with Mather. He takes the back room that would look out to the alley. It looks like the original master bedroom—his parent's old room, maybe. I begin in searching Emmerich's bedroom, a corner room with a view over the front porch to the street. At least, for now, I assume it's his bedroom, because I find some open mail on the dresser with his name and this address on it. I put a couple of those letters in a pile to be taken. The judge always likes to see some form of mail matter, or documents, which verifies we hit the right place.

The slate gray overcast clouds do not allow much light. The barren walls are painted a light blue and the vanity mirror above the dresser is the only item hanging on the walls. The bed is neatly made—an art deco style light wood nightstand beside it, with a reading lamp and cordless phone. The dresser drawers are neatly stacked with name brand undergarments, socks and polo shirts.

The walk-in closet is meticulous in its arrangement with shirts, slacks and jackets; three levels of shoes on a chrome rack. Wooden shelves line two corners of the wall from floor to ceiling, with squarely folded jeans, khakis and sweaters. Another shelf stretches along the top, with well-balanced stacks of shoe boxes and file boxes.

Aside from the regularity of form, this is a room void of personality. That is an expression in itself. It is certainly one of the nicest places I have ever searched.

I sort through documents, papers, receipts and photographs recovered from some of the shoe boxes. I'm confident that this is his room.

Marv and the office crew clear their scene, having imaged the necessary hard drives and seized the relative documents.

There's nothing here. I'm just going through the motions, along with Mather, who is focusing his attention on the dresser drawers that I already looked through before I started on these little shoe boxes.

I have a pile on the floor of what I'll take—old childhood photographs of Emmerich and Bergine, posing together with peculiar smiles; phone records and work-related documents. I come across photographs of people I can safely assume are his parents. The mother is easy. She stands firm, an inverted smile, her son dutifully by her side. She looks as I imagined her. No smile on Daniel's young face. The father either. I find only one other picture. It is a younger Emmerich—early twenties—arm in arm with an attractive young woman. It does not appear to be a closeness that comes from friendship. It is something more, a familiar look they share—maybe love. They are standing on a porch, and Bergine is there, off to the side, leaning against a cast iron railing surrounding the porch, like a distant shadow, an elusive figure. She is a pretty woman and the look on Emmerich's face does not portray the image of the Emmerich I am familiar with. I know that look. I had it once. I am almost sickened to find a comparison between us, and, even moreso, to be brought back to a time when I had a similar look and the feeling behind it.

I drop the photo with my pile of items to go.

I'm sitting here on the floor with my back aching and a giddy head, going through Emmerich's family photos, most of which I won't take, because they are useless to me. All except for that one of Emmerich with that pretty girl and Bergine in the background. That one doesn't seem to belong with the others.

I'm tired. Let's get this over with.

I carefully search the rest of the shoebox. At the bottom I Find wrinkled documents, as if they were tossed, then recovered and folded nice and neat. I examine them.

GED.

The man of great means has a GED. His name's right there. He didn't even get through high school.

How great is that?

❄

THE SEARCH OF HIS home was a great disappointment, though it'll take a couple of days for Marv to get through everything he's got. Still, it's something I had to do. Leads I had to exhaust.

But I don't feel this is over.

I sit hunched on the chair, staring through the monitor on the desk. I've already closed the report out. All that is left are the blurry icons on a blue screen. Now all I have to do is stand; make my way out the door. Just stand up and move. The cold air will slap my face before the drive home, give me that extra push. But I can't do it. I am lost. Adrift in a heavy sea of indecision, and the way I'm looking at this monitor, it's as though I'm searching for that glimmering distant star that'll set me back on course.

The sleepless nights are catching up to me. They have caught up to me. I have enough sense to realize that.

So move!

"Go home," I hear a voice behind me say, and I snap to—out of my seat. The chair rolls out from under me, and I drop to one knee.

Crack! That's the sound of my knee on the hard tile floor. But I think the sound is an echo in my body made louder in my head. At least, I hope that's what it was, or I'll feel it later.

"Are you all right?" the voice says.

I turn. It's Hattie.

Great. What's the Lieutenant gonna think now. He scared me out of my chair, and I fell on the floor.

"You caught me off guard" is all I can think of saying as I straighten myself up with a slight grimace. I'm afraid to sit back down. The chair might get away from me again.

"It's time for you to go home. You can finish up tomorrow."

"I'm finished," I say knowing how that must sound coming out of my mouth, but I was only referring to the paper work.

"I'll see you tomorrow, then."

I nod, unresisting and a little embarrassed.

"I'll take you off the book," he says kindly.

TWELVE

I'M THINKING ABOUT THAT time with Clem, when we were looking over the Potomac to that portion of land thick with trees, stretching along the river's edge on the Virginia side. It was only a patch of land across the river and a glance to the right or to the left would quickly reveal the presence of man. But there was a greater landscape there for her. I could see it in her face. That view across the river to that little stretch of land made vast and rich through her green eyes. It is a look this mind can turn to and remember with clarity, and find comfort there.

When I wake up I realize I have slept.

The shower is hot. I step out, towel myself dry and resolve to go to work with green eyes.

It is unfortunate that in taking his own life, Bergine took the answers to some good questions with him. I'm confident I know the answers to some of them. I'm certain that Bergine was lying about dating Amy, and they never met through a class of his. I am downgraded to 'somewhat' confident that

Emmerich had something to do with the murders, and whether he was actively involved, I am not sure.

There is nothing that connects him with certainty to either of them. Emmerich was the one dating Amy Noyes, though, and all the while duping the follower Bergine into letting him use his name and cell. Why Bergine allowed this, I don't know. Maybe it was a game they played with women—a game that may have started with Evelyn Jackson, or before. Rucker's probably right about that—just a couple of sickos. Their stories were well-rehearsed. I'll give them that. But as it is, the course of these events would not have played out as they did if Bergine had not committed suicide. Who knows how hard it would have been to close the earlier case otherwise? Or easy—maybe Bergine would have broken, given up everything. What's the point in getting into all this? I'll take the administrative closures over the unanswered questions for now. Let's leave it at that.

And now there's Aletheia Wynn. Where is she?

I'll try to be as patient as my dead victims. They don't complain. They know at the end, whether there is a conclusion or not in the life that goes on without them, that the one responsible will eventually meet the same end. Everyone takes a last breath.

Armed with this new intent, I find my most comfortable well-washed brown sweater, loose fitting jeans and reliable ¾ length leather coat and make my way back to the trenches.

Detective Beachballbelly greets me the moment I

walk into the office with, "You got an irate customer on the line. Third times he's called. I was about to hit you on the pager, get this guy off my back."

"Who is it?" I ask, while taking my jacket off.

"Wouldn't say."

I get to my space, rest my jacket over the back of the chair and push the line that's on hold.

"Hello," I say.

No response. The air is dead.

"Hello," I try again.

Nothing.

"How long has this guy been on hold?" I ask Beachballbelly somewhere over the cubicle.

"Called just before you walked in!" he belts, like he's hovering some distance away.

"He's not there now," I say.

"You know how they get."

Irate customer? I haven't had one of those since the district days and all those live victims. But then, irate customer here might mean family member of the deceased or something like that. He'll call back or call an official to complain. Either way, I'll hear something. Of that I'm sure.

The disappearance of Aletheia Wynn took me out of the loop for a while. According to Hattie and Rucker, until a body's discovered, it's not something we can put too much time into. 'Closures, baby.'

Next week I'll be back on regular rotation with Mather and the rest of the Squad. Back to day work. I check the calendar on the computer. *New Year's*

Day falls on Monday. A mental sigh of relief when I realize I'll be off midnights for New Year's Eve. All those bullets falling like rain at the stroke of midnight might find one body to rest in. If that happens, Beachballbelly and his Squad are up. They start midnights when we're on day work.

I look at some of the photographs taken from Emmerich's home. A few pictures of him and Bergine in their youth and only a couple of them together as adults. What use are they? The only purpose they serve is justifying an otherwise unsuccessful search warrant by seizing items that show a relationship with Bergine. I shove them back in the protective plastic sleeve before I get too wrapped up in self doubt.

I think about calling Marv. It might be too soon, though. He's got my pager and my cell anyway and if he did manage to recover something substantial he'd hit me. This is what I'm thinking, but I still give him a call at the office. It rings four times before he picks up.

It doesn't sound promising.

"Nothing here so far on your boy Bergine. Got some good deleted sent and received e-mails off that Emmerich character's hard drive; looks like some racy correspondence with a couple women, but not any of the names you gave me to look for. He also stored a lot of JPEGS—normal stuff, not like he was trying to hide anything."

"What kind of pictures?"

"Him with a couple of other women, posing in bars, what looks like his residence. Very pretty women with that 'I got lots of money' look. Come see for yourself. I'm still searching this stuff, but you can come take what I've already got."

"I'll be there in a few," I tell him. After I hang up, I leave.

WHEN I GET THERE, he walks me through a little of what he's got and how much more he has to go through. I look at the color printouts of the photos. Marv was right. They're very pretty women and certainly don't look like escorts, but then who am I to say. One of them, a silky brunette sitting on a bar stool at some expensive bar with her head cocked to the side, laughs toward the camera. Emmerich is standing over her left shoulder, head arched forward, looking toward the side of her face with an ambiguous smile and hair falling in just the right places. His forehead is shiny, and he's holding a champagne glass in his right hand. I see photos with the same woman in different locations at different times, and in all of them she looks as if she is comfortably familiar with him. Another woman, just as beautiful, with the same poses as the brunette, like they went to the same snob academy or modeling agency.

I look through a small stack of e-mails. There are a couple to and from women who have sexy names, like this one:

Dear Tanya: I will be in NY *on a business trip later this month and was hoping to have an opportunity to see you. I am planning to arrive September 3rd and will be in* NY *for only a few days. I am a Corporate Attorney living in* DC *and am on a trip out to* NY*. I have included my cell # and a few photos for you to look at. I am looking forward to your response and a thousand possibilities. Daniel*

Corporate Attorney?

This guy just gets better and better.

What's greater yet is that the cell number he included belonged to William Bergine.

I call Morgan for some more subpoenas.

Back at the office the Admin Sarge sneaks up on me and tells me I have a disgruntled visitor standing in the foyer.

"Said his name's Daniel Emmers or something like that," the Sarge says.

HE IS GLANCING TOWARD the ground with his hands in his pockets and an expression indicating displeasure. He looks up, having noticed my approach through the glass front door. I turn the security latch and open it.

"Daniel," I say in a familiar way and as if his appearance is no big deal.

"I'd like to talk to you," he says firmly.

"Come in."

He walks into the hallway, stands before me like he can't wait.

"You called my mother," he says in that same manner, but with an odd look of disbelief. "What gives you the right to call my mother and bring her into this mess?"

I'm rarely taken by surprise in this business so it takes me a moment—not long, just a second or two.

"Why don't you come with me to one of our interview rooms, where it's more comfortable," I say directing him with a turn of my head.

During the short walk to the interview room, I can't help but wonder how he can be more upset with my having called his mother than with our busting in his front door, or serving papers on his associates at work to search the computers. That should've been a great scandal, at the very least richly embarrassing. Instead, he is angry because of a phone interview I had with his mother.

I thank God for mothers sometimes, sweet useful mothers, what a great tool they can be.

And to top that off, he's here alone—no lawyer, no friendly back-up companion. Just him all by his lonesome.

That's interesting.

It can be a good sign. He's worried, but doesn't want to show it by having a lawyer. He's fishing for information, and he needs to do that alone. A guy like him shows up with a lawyer, it's sending the wrong message. Let's see what he has to say, though.

I could be wrong about everything.

He sits where he sat the last time we spoke, straightens himself in the chair.

"I can't imagine how a murder investigation involving a former friend of mine would lead you to call my mother," he says immediately after sitting.

"A lot of unanswered questions is how. I tried to find you. You weren't around."

"I was in New York for a couple of days. I got home late last night. I don't understand what you're doing. Before I left for New York, it was on the news that this case was solved."

I must have missed that. That's what I want to say, but I don't. I honestly did miss it. It must have been one of those great TV moments for Rucker.

He continues, "They didn't give a lot of the details, but it was obvious they were talking about William. They mentioned the suicide. The case is closed, isn't it? So why are you calling my mother?"

"When did you speak with your mom?" I ask as I sit down.

"I spoke to my *mom* this morning," he says with an emphasis on 'mom' obviously mocking my usage of it.

"So I assume while you were in New York someone from your office contacted you about the search warrants?"

"Yes. And I *assume* you expected that information to disrupt my trip?"

There he goes again with his surprising comeback statements. "Well, as I said, there are still some questions that need to be answered. Don't always believe what you hear on the news. The case isn't closed."

"The case is not closed?" he asks, leaning forward in the chair.

"No," I say convincingly because in my mind it is not closed.

He relaxes again. "Listen, Detective Simeon, I understand your position. I even understand the necessity of your having to destroy my door and search my home and office, for that matter. That makes sense because I wasn't home at the time and because of my connection to William, but you could have asked me first, I would have given you permission to search. If there is some evidence you think William left behind and for some reason you think it's at my home or office, then you should've asked. There's nothing I'm trying to hide. All that warrant, kicking-in-the-door business wasn't necessary. And I was very disturbed with the mess you left for me, by the way. A close friend of mine, who happens to be an attorney, informed me I have a good complaint if I wanted to pursue that sort of thing, which I don't. I'm not about to waste everyone's time and money on something that trivial."

"I apologize for the mess. Some of the guys are a little overly enthusiastic, and we're really not paid to clean up after. We appreciate your not going forward with a complaint." I say this only to appease him. I could care less whether he complains or not.

"So why is this thing still being investigated? What are you looking for?"

I was right, he is fishing.

"I can't get into all the details with you Daniel, as much as I'd like to."

"So are you suggesting William is not the murderer?"

"I never said that. I believe there's more to this investigation."

"What doesn't make sense is the connection you see between this investigation and my mother."

The mother again.

"Your mother was able to provide some good background information is all. She was actually very helpful."

"Helpful? Please. That's not the impression I got after talking to her. It was quite the opposite, and, according to her the phone call was inappropriate and disruptive. She had a difficult time getting on with the rest of her day after it. And she didn't understand why in the world you would call her about some murder investigation related to William."

"Let me just say that your mother was very helpful in ways she may not fully realize."

His presence here being the obvious result, but I'll just keep that to myself. I don't want to piss him off that much—not yet, anyway.

"What? What does that mean? Is that a not so subtle attempt at being cryptic? The way you people operate amazes me. You know there is nothing my mother can offer you. That is very unprofessional and—"

"I'm just doing my job, that's all. I'm following up on some new leads. Don't be so paranoid."

"You think I'm being paranoid? That's rich. In fact, if you think about how cooperative and patient I've been despite your actions—"

He doesn't ask about the new leads. Good.

"Wrong choice of words then. Let's try to start over. Was that you who tried to call me earlier today?"

"Yes. A couple of times and I finally gave up. I was on hold for twenty minutes one time." He looks up to the camera on the wall as if he suddenly remembers its presence. "Is this thing recording, by the way?"

"No."

"You have to tell me if it is, you know."

"I'd tell you if it is, and it's not. If you see a little blinking red light, then it's recording. Why would you worry about something like that, anyway? You're here voluntarily. And I don't see you in handcuffs." I smile as comfortable a half smile as this face can muster.

"Of course, I'm here to help, but I'd rather keep that between the two of us."

"It's not recording," I assure him. "So you taking some time off work?" I ask trying to turn the conversation around.

"Just one week. I'm too busy to take more than that."

"Why New York?"

"I like New York, and I have a few friends there."

"I'm glad you showed up, even if it was under the

wrong circumstances. I still feel there's so much you can help me with. I also wanted to apologize for jumping on you the way I did when we last spoke. It's nothing personal, just the nature of the job. But I've already said that."

He nods in acceptance of my apology and I know he wants an additional apology for the call to his mom. That won't happen. I need to let that churn inside his gut for a while.

"As I have said, I am more upset with the distress this has caused my mother."

I'm pleased with myself for reading that right. After a thoughtful pause he adds, "I take it you've searched William's laptop and computer by now?"

"The ones at your office," I say knowing he didn't mean those, but the laptop belonging to William—the one he mentioned during the last interview. Then the image of fishing comes into my head again, and I feel like he's trying to hook me, after setting the bait at the last interview. How stupid he must think we are.

"Well, yes, those as well, but I was referring to his personal laptop. You remember when I told you about his laptop, don't you? How he kept it with him at all times, like it was a child."

"Yes, that's right. I remember. 'Like a child' was an interesting metaphor. Our forensics guys are still searching it. They're so overwhelmed with cases over there, but they have shown me some preliminary stuff, and it looks interesting. That's one thing

I wanted to talk to you about. Maybe you can help me with."

He nods again and I realize there are different levels of Emmerich nods. I interpret this one as something like 'Yes, I can be very helpful'. It is a little slower than the previous assenting nod and more deliberate.

"Anything I can do, but I also came for another reason. That court document you left at my home that listed certain things you took—"

"The warrant," I advise him.

"The warrant then. Well, it was very vague. You see, you wrote on it the things that you took like, 'photos' and 'assorted papers' and I don't even know what photos you took, and I can't imagine why you would take any photos to begin with. And then 'assorted papers—what do you mean by 'assorted papers'. I would like to know specifically what 'assorted papers' were taken and the significance of taking them."

"I'll see if I can put something together for you. It's in evidence, though, so it might take me a couple of days."

"Evidence? Why on earth would that be considered evidence? I know for a fact there was nothing in my home that could be considered evidence."

"Daniel, until I know otherwise, everything will be listed as evidence, at least until we've had a chance to sort through it all."

"What do you expect to find? You know there's nothing there."

"It won't take long."

"Can you, at least, get me a list of exactly what you took from my home?" he politely demands.

"I'll see what I can do. What about your office? You good with that?"

"I haven't been to the office yet," he says awkwardly. "Some of the photos from my home are rather sentimental, though."

"Pictures of you and William?"

"Yes, believe it or not, among other things."

And I remember the GED documents. I didn't take those, but he has to know I saw them.

"Well, it is a little hard to believe, considering how you talk about him sometimes," I say referring to William.

"I've known him all my life, detective. Despite the anger and pain he has brought me, there is that bond."

"You can say that, but the truth is you want me to believe he did all this alone. And really, you can say anything you want about him because he's not here to defend himself."

"That's cruel, but I expect that of you. You do have a mean side about you, after all. Did all the stress, related to your job do that to you? It must be so difficult." He says in a rather lofty-minded way.

He's either avoiding what I said about William having an accomplice, or it went right over his head.

My good side smiles, then I say, "We're stepping backwards again and I'll be the first to admit it. We should keep in mind the purpose of our meeting.

Amy Noyes was murdered. You have to understand that the grief a family goes through from a death that comes naturally passes, but when a life is taken like this, the family never finds rest, until the case is solved. That's what we have to focus on here. Nothing else."

"Again, I can't imagine all the stress it must cause you," he pursues.

"I do my time here, just like you do at your job. Afterwards, I go home and sleep comfortably, like a little baby" I lie. "How are your nights?"

He doesn't reply, just looks at my left side like it should make me uncomfortable. In fact, it does. My left upper lip twitches the palsy twitch. I press my finger against it, resting my chin in the palm of my hand as if I am pondering. He knows I'm trying to conceal the twitch.

I can only hope my left eye does not start tearing.

He keeps avoiding the point. I so much as told him I believe there's a second suspect, which is something that only helps to confirm the suspicion in my mind.

"I do want you to know that even though William was a lifelong friend, I would not hesitate to give you any information or evidence that would help you close this thing."

Thing? What kind of word is 'thing' for an act of murder?

"By the way, you keep mentioning his laptop. You have a gut feeling he kept some kind of evidence on it?"

He sits back, a moment of contemplative pause. "I do," he says with certainty.

"That's why I need you here. What about the computers at your office? What do you think we'll find on them?"

He hesitates, and I sense it is deliberate. "I hope, for the sake of my company, he didn't leave anything illegal on any of those computers. And if he did, I certainly hope you won't hold me or anyone at my company responsible."

"What do you think he might have left on his laptop, or your computers at work?"

"I honestly don't know," he says while slowly shaking his head back and forth a few times.

"Give me a second. I want to get the case jacket—something to show you," I say as I lift myself out of the chair. "I'll be right back." I smile with a sort of weak wink as I walk out, like this is something he'll want to wait for.

I pull the case jacket out of my briefcase.

Before I return, I go to the monitor room and watch him on the little screen. Only for a minute or two.

He sits there, composed and still, with an occasional turn of his head toward the wall, as if he senses me on the other side. He looks back up at the camera. I am sure he expects to see a red blinking light suddenly appear.

I return to him, sit back down and rest the case jacket on my lap, open it in such a way that he cannot see the contents.

"As you can see, this thing's getting pretty thick."

I find the copies of the pictures of him posing with pretty girls that were recovered from his computer. I display them on the table before him.

I cannot read his face. It is like the gaze he has in one of those pictures, where he is focused on some distant, perhaps nonexistent, empty place, in his head.

"Who are these girls?" I ask casually, trying not to sound prying or suspicious.

He continues to examine the pictures, maybe taking a little bit too much time, and then lifts his head and attempts eye contact. "These are some girls I've dated in the past."

"Where were the pictures taken?"

"I don't remember, some at bars, hotels, places like that. Just places we frequent. Why?"

I can sense his discomfort.

"I know a lot of the spots here in DC, and I don't recognize any of the locations in the pictures. That is, unless, these are the *types* of places people like me would have a hard time getting into without a lifetime membership or an escort."

"No. They are just regular places."

"Were these taken in New York, or something?"

"Yes, they are friends of mine there."

"Very pretty women." I pick up the picture with the silky-haired brunette. "What's her name?"

His lips seem to tighten a bit, like it's his turn

to twitch—not something he can control. "Why is this important? There's no need to bring my New York friends into this. They have nothing to do with William."

"Daniel, I am not trying to disrupt your life, no matter what you might think. You have to understand that the nature of my work is finding things and ruling out what is not important. I don't know what is and what is not relevant until I look into it. It is unfortunate that sometimes it will cause embarrassment to people like you or your family and friends. Right now, it's just between the two of us. Help me out here, or I'll be forced to show these pictures around, see if I can get these women identified that way."

"Well, I can tell you that you can rule them out. They are just friends I see on occasion when I'm in New York."

"I need their names and contact information. For all I know, and for all you know for that matter, William got a hold of them, too."

He belts out a laugh like someone would a burp. "I can assure you that William did not hurt any of these *women*."

"I'll need to verify that. And I'm sure you'd want me to, as well. Aren't you concerned with the safety of your friends?"

"But I'm telling you—they're fine. I've spoken with them since William's death, and they were very much alive."

I pick up the pictures one at a time. "That's all right." I slip them back in the case jacket, pull out the one photo of him, Bergine and the pretty girl he is arm in arm with. The one from his past.

"Who's this pretty girl? And that's Bergine back there, right?"

"Why would you take that photograph from my house? That's very personal and has nothing to do with anything related to this so-called investigation of yours."

"She an old girlfriend?" I ask.

He doesn't answer and I sense that I may have made a mistake by displaying it and maybe even moreso by taking it. I don't want to provoke the wrong kind of anger. It might be his Priscilla.

He stiffens abruptly, "She has nothing to do with anything. I was engaged once, but that's all in the past. Oh, and she's very much alive and, from what I hear, comfortably married."

"I'm not worried about this photo," I assure him because I realize I'm losing him and this is not the right path. Call it a second sense, maybe something uncomfortably familiar and so I decide I'm not going there. I gently place the photograph back in the jacket. "You're right, it has nothing to do with the investigation. We'll keep it here for the time being, and I'll make sure you get it back once this is all over with."

"Take your time," he replies with a familiar coldness.

"I appreciate that," I tell him. I realize I need to get this conversation back on track and so I say, "I don't want to get into another argument with you, but I'd want you to know what I'm doing so you're not taken by surprise. I'm trying to be straight with you."

No reaction.

I pull out a subpoena from the jacket.

I show him the subpoena. "This is a subpoena. As you can see, it directs the person who is being served to provide the information requested. In this case, it's subscriber information to several of these e-mail addresses we recovered from your personal computer at your office. I have several more of these subpoenas with several more e-mail addresses and unlisted phone numbers, which are usually cell phones. In fact, just before you got here, I faxed several of them out." I show him some of the fax confirmation sheets. "They don't take long to come back. All I want to do here is to let you know I'm not trying to trick you out of information, that's why I'm showing you what I'm doing. I don't usually do this sort of thing, but I'm not about to treat you like some common thug, because I know you're here to help. Right?"

A reluctant slight nod.

"I'm going to find out who these girls are and probably other acquaintances too, and then I'm going to call every one of them, or you can just tell me who they are, where they live and when you last spoke, and maybe we can avoid having to put your name out there like that."

He rests his elbows on the table and leans toward me. "It is obvious your people had the time to search my computer, so I find it hard to believe you haven't searched William's. I don't know what it will take to convince you that maybe you need to focus a little more time and energy there instead of wasting it on this nonsense."

"Your gut feeling again?"

"Yes, detective," he says with such conviction I know he knows about what we have already found on the laptop.

I pull out the Tanya e-mail and set it on the table. "Tell me about this."

The right side of his mouth tightens just ever so slightly:

I say, "This reads very much like soliciting an Escort, in my opinion. I have her e-mail address, so I already know."

"And you said you weren't going to trick me."

"There are times when I'll ask you something I already know the answer to and that is only for the purpose of judging your honesty. If you're here to help, how can I trust any information you give me if you can't even tell me the truth about the women you see in New York."

"Then you got me. I sometimes hire escorts when I'm on out of town business. They look good at my side, at some of those new client business dinners my company's so proud of hosting. I'm sure you already know this. You were only waiting for the right moment to pounce."

"Why couldn't you tell me about the escorts in the

beginning? It's not such a big deal. Why so evasive?"

"You already know the answer to that. Don't try to be so coy. This Amy girl was also an escort, and I was just scared. That's the truth. I didn't want you to think there might be some kind of connection with her death. Because there is not."

"So when we contact all these women, what are they going to say?"

"I think you know the answer to that, too."

"Okay, then I'll answer and you tell me if I'm right. They're all escorts?"

"They are. And they are all live escorts, if that's going to be your next question."

"That wasn't going to be my next question, but I'll be sure to check into it. Don't worry. Why did you use William's cell phone with all these women?"

He straightens in his chair, not uncomfortably, more like strengthening his posture at a conference table before his turn to speak.

"Because William didn't have as much to lose as I do. And I don't like these women having my information. You never know what they might do with it."

"Come on, what businessman cares about your getting with prostitutes every now and then? And as far as the escorts are concerned, I would think they're more interested in maintaining you as a good client instead of getting your information and involving themselves in identity theft or something petty like that. Is that what you were thinking, they were going to steal your information, open up a Macy's account?"

I say, offering him some things to work with, hopefully open him up a bit.

"They aren't prostitutes, first off and secondly, they are in the business of making money. Who knows what they're capable of doing."

"They offer sexual favors?"

"I suppose some of them do."

"Come on, Daniel." I pick up the e-mail and read from it, "'*I am looking forward to your response and a thousand possibilities.*' Give me a break."

"What can I say," he tries to smile shyly, but it comes out looking vulgar.

"You can say the truth. In other words, your business associates would frown on your extracurricular activities?"

"They might. But mostly it's just my own private business I'd rather keep to myself."

"I mean, you're a good looking guy. Why do you have to pay for it?"

"I don't have to pay for it. I choose to. It's easier that way and less of a burden."

"I can understand that. It's a control thing."

"It has nothing to do with control. It's just like I told you, nothing more. Don't try to make this what it isn't."

"Well, now that this is out of the way, let's get back to William."

"Thank you."

"You have anything to do with setting him up with Amy Noyes?"

"No. Of course not. He found her on his own. I'm afraid she was—how can I put this—"

"Not high class enough for you?"

"I wasn't going to put it that way, but yes. William couldn't afford a quarter of an hour with a woman like Tanya or any of the other women I see, for that matter."

"Did you ever set him up with any of the expensive ones, or any other cheap dates, just to help a buddy out?"

"I may have," he says then reconsiders. "Yes, on occasion I've helped him out. He had needs that were hard to fulfill otherwise. Unfortunately, what I mean by that is his looks and his attitude kept most normal women at arm's length, but mostly beyond. And let's just say, I would help him out in an effort to keep him off the street."

"Explain that."

"Please, you know what I mean."

"Hookers?"

"Yes."

"Why don't you just say that then? You're the one being cryptic."

He doesn't respond.

"Why did you think it was your duty to keep him off the street?"

"I'll try not to be vague this time. As you know, the streets of DC can be dangerous, especially his neighborhood. Those drug-addicted hookers can be, as well."

"You were worried he might get AIDS or something like that, maybe be robbed? Is that it?"

"You're a good detective, despite your mean side."

"There you go again," I say lightly.

"Have you considered acupuncture?" He asks, either feeling the need to bring this to a personal level or just trying to make up for having, in his mind, hurt my feelings before.

More likely, he's just trying to get off the subject.

"Naw, I'm sort of adjusting to the new look. I think it works for me. Some people even feel sorry for me and tell me everything I want to know."

He burps another laugh.

"Now that we've opened up to some real facts, tell me why you think William would kill Amy?"

"I don't know. Maybe because he snapped, because he couldn't truly have her unless he paid for it. I wish I knew the answer to that. I really do."

"That's interesting—actually a pretty astute observation. Did William have any other girls in his life? I mean ones he saw on a regular basis, even normal girls?"

"Normal," he chuckles. He considers this, but then shakes his head. "I don't know –"

"He never saw anyone else on a regular basis? In all the years you'd known him. Is that what you're telling me? Maybe someone he met at UDC?"

His forehead wrinkles, and he nods, like he all of a sudden remembers.

"Yes. In fact, there was someone. I don't know

whatever became of her, though."

"What was her name?"

"I don't remember."

"Did you ever meet her?"

"That was back when we weren't really talking much. I can't help you there, I'm afraid."

"Back when? How long ago?

He shakes his head like he's having a hard time remembering. I realize he's not all that difficult to figure out, despite all the nods and gestures. He's lying. And there's only one reason for that.

"What? A year ago? Two years ago?" I persist.

"Around two years ago maybe. Something like that."

"But you did meet her?"

"Once or twice."

"Where did they meet?"

"I really don't know—the university maybe. I'm sorry. I wish I could be of more help to you."

"What did you say her name was?" I ask.

"I didn't and I really don't remember much about her."

"Can you describe her?"

He shakes his head again like he's at a loss.

"Help me out here—White girl? Hispanic? Black girl? Age range?"

He's been trying desperately to lead me to William as Amy's killer, so if he knows about Evelyn then he would try to lead me there, too. But he's avoiding Evelyn for the same reason he's avoiding asking any questions about a possible second suspect and the way he avoided the New York escorts until I confronted him with what I knew.

"You remember what I said earlier," I tell him. "That sometimes I'd ask you questions I already know the answers to just to test your truthfulness? See if you're somebody I can work with?"

He nods a very reluctant nod. I decide on that moment to reach into the jacket where I find the death photo of Evelyn Jackson. I slide it across the table like a playing card. He looks at it.

"Oh my god," he says as he quickly looks up to me. "He killed her, too?"

"Tell me about this girl."

"I—I don't know. I don't know who this girl is. I just assumed after you showed me the photo it was someone else he killed."

"There was a lot of evidence left behind on this scene. Don't do this to yourself, Daniel. Why do you think I've been looking for you so hard? I know all about this girl. I'm just trying to give you the benefit of the doubt here, that's all."

His face sinks a bit, and now I know I'm on the right track, but now I'm afraid he'll decide to turn the other way, maybe lawyer up and walk out the door. I decide to offer him a solution.

"He was your best friend and he did some awful things. You feel guilty because you knew about it. I can explain that to the prosecutor. It's easy."

"That's nonsense," he says.

"Why is that nonsense? So what is it? You can't be

protecting William, he's dead, and you've been trying to convince me he's the sole killer, anyway. Don't make this any rougher than it has to be. Help me out here, so we can put this whole business to rest. You're just making yourself more involved than you need to be."

"I had nothing to do with any of this."

"I told you that's what I believe, didn't I?"

"I don't know anything more than I have told you."

"I'm trying to help you, but it's piling up against you. It's looking more and more like you're the only one connected to everything here and poor old William was just a dupe."

"If anyone is a dupe, it's me."

"Okay, talk to me. Why?"

"William was crazy. I'm sure you saw all the medication he was on. Have you talked to his doctor?"

"Yes."

"Then you know what kind of shape he was in, mentally, I mean. He was manic. He was obsessive compulsive. He could be very violent at times. I was terrified of him most of the time."

"I can tell you, based on all the experience I have, that telling the truth can fix a lot of things. If we connect everything together without your help, it will be worse. Just tell me about the girl in this photo," I point to the picture of Evelyn Jackson.

He doesn't look at the photo. He is fixed on me, looking right through me.

"Tell me about her, about Evelyn," I try again.

I lift up the photo and show it to him so he can't escape it. He doesn't look away from it. It doesn't even seem to affect him. I set it back down and his eyes close slowly and open again. It is like his head dropped, but internally.

"Tell me about Amy?"

He slowly shakes his head back and forth, but not like he is overcome with painful memories. Coupled with the expression he has, it is more like this whole thing and every question asked is a terrible inconvenience.

"Here it is. This is the truth. He met her at a strip club. At that time she was just a part time Escort, more or less in his price range. He still needed a little financial help from me from time to time. William became obsessed with her, just like I told you. He was crazy. That's all. I should have just gone to the police in the beginning. I realize that now."

"Obsession isn't a crime. Why did you feel you needed to go to the police?"

"Isn't it obvious? Maybe I could have prevented what happened?"

"What makes you think you could have prevented it?"

"I don't know. I'm not a detective. He was just acting really crazy, more than usual. I should have seen what was coming."

"What is your impression as to why he killed Amy?"

"I suppose because she didn't want him anymore. I mean as a customer. He became too obsessed with her, to the point of stalking her. At least that's –" He stops himself.

"At least that's what?" Before he has a chance to reply I ask, "That's what she told you?"

"Maybe I talked to her once or twice. I'll admit that."

"So tell me, why do you think it's so important to search William's laptop?"

"Is this where you reach into your little magic box and surprise me with something?" he asks playfully.

I look at him for a second because I am genuinely surprised with his question and the light tone in which he asked it.

"Not this time."

I sit quietly for a moment with the hope he will reply and suggest something—even another silly explanation. *I love those silly explanations.* They offer you so much to work with. But all he does is sit quietly, in that patronizing way with that smart face I feel myself wanting to slowly peel away to find the evil I know exists.

"You know I talked to your mom for a long time, and I have to tell you, I can fully understand how you turned out the way you did."

His brow furrows, and the well lubricated thin skin under his eyes reddens. It's a shiny, oily red color. That's the first sign of anger I have seen on him. With all the buttons I've been trying to push to get a truly revealing reaction, the only one that does, is dear *mom*.

"It's just like William's suicide. He couldn't run

from that. It was in his genes."

"Who do you think you are, bringing her into this?"

"You honestly think I'm going to forget about the conversation I had with your mom?"

He's quiet now. He is still angry, even though his face doesn't show it now.

"I'll tell you what I think," I say calmly. "I think you're a murderer. Don't forget, I've been through your house. I'm pretty good at piecing together a personality, a life. I've made a career of it. But we don't need to go into all that. I know you were doing a little more with Amy than just talking to her occasionally. Probably with Evelyn, too. The best thing you can do right now is tell the truth about everything. It's a lot easier than the Warrant Squad showing up at your home at five in the morning or at your office when you least expect it." Obviously, I don't have a warrant for his arrest, but I'm hoping to get a reaction, make him think I have more than I really do.

"I told you William was the one seeing her, not me."

Not the reaction I expected.

"Then why would a witness who worked with Amy pick your picture and tell me that you were William Bergine?"

And there he goes shaking his head again with that winning smile.

"This is funny?" I ask.

"No, not it all. I'm just wondering where that came from and how long you were waiting to use it. You don't have a witness," he says with a business-like seriousness. “You’re just trying to trick me again.”

“I don’t trick people. That’s not my game.”

“Obviously, I’m not under arrest, right?”

“Be patient.”

“Well, then. I think I’ve offered you all I can offer. Good night. I’m tired. Should I show myself out?”

He actually takes me by surprise, but I hide it well. “Are you sure you want to walk out like this, not knowing what I might know?”

“I can walk with ease,” he says.

“Next time we talk you won’t have that luxury.”

I escort him to the door, open it and before he exits I say, “You’re my special project Emmerich, even if it takes my whole career,” I say as if saying it will bring me comfort.

He doesn’t respond. I watch him walk across the parking lot and out of sight.

❄

THE WINDOW IS OPEN just enough to let the cold air push in. Brings life to my fallen side. I like the smell of cold air just before snow falls. I like being drawn inside myself, then being drawn out again—something like hope. The bleakness of winter brings out the best in me. That’s why I decide to take a drive after my interview with Emmerich.

Emmerich is not a man who would easily confess, even when confronted with the most incriminating evidence. He’d still fight and find a way to justify it. He is a thinly veiled man stricken with a glorified self image created over time. Lord knows how much time.

I allowed too much in too soon. Patience should have prevailed over a selfish desire to get a quick reaction. It's funny how these things work. There is street justice, but it only works for the Grims of the world, not for victims like Amy and Evelyn. You'll never find someone like Emmerich with his face down in the gutter, spent 9mm casings surrounding his body.

I drive to the scene where Amy Noyes' body was discovered—perhaps an attempt to find inspiration. No, simply three hours to kill and nothing better to do. I convince myself I need inspiration. There's less guilt.

I park the car along the wooded edge and walk a short distance to an open area that leads to the muddy bank of the Anacostia River near where her body was discovered. My fully charged Streamlight shows me the way again. Deep tire treads and foot prints, like healing scars on the face of a frozen landscape—the remnants of our presence. Ahead is the Anacostia River. Darkness besets me, as I shift the beam of light from the area ahead of my feet and to the icy river.

Do I expect to find Aletheia Wynn's body here?

New, thinner ice has formed where the divers worked, searching for evidence in the dark, murky water. I bring light back to land. What do I expect to find now? The trees, wind and all this organized matter thriving along this river held her body. Parts of the body still remain, caught like fossils in the stone-like mud beneath my feet. Could something else be revealed before the ice melts away?

After I feel enough time has passed to pacify a guilt-ridden spirit, I walk back to the car. I need to find another spot to kill time, someplace busy where I am forced out of abstract thought.

I unlock the door and hear something to my right—steps against a crunching surface. I turn.

"Emmerich?" I say, shocking myself.

He's standing at the rear bumper of my vehicle at arm's length, a revolver pointed toward my head.

My hand instinctively pulls my coat back, unsnaps the holster, and grips my weapon.

"You shouldn't have called my mother," he says calmly. Comical—

"Wait," I say.

The muzzle flash from his gun, bright, silent. I turn to react. A sudden intense burning and pressure on the left side of my face, searing and it throws me back, but doesn't drop me. I was hit. My ears are ringing. I see him move forward, gun still drawn. I reach for his revolver with my left hand—manage to slap his arm down. I see the muzzle flash from his gun again. My right thigh burns now. I lunge again, manage to wrap my hand around the gun, cradle the cylinder and the hammer firmly. His face, has an odd look, fixed on my face like I shouldn't be doing this—I shouldn't be standing. *Does he know something I don't?* I can feel the hammer of the revolver he is holding pulling away from my pinky. He tries to punch me on the right side of my head and misses. It's a child-like, weak swing that grazes the whiskers on my chin. I kick his knee and he buckles but doesn't fall, the revolver still held firmly, but the cylinder moves and I feel the hammer push out, away from my pressing finger. It slams back to find the tip of my little finger instead of the chambered round. I scream. It's a deep-throated yowl with spits of blood. The pain throws me as the great pressure against the tip of my finger is like a sledge hammer, but I still struggle to find and finally get a grip on my weapon—pulled out quickly, despite all this clothing. Tucked against my side, I fire. Several times. The muzzle flashes, and rounds re-chamber—my weapon tight against my side firing repeatedly. I hear the shots, loud echoing pops. One shot, though...the last shot, finds his head. I see the contact. His head cocks back, slightly, but he remains upright, silent stunned and motionless. Thick deep blood oozes from the center of his forehead, trails down to the nape of his nose to the inside of his left open eye. I shout—something directed to him, like a command, an order, "Drop!" My blood spatters on his face. He releases the grip on the revolver and the weight of the gun attached to the tip of my finger drops it to my side, like a swinging pendulum coming to a sudden halt. He falls hard on the ground. Beside my feet. I aim, the top of his head, but for some reason don't pull the trigger. How would that look? *What an odd thing to think.* My finger slowly releases pressure on the trigger of my weapon. I don't shoot. I am diverted as I try to lift my left hand and notice the revolver attached to the tip of my pinky crunched and flattened by the hammer. Funny looking. 'Radio', I remember and then realize the blood I am swallowing, like thick syrup mixed with little jagged rocks down my throat. Too much blood I think. There is blood on the ground surrounding his head. I step back and pain like a burning hot poker shooting through my left leg into bone. I lose my footing—a wave, an earthquake under my feet and I'm suddenly light headed. I lose myself and fall.

The ground is hard. The right side of my face hits—stuns me and I struggle to get up, not to go out. The ground is frozen. I can see Emmerich's arm stretched below my feet. There's no movement. I feel something heavy drop from the roof of my mouth and hit the middle of my tongue. Bone? A tooth? It slides down and off my tongue. I gag, try to spit, but can't. I let it fall to the side of my tongue and then let the tip of my tongue find it and push it out my mouth. It slides down my chin thick with saliva or blood and to the ground at the tip of my nose. Oddly enough, I focus on it. It looks like a bullet, mushroomed out, split.

A bullet? Isn't that something?

Blood, like deep red lava flowing before my eyes, slowly it moves across the cold ground—trails down to fill a scar.

THIRTEEN

IN A DREAM I die. And for a brief moment, before my eyes close for the last time, I feel my loss. And it's not the whole of my life nor the loves and all that I hold dear. It's simply breath.

Voices, like demons, odd voices, octaves lower than they should be. There is bright Fluorescent light and an acoustic ceiling.

An IV hanging, tubes trailing down to my right hand, taped over is what I notice next. The last thing I remember is standing over Salty Dog's body and the ground, how cold the ground must have been. His face was stuck to the icy cement. The cheek pulled out when the body was lifted. The skin peeled and the blood was shiny, the color of red grape. Then I remember.

"You're at Med Star," an unfamiliar female voice says.

I must have spoke.

I focus and notice someone who appears to be a nurse beside me. She has very dark skin. It shines.

"Don't try to talk. Your mouth is wired shut."

I lift my left hand, weakly and touch my face. It's bandaged thick with gauze. I run my thumb across my face. I can't feel my skin. I am weightless, a good feeling.

I try to speak, but my mouth doesn't open. I mumble what I hope she can understand as, "Face."

"It will take some time," she says. "The doctor will be in shortly. Everything is fine."

I drift off—fall away and I think the last thing I say through clenched teeth is, "My gun."

When I wake up, I see Mather sipping take-out coffee. Days, that feel like disconnected episodes, have passed. Mather told me I somehow managed to get to my radio, call out a priority. "Pretty unintelligible," according to Mather, but help managed to find me.

A doctor is studying the parts of my body.

"You are fortunate," he says. "The mandible is one of the strongest bones in the body."

A few new teeth, rebuilt jaw and a couple of nice scars is what I was originally told. The second shot struck my thigh and fractured my femur, narrowly missing my femoral artery.

Mather is still shocked that I refused the bullet fragments, especially the one I spit out. Why would I want a souvenir of something I will be fighting to forget?

I'd like to think it all happened the way it was supposed to. The wind was at my back or something silly like that. I will be left with more unwanted images now. They are equal to scars. I'll always remember the blood trailing down Emmerich's forehead and then like a shadow over his left eye.

FOURTEEN

I'VE BEEN CLOSED IN too long, but I have a new face, mostly my old face back to normal. Ironic that it took a bullet through the left side to rid me of the burden of Bell's palsy. There are some side effects, but no drooping and I can close both eyes. There will always be a slightly crooked smile. I can live with that.

The vast, dark clouds look like they carry a well-needed downpour—the storm that will mark the end of spring is expected to pass over quickly. I drive to Celeste's home with all of Scanns' work belongings in the trunk of my car.

She greets me at the front door, and holds it open for me as I carry the boxes in. I set them down beside a recliner in her living room. The items packed neatly in these boxes once occupied a comfortable place around Scanns' work space. Whether they stay packed or not is of no consequence. The contained memories are where they belong.

Seeing Celeste isn't as painful as I thought. We visit for a short while. I don't talk about the circumstances that led to my long hospital stay. I won't burden Celeste with something that I know will remind her of the job her husband did, and what she feels led to his death.

After a while we hug and share a comfortable smile. I walk to the car, look back and feel like something connects us for life. She waves and closes the door behind her.

I cross over the 14th Street Bridge back to DC. A sudden craving comes over me. But before I make my way to a secret spot I used to hit for a roast beef sandwich back in the district days, I take a drive to North Capitol and New York Avenues.

Sure enough, fat fingers is sitting on the same blue crate and eating crabs out of a bucket. All of the addicts wander back and forth, grinding their teeth, scratching their arms, almost brushing against regular pedestrians, like passing ghosts.

I double park in front of the liquor store. Grim Junior is still holding his spot as if he never left, drinking an orange soda. Some things never change. Sometimes that's a good thing.

I hit the hazard lights and push the button to slide down the front passenger side window. Grim Junior has already noticed me inside the car. He steps up, stoops down and leans his head toward the open window.

"This ain't no detective car," he says. "You back to jump out?"

"No, those days are gone. This is my own car."

"You move into my neighborhood?"

"No, but I'll consider it if you want me to."

"That's arright. Looks like you getting' your face back. "

"Yeah, I've been getting a bit of rest lately. That's all my face needed."

"So I guess I figured you wrong Sim, or is the reason I didn't see you again after that day because you went and got yourself some rest on some beach somewheres?"

"You didn't figure me wrong. You never would have said what you did if you had. If I wanted to get you on that, I'd of found a way. Besides, if it were DC Superior Court, your brother's shooter would be out by now. The case is gone Grim, tucked away nice and neat in a spot that'll be hard to find."

He shoots me a nod like that's all right.

"You ever had yourself the best roast beef sandwich in Washington, DC, Grim?"

"Naw man. I don't know no place like that."

"I think it's something you should consider cause you never know when your times up."

He chuckles. "You figurin' my time's almost up? Somethin' I should know?"

"No, but I'm not the one in control."

"An' why you think I'd care about the best roast beef sandwich in DC?"

"Man, you would if you only knew."

"Where can I get me one of these sandwiches?"

"Hop in. It's not far from here. No strings attached.

There's nothing I want from you. Like I said, 7th and O is ancient history."

"I ain't getting in no car with you, Sim. How'd that look?"

"Your brother never had a problem because he knew who called the shots. So you don't call the shots around here?"

He huffs like I should know better than to ask a question like that.

"There's nothing I want from you Grim. This isn't some kind of trick."

He hesitates. This is not common. It certainly is not common for me, but I got an urge for uncommon company and a killer roast beef sandwich.

"My treat. Something you can tell your brother when your time comes."

"My time ain't gonna come that soon so it better be a damn good sandwich."

He looks around, makes sure his boys aren't watching, snickers and hops in.

It's a tiny hole-in-the-wall with dirty windows and an aging tin awning, sitting alone at the cut, off an alley on New York Avenue, near 5th.

Looking at it from the outside, if you're not one of the enlightened few, you might quiver at the thought of eating something out of this place. The outward appearance is deceptive. I was hesitant the first time I was brought here. In fact, I think it was Scanns who introduced me.

Grim shakes his head like this can't be the place.

The same large man shaves thick slices off a hunk of meat resting in a pan of its own juices, lightly dips the top portion of a Kaiser roll in the pan. He scoops the pile of slices and presses them between the Kaiser rolls and into a Styrofoam container. In anticipation of the mess I'm about to make, I grab a stack of napkins off the counter—about a dozen, maybe more.

We walk back to the car.

My front side is adorned with napkins. I haven't been able to eat a sandwich like this in a long time. I notice Grim through the corner of my eye as he takes his first bite. I think what I notice on him, unlike his brother, is a smile.

It is quiet outside with only an occasional sign of life, a welcome idleness brought to this city by that brief time after rush-hour when all those hard at work little cells take their leave. A peaceful stillness made by their absence.

We sit there and eat without saying a word. As much as I want to know what it was that happened that led to the murder of his cousin, I don't ask. Oddly there's a certain comfort in that—a common bond that only I can realize, and never share. Grim's street justice was for his cousin. Strangely enough, I got mine too. Not the easy way, though. I'll never know what really happened.

I am sure that Alethea Wynn is being held at the mercy of the Anacostia. The river has a strong current that flows into the Potomac, where the Cherry trees line up along grassy inclines. They will blossom soon, signing off on the dead season with an outburst of pale pink and white.

About the Author

DAVID SWINSON SPENT THE EARLY 1980S as a punk rocker in Los Angeles, booking acts like Social Distortion, Nick Cave, John Cale, Chris Isaac and the Red Hot Chili Peppers into clubs and producing spoken word events with Hunter S. Thompson, Dr. Timothy Leary, John Waters and Jim Carroll. He produced the cult classic film "Roadside Prophets," starring John Doe of X and Adam Horovitz of the Beastie Boys and featuring Timothy Leary, John Cusack, David Carradine and Arlo Guthrie.

In 1994, Swinson returned to his hometown of Washington DC to enter the Police Academy. He worked as an undercover narcotics officer, and worked robbery and homicide details, and in 2000 was promoted to the Special Investigations Bureau/Major Crimes, becoming the lead investigator in the District of Columbia for serial burglaries, high profile cases and organized criminal operations related to narco-fencing. He was often called upon by the Federal Bureau of Investigation, United States Secret Service, The Treasury Department and The United States Attorney's Office for assistance with sensitive cases.

Swinson retired from the MPDC after 16 years. This is his first novel.

54797915R00207

Made in the USA
Lexington, KY
28 August 2016